THE ELEVENTH HOUR

ALL THE OTHER GODS · 1

To those who have questioned their own magic and doubted their abilities. May this book be a testament to the extraordinary power that lies within you.

THE ELEVENTH HOUR

ALL THE OTHER GODS · 1

Prologue
Alfred Mandrake

June 30, 1996
Alfred Mandrake
Hampshire "The Hidden Borough" of New York

In hindsight, Alfred shouldn't have entered the speakeasy to meet with his loyalists that day. He had only chosen to because he wanted to prove that the Mandrake family remained strong in the wake of the upcoming betrothal ceremony, but the weather tonight was insufferable. The rose bushes at the entrance had wilted, and the stray cats wandering the nearby alleys were huddled together for warmth.

"Strange weather," Malicent said. His younger brother stared up at the gray clouds in the sky. "Even for Hampshire."

"*Especially* for Hampshire," Alfred corrected. As they both gazed skyward, he noticed the clouds moving erratically, as if they were concealing something. "We should head indoors."

"Yes," Malicent said, still looking up at the sky. "After you."

Alfred nodded. He knew there was something lurking in the clouds, and then, as if on cue, a massive wing cut through the cloud cover, confirming his worst fears.

Dragon, he thought. *And a rather large one at that.* It concerned him more than he was willing to let on. Alfred wasn't sure his brother could see it, but he knew the Dimitri family wouldn't be so bold as to attack him in Eaton—it was a neutral city.

Their great-grandfather, Mason Mandrake, had come to an agreement with Police Commissioner Ward before either party's passing to ensure it was a safe area for the wizarding community. It was one of the Sacred Thirty-Eight treaties and the first Alfred had learned about in childhood. Eaton was Hampshire's only city that could be used for entry into the non-magical boroughs of New York, with Queens to the west and Brooklyn to the east. Every security measure around Hampshire assured that non-magical beings couldn't access it without a magical escort—and those were rare cases. After all, Magicks weren't exactly eager to marry non-magicks—or mundanes, as most called humans. It was impractical for all involved, but Alfred had seen it as worthwhile for his third marriage. He had been a widower twice—though he'd been estranged and then subsequently divorced from his second wife prior to her death during the birth of their second son, his third son—and now a married man once more. In truth, he felt nothing more could be expected of him. Alfred was the eldest of four brothers and had performed his duty two times over. Therefore, he deemed it was only right his third marriage was purely for love.

Thus, making their meeting tonight imperative. As if he was duty bound to marry his only daughter to the Carmines's son to keep the wizarding world from falling into an all-out war, he would at least meet the young man first.

The Sun Club was where many of the sacred treaties were made. It was Mandrake property and, therefore, heavily warded with every protection spell known to wizard-kind. If anyone attempted to cast a lethal spell indoors, it would rebound and consequently kill the caster. Which was rather unfortunate for the few drunken hot-blooded American wizards that wandered in.

Alfred took out his wand and waved it over the lock. It creaked open, and he stepped inside, his brother following closely.

The door slammed shut abruptly, and the wards sealed once more. Alfred strolled calmly through the dimly lit corridor until they were near the main dining room. The room's yellow light shone gold, complimenting the rich red walls that seemed to echo the numerous voices of the lively patrons. The tables were evenly dispersed throughout the room and filled with smiling patrons ordering off the menu. Drinks came from the bar, but food came from the kitchens in the back. The bar took up a corner of the room, and even the barstools were full.

Patrons who noticed him enter smiled at him, and Alfred nodded at them politely. He counted at least forty-four guests tonight, and it was only ten o'clock. He expected it'd fill up the closer it got to midnight.

Most present were young witches invited into the club by the bouncer, likely seeking eligible partners. The bouncer was Jaime, the second son of Vincent Augustine, the Head of the Augustine family. The Augustines had been loyal to the Mandrake family for ten generations. Jaime was bald and the tallest and palest of Vincent's six children. He and his elder brother, Duncan, typically managed security at the club. Alfred imagined that Duncan had gone to manage the lower floor of the club, where three separate rooms hosted live acts that guests could dance to and would need constant surveillance. But Duncan knew how to divvy up the guards.

"Mr. Mandrake," Vincent Augustine said, bowing in respect.

"Vincent, it's good to see you," Alfred greeted.

"Where's Carmine?" Malicent asked abruptly.

Alfred almost wished to excuse his brother, but Malicent had never been one for formalities. And, of course, he was right; they had business to attend to.

"Carmine, yes, of course," Vincent said. "I escorted him to the tables in the VIP room with his son. I didn't want anyone to disturb your meeting," he continued, and Alfred smiled approvingly. "They're right this way."

Vincent escorted them to the back, passing by the security that held up the back curtain to reveal two brown leather couches accompanied by armchairs and tables. The lights here were brighter and reflected in the square mirrors on the walls. Behind them, the wallpaper was beige and brown, though the beige looked golden in this light. In the corner, two young men played pool, one of which was his future son-in-law Mordecai Carmine.

His father, Joseph Carmine, sat on one couch in a gray suit, holding his belly as it rumbled with laughter at something Eric Graves had said. Both heads of their respective households appeared in high spirits. Eric was tall with a pale, pointed face, slate gray eyes, and golden hair that came to his shoulders. He wore an all-white ensemble with the matching blazer lain on the arm of the leather couch he sat on.

"Ah, Alfred," Joseph said, wiping a tear from his eye. "You simply must hear the story Eric has just told. He encountered the funniest human in Manhattan today."

"Manhattan?" Malicent repeated, taking a seat in an armchair. "You have business in Manhattan?"

"*Yes.* According to the humans, I have a son on the way," Eric explained, picking up a glass of scotch from the table between him and Joseph. "It's been proven through both magical and non-magical means that I'm the wretched thing's father."

"Well, you can't expect much when you play with fire," Malicent said. "And how's Martha taking it?"

Eric laughed dryly. "Martha won't be hearing anything about it. My lawyers will be in contact with the young woman soon enough. Of course, I'll cover the medical expenses and include a small inheritance for the child."

"And if they have magic?" Malicent asked.

"*If?*" Joseph repeated before letting out a bark of laughter. "There has never been a non-magical Graves. Boy or girl, that child will have magic."

"You will be taking the child in then," Alfred said to Eric.

Alfred did not like to intrude on personal matters, but a child living a life of bastardy among the wizarding world wouldn't be treated well. To be a bastard was to be marked for life. It kept many from getting housing or employment. If Eric claimed them—as Alfred had done with the four sons he'd fathered during his separation from his second wife— then the child would have a chance when they were inducted into the wizarding world. And that was *if* they had magic, as even the strongest magical bloodlines could fail.

Being *mundane* was not a crime, but it simply wouldn't necessitate them being brought into the magical world.

Eric sighed. "Well, I wouldn't leave them to rot," he answered, taking another sip from his drink.

"Atta boy, and then you'll have time to explain to your missus," Joseph said, nodding to himself. "Five years—*seven* if you're lucky."

"Claiming him is the right thing to do," Alfred told Eric.

Eric muttered something in Gaelic. "It'll be a relief to have another son," Eric said with a wry smile. "Perhaps I'll be able to sway the Wrens to wed their newborn daughter to him. Take another loyalist faction from the Dimitri family."

"Yes, and I wouldn't mind helping you," Joseph said, taking a pint of beer from the waiter, "once my boy is wed to your daughter, Alfred. The Dimitris are my distant cousins, but the Wrens have been slighted by them. I received a very unsettling letter from Norman the other morning."

"They could defect," Malicent said, giving Alfred a knowing look.

Alfred knew Joseph was starting the proceedings, no matter how slyly he was trying to go about it. The head of the Wren household, Norman, had maintained a close friendship with Joseph for years. The Wren family controlled Gates Village, the City of Gates, known for its trade routes. An alliance with them would destabilize trade for the Dimitri family. If the Wrens defected, others would follow. The Dimitris could quickly lose their stronghold in the Big Three and fall into obscurity. It would be a big win for the Mandrakes.

Alfred cleared his throat and said, "Yes, I'd daresay she's looking forward to it."

Joseph nodded silently. "I'm glad to hear it," he said with a smile. "As much of an honor it is for my son to be wedding your daughter—and I say this with the utmost respect—I wouldn't want to marry my son to a woman who couldn't stand the sight of him."

"Well, I assure you, Hermione has been preparing for this for years," Alfred said.

Alfred looked over at the two young men playing pool. Tall and dark haired, Mordecai was well-built and well versed in charms; Alfred could trust him with his daughter's safety—if it ever came to that. Though he had been sure to give Hermione the best magical tutors money could buy, he wanted her to have a bodyguard if the worst-case scenario were to ever happen. If he weren't here, he didn't want her to be alone. Because if he were struck down, her brothers would soon follow. This marriage wouldn't be her undoing—she had been taught the importance of family and duty, the same as himself. He'd hoped that his wife could forgive him for that. But even he hadn't been above duty, and the Carmines were a loyal ally. And he hadn't heard a single word of criticism about the boy's character, only an unending chorus of praises. As for the smaller, spindly Graves boy, Elliot, who was laughing and snorting beside Mordecai, Alfred had heard rumors about his escapades. From the wenches he'd impregnated in brothels to the gambling debts he owed to the Egleston family. Simply put, Alfred was glad the boy wouldn't become the next head of the Graves family.

"I suppose introductions are in order," Joseph said with a

bark of laughter. "Boy! Come present yourself to Lord Mandrake."

Mordecai jumped at his father's request, shooting upright from his hunched position. After putting away the pool stick, he walked over and stopped before Alfred. Mordecai bowed his head with a tight-lipped smile.

"Good evening, sir. I am honored to have been chosen to marry your daughter, and I look forward to the day I join your family," Mordecai said formally.

Alfred looked at the boy. He noted his rolled-up sleeves had ink splatters on them and his black vest was folding at the bottom. His pants were the only thing that seemed perfectly tailored. Sweat beaded on his forehead, and fear flashed in his green eyes. He favored his mother in looks, and Alfred assumed most of his upbringing came from her. Joseph spent too much time hanging around the Barley family's gentleman's clubs to be an attentive father. But Alfred had some difficulty in reshaping the mindsets of his loyalists. Most of the men were old-fashioned and believed that women should handle the child-rearing, requiring them to be both nurturing and partial disciplinarians.

Mordecai was the heir apparent of the Carmine family, and Alfred was beginning to think that it may have been better that Joseph hadn't had as much involvement with the young man's upbringing—or that of his other seven sons. Perhaps there was a chance that Mordecai and Hermione would take a more modern approach, as he hoped his daughter would still be able to pursue her art.

Hermione was a fine painter. She had painted a portrait of Alfred and Isabel as a gift for his birthday, and he'd hung it proudly over the mantle. And as much as he desired his daughter to perform her duties, he did not want her to lose who she was. That was where he differed from his own father.

"I look forward to it as well," Alfred finally said, and the boy let out a breath he appeared to have been holding. "Perhaps we can get better acquainted at the garden party this Saturday."

Mordecai smiled. "Yes, of course—"

Joseph cleared his throat as if to tell his son not to be too eager. Mordecai seemed to gather his senses and nodded. But Alfred was happy that the boy wanted to please him.

"Will Hermione be attending as well?" Mordecai asked.

The question made Alfred smile and Joseph cough. Mordecai messed with his hair and smiled nervously at Alfred.

"Yes," Alfred said, suddenly feeling in high spirits. "Yes, she will be."

Mordecai smiled. "Does she really paint as well as they say?"

Alfred nodded. "Well, as her father, I may be a bit biased, but I'm never one to discredit the truth."

"Well, I fear I'm no good at painting, but I would very much like to see hers," Mordecai said lowly. "My mother often says that it's important to know a woman's interest, especially in the case that the woman is your wife—"

"Oh, be quiet!" Joseph said, interrupting his son. "Do you truly believe that Lord Mandrake wishes to be bored to death with your mother's silly little teachings?"

Mordecai fell silent for a moment, appearing disheartened.

"Well, I'm sure Hermione would love to show someone

else her work besides an old fart like me," Alfred told Mordecai, eliciting a smile from the young man. "And there will be plenty of her art on display in the gardens. And plenty more to look forward to in the future, I'm sure."

Mordecai nodded.

"Then everything is settled?" Joseph asked.

"Yes," Alfred answered, looking at Mordecai again. "Our children will meet on the first of July and then marry on the fifteenth, as it has been agreed upon for decades."

Joseph nodded slowly as if he were considering whether the transaction met his approval. Alfred held his hand out to Mordecai. "I look forward to speaking to you more, Mordecai."

"Yes, sir," Mordecai said, giving Alfred a firm handshake.

When it was done, he turned to Joseph, who was standing and holding up his hands as though he were rejoicing.

"This is wonderful," Joseph said, clapping his hands together. "Simply wonderful! Our families coming together into union, as your grandfather predicted they would. This will be a great wedding that all the Carmines will attend—and perhaps the Wrens too." Joseph concluded with a wink. "We must celebrate! I will order us a round of beers."

Alfred nodded and sat down on the couch beside Eric.

"Hmph . . ." Eric said thoughtfully, and Alfred looked toward him.

While he didn't approve of Eric's infidelity, Eric had served as an advisor to him for most of his time as the Ruler of Merlin, a title he didn't often use but was his official claim. Alfred, Head of the Mandrake Family, Ruler of Merlin—Merlin being their magical ancestor, who hadn't been written into history as a criminal, and the namesake for the county of Hampshire they controlled. The pure Merlin blood flowing through his veins had given them six of the fourteen loyalist families that followed him now—war had given the Mandrake family the others. War had killed four of his uncles and many of his cousins. War had given his father the title before him.

And though he rarely drank, he drank tonight in honor of preventing the start of another war.

The Father. The Son. The Hidden Borough.

July 1, 1996
Hermione Mandrake
Hampshire "The Hidden Borough" of New York

All fourteen families had received invitations to Hermione's twenty-first birthday, to be celebrated on the first of July, so that her betrothal could be announced on the fourth a minute before midnight in accordance with tradition.

Her mother, Isabel, recited these proceedings daily and had started repeating it more frantically as though it were some sort of divine incantation that would make Hermione fall in love with the Carmine's son at first sight. That was unlikely, but she'd grow to love him—Hermione had promised herself that. The Carmine family produced by far the most handsome men of the wizarding community's noble families, and Mordecai was no exception. The framed photograph of him that her mother held was proof of that, though that didn't stop Isabel from grimacing down at it.

Hermione glanced up at her lady's maid, Cressida, who didn't return her gaze. Instead, the brown modelesque elf continued diligently working on Hermione's curly hair, straightening each section to perfection but moving slower than usual. Cressida's own hair was dark and cornrowed and certainly more well-kept than the curly bun Hermione had chosen to wear overnight. Unfortunately, that had caused some tangling. While Hermione may have thought the silent uncertainty in Cressida's eyes was directed toward her due to the state of her hair, she could safely assume it was toward her mother because of her mother's morning tirade. However, Cressida would never raise her concerns without someone probing her. Most elves weren't discreet with their emotions, nor did they bite their tongue when stating their *opinions*, though the few Hermione's family associated with weren't in Cressida's economic position.

The elf was in no better position now than her mother Isabel was when she'd married her father, Alfred Mandrake. Before she was Isabel Mandrake, she was a non-magical African American librarian working in the New York Public Library who came across magic by accident. Though she couldn't practice it, she'd fallen deeply in love with it—and Hermione's father, despite not knowing everything about his family. A love he fully returned.

Isabel had known they were Caucasian, wealthy, and owned Mandrake Enterprises. She had been shocked when she'd seen him dueling a man in a subway station—their wands drawn, shouting strange words, sending curses at one another—but even after, she was swept up in romance. How could she have predicted that the Mandrake family was a powerful wizarding noble family?

Traditionally speaking, Alfred should've never married Isabel. She was his third marriage, and any marriage that took place was meant to be between the allied families to strengthen their house. To maintain law and order within the wizarding community. Alfred straying from tradition caused the loss of two loyal families.

The Bane and Bishop families were offended by his quick dismissal of their daughters after his second wife's death, and consequently, his decision had created a feud. And the Dimitri family had risen to be the second most powerful family in New York when the Bishop family assimilated into their ranks. The smaller families weren't as much of a threat to the Mandrakes. They were still the most powerful family of the Big Three. The Banes came in third and were trying to get a meeting with her father to settle a dispute inland. They were currently warring with the Petra family on Long Island, so Hermione reckoned the Banes family's days were numbered. Petra would move up to third, and a new family would ascend into the Big Three. And the cycle of violence would continue.

But that was Hermione's least pressing concern. Her birthday party represented more than another revolution around the sun, it would determine the security of the Mandrake family.

The Treaty of 1910 between the Mandrakes and Carmines was due to be reassessed in 1992. But thanks to Hermione's timely birth and her father's quick thinking, they'd created a temporary agreement to a marriage that'd reaffirm their treaty. Thus, she would marry on July 15, 1996, ten days after her twenty-first birthday.

This new treaty would keep the Carmines from aligning themselves with their distant cousins, the Dimitris.

But duty is bound in blood, Hermione thought to herself. And they could still lose the Carmines. So everything had to be perfect—including herself.

Hermione looked at herself in the mirror. Her hair was nearly finished, but her skin looked rather dull. She couldn't meet her future husband this way. She needed to look her best. If he didn't marry her, it could mean war.

Cressida pulled a small bottle from her pocket and set it on the vanity in front of Hermione. Hermione nearly laughed after reading the label; *drink me,* it said. She hadn't read *Alice's Adventures in Wonderland* in quite some time, but the thought of it always made her smile. Hermione gulped down the potion slowly, doing her best to ignore the tangy copper taste as her stomach seized slightly. She forced herself to shake off the feeling.

Then she looked back into the mirror and watched her dark brown eyes shimmer for a moment as the magic passed through her veins, snaking over her brown skin and reaching all the way to the tips of her toes. Her skin looked refreshed, as though she hadn't missed a single night's sleep. But over the past week, she hadn't slept more than three hours a night. She was anxious and exhausted.

"Mom," Hermione said softly, drawing her mother's attention. "You really don't have to stay while I get ready."

Her mother sighed. "You can hardly expect me not to. How else should a mother react when her husband has promised to throw her only child to the wolves?"

"We knew this was coming," Hermione said.

Her mother shook her head.

"That doesn't make it right," she said, her voice just above a whisper. Then she looked to Cressida, who was finishing the second of two small braids that would frame Hermione's face. "Perhaps a necklace as well."

Her mother stood from the bed and unceremoniously tossed the framed portrait onto a pillow. Then she crossed the room to select a necklace from a jewelry box on Hermione's dresser.

By the time her mother settled on one, Cressida had finished Hermione's hair and makeup. The necklace was silver with a diamond teardrop pendant, and Hermione was quite sure it wasn't part of her collection as Cressida clasped it around her neck.

Her mother kissed Hermione on the cheek. "Happy birthday, darling," she whispered, squeezing her shoulders.

"Thanks, Mom," Hermione said, admiring the necklace.

After her mother left, she was finally ready to get dressed. Hermione slipped into a black dress, and though she wasn't attending a funeral, she felt it suited the occasion.

The servants bowed their heads as they passed her, not in fear of her but as a sign of respect. Also because her eldest brother was standing at the top of the grand staircase, waiting for something, grimacing down at the sea of people streaming through the front doors.

Gianni Matias Mandrake was technically her half brother, but Mandrake loyalists refused to acknowledge the difference, as they were siblings or they weren't. But he was of pure Merlin blood. He had strong Merlin features, with blue eyes and black hair. He was over six feet tall, like their father, and pale, courtesy of his mother, Fonda Abbot, who was also a descendant of House Merlin. Their father's cousin and first wife, Fonda, had died giving birth to their twin sons.

Loyalists from older families marveled at the heir apparent and were constantly scheming to wed their daughters to him. They didn't balk at a chance to bow humbly before him. And she hated to admit it, but she envied him for it. Pure Merlin blood was something all her half brothers shared, including the *bastards,* those conceived through a tryst with her father. Her father had legitimized all of them to put rumors to rest, though it made no difference in how they saw them.

Admittedly, being a true-born child of the Mandrake family helped Hermione some, as it kept her from being looked down upon. Truthfully, she pitied most of her "bastard-born" half siblings, though they all shared the burden of the serpent. A proud creature that had represented the Mandrake family since it was founded.

"Oh, there you are," Gianni said, looking her over. "Why are you wearing black? Do you mean to insult them?"

"No—I mean, not really," she said. Hermione huffed out air. When she'd chosen the dress, she'd felt as though she were walking to her execution. "Can you believe all these people came?"

It was a rhetorical question, but Gianni didn't much care.

He shook his head and mumbled *petite souris,* little mouse, his nickname for her since she was five. She was more timid back then.

He can't be too angry, she thought, looking up at him, hopeful.

Gianni looked at her and said, "If they ask, you tell them you had nothing else to wear."

Hermione nodded silently. "Yeah, good idea."

He sighed and offered her his arm.

"Come on," Gianni said, and she took his arm.

"Were you waiting for me?" Hermione asked softly as they began their descent down the stairs.

Gianni smirked. "Well, you can hardly expect me to let you walk into the lion's den alone."

She knew he meant it as a joke, but nausea still seized her stomach.

"Hey," Gianni said softly, drawing her attention. "It's going to be okay."

"What if he doesn't like me?"

"He'd be a fool not to," he said.

When they reached the bottom of the stairs, Gianni turned them into the living room and greeted a few guests on their way out to the gardens. The sweet smell of roses pricked her nose as she finally released Gianni's arm and stared out onto the garden, with its perfectly paved paths and statues lining the hedges. Her father had even assured her that some of her paintings were on display, clearly wanting to show the Carmine family that she had a talent. She was also trained to play piano but was glad she didn't have to play anything. Nearby, a gardener was tending to the flower beds while visitors gazed into the fountain at the center, perhaps hoping to catch a glimpse of one of Merlin's memories. But many of her ancestors tossed a memory into that fountain, telling their stories long after their death. Hermione herself had watched memories of Damon Mandrake the First win the Battle of the Three and another of his wedding ceremony with Amada

Torneau, the marriage that made the Mandrakes the most powerful noble family in the wizarding world. And her marriage was meant to help maintain that power.

"Aye, Gianni!" a young man called, waving at him.

Gianni smiled and waved back at him.

Hermione looked up at Gianni. "Well, don't let me hold you," she said sweetly.

"No, we don't have time," he said, shaking his head.

"We have plenty of time, Gianni. Besides, you never spend any time with your friends anymore. I promise, I won't move from this spot," Hermione said, hoping he'd budge.

Gianni sighed. "All right, but I won't be long ju—just stay nearby."

Hermione nodded, and her elder half brother walked away. She let out a sigh of relief. *Just a few minutes of freedom*, she told herself, looking around. *Only a few minutes.*

She strolled over to the fountain and took a seat on a spot that wasn't damp, though she doubted anyone would notice a damp spot on a black dress. Hermione looked into the water at her reflection until it was replaced by another image, a memory; Damon Mandrake rallying his men for the final push against the Dimitri family, his words were warbled at this distance, but she didn't dare to lean in closer—lest she fall in and have to retreat inside to make herself presentable. If she ran into the gawking gulls of the Graves family, she wouldn't hear the end of it until the day she died—*Oh dear, did you hear about Hermione Mandrake? She was pampered and primed to perfection, and then she fell into her family's fountain before meeting her husband, the poor dear. She's ever so lucky he hadn't seen her yet, otherwise I couldn't imagine the engagement going on.*

Hermione rolled her eyes. Her options for friends within the noble families were limited on account of her age, as there were so few she could relate to. A few years younger or older, depending on their life stage, they could have little to nothing to talk about. She spent most of her time accompanied by Phaedra Thistle and Melody Fauntleroy, though neither had arrived at the party as of yet.

"Well, you've got some nerve," a deep, familiar voice said in a grim tone.

Hermione gulped and turned to face him.

"Uncle Rowan, it's so good to see you," Hermione said, hoping his expression would soften.

It didn't. In fact, his already contorted pale face grew more unpleasant as his scowl deepened and the snarl on his lips harshened. His eyes were nearly black, and the long brown beard on his face matched his shoulder-length brown hair. He was muscular and looked as though he should be carrying an axe rather than a wand.

"Humph . . ." Rowan responded, giving her a narrow-eyed appraisal.

"How have you been?" she asked calmly.

"Actions have consequences, Hermione," he said sternly. "The future of our house hangs in the balance, and it isn't only your father that needs to be careful today."

Hermione was taken aback by his statement. Had her gazing into the water frustrated him?

"I know—"

"Then why are you dressed as though you're attending a funeral?"

She stammered for a moment. "I ran out of clothes—"

"Ran out of clothes? Are your elves not tending to laundry properly?"

"No, they have been—"

"Then why, pray tell—"

"Allow her to breathe a moment, Uncle," a familiar male voice retorted. "She's anxious as any young woman would be in her place. In fact, I recall Uncle Malicent saying Alison was nervous when she *unexpectedly* bedded father all those years ago."

Christian Carlisle was her father's third-born son and firstborn bastard. His ivory skin and brown hair were reminiscent of his mother, but the strength of his jawline, tall stature, and piercing blue eyes were a gift from their father. But while Christian had a knack for getting into trouble, he also had a knack for getting Hermione out of it.

"Mind your tongue, boy," Rowan said sharply. "Know your place. Alison did her duties without insult or complaint to this family. She had nothing but respect for your father and was *murdered* for her loyalty—while you are nothing more than the bastard of Kassandra Graves."

Rowan glared down at Hermione. He was known for his brutish nature, but today was the first time his snarl was directed at her.

"Our time is short," said a stern voice, which she was relieved to hear. "We need to move on now, Uncle."

Hermione felt a hand on her upper back, and she turned to see Gianni, who was glaring at their uncle. Rowan shifted under Gianni's gaze, appearing intimidated by her older half brother. Though their uncle was a decade Gianni's senior, he was a few inches shorter and not the Mandrake family heir.

And as heir apparent, Gianni was delegated a certain

level of respect which superseded his uncles, but not the head of house—their father—as it was with other heir apparents. Heir apparents were learning from their fathers to take over their respective families. For Rowan to disrespect him was to disrespect the family itself.

"Of course, Gianni," said Rowan with a small bow. "My apologies for holding you," he said to her.

Hermione nodded silently, and Gianni led her away from the two men.

"Thank you," she said lowly.

Gianni nodded. "I think Uncle Rowan was just looking for someone's head to bite off today. Don't take it personally."

Hermione tried to laugh it off but couldn't shake the feeling that it was personal for her uncle. She'd always had the feeling that Rowan didn't like her, whether it was for the way she was presently dressed or simply being a half-blooded Merlin—she was banking on the latter.

"Well, this time I'll leave you with more pleasant company while I ask Mr. Graves where our father is. Perhaps someone that'll scare Rowan away," Gianni joked.

Hermione smiled at the thought.

In truth, she would happily take any company that kept their uncle at bay. However, her present company would've been preferred. But she didn't much feel like strolling aimlessly around the garden in search of her father. Hermione was quite sure every loyalist family would stop her to give their congratulations or well wishes on her pending nuptials. And today, she would rather not hear them. It was the first time she would publicly meet her husband-to-be, likely the *only* time she would see him before the wedding. As far as she knew, the only thing they shared in common was their intertwined noble families' history and that they were spokes on a wheel. Merely tools to keep a never-ending cycle going. Though her father was grasping for greater power now that he was involved in politics.

"Ah, here we are," Gianni said. "Grandfather, how are you feeling?"

The old man grumbled and shifted on the bench with a bare-knuckled grip on his cane. Their grandfather, Thomas Mandrake, was not a crabby old man, but he had the appearance of one. His skin had paled and wrinkled like old paper and stretched over his thin body and brittle bones from growing old. In his younger years, he stood tall at six feet, but in his seventies, he'd lost the lower portion of his left leg in a duel, which he slowly adapted to. Nowadays, he spent more time hunched over. As he aged, his hair had turned a pale silver, and its length rivaled that of his beard. In truth, if he had chosen to wear wizard robes rather than a suit, he would have looked like Merlin himself.

"Ninety years young," Thomas said before letting out a laugh. "I'm lucky to keep these old bones working most days. What can I help you with, Gianni?"

Gianni smiled at him. "I was wondering if it was alright if I left Hermione with you. Seems like Uncle Rowan has it out for her today."

"Ugh," Thomas groaned. "Of course he does. That one has always been a bit rough around the edges," he said, looking up at Hermione. "You'll be no bother."

Hermione gave him a small smile and took a seat beside him, allowing Gianni to search for their father.

"Come on, stand tall little soldier," Thomas said, nudging her. "No need to let the likes of Rowan get to you. Between us, I always thought the whole blood purity thing was ridiculous. I often doubt Merlin cared for it. Nothing in his journals makes me picture a wizard worried about his bloodline." He shook his head slowly. "I'm not sure where I went wrong with that boy."

"I'm quite sure it had nothing to do with you," Hermione said softly.

"Yes, quite sure is good," Thomas said, pulling out a silver pocket watch and checking the time. "I wonder if your beau is late."

"He's hardly my beau," Hermione said.

Her breath caught in her throat. She immediately regretted having said it.

"Oh dear, I didn't mean—"

"Eh, of course you did," Thomas said in a bored tone. "You're about to embark on one of the most important journies of your life with a total stranger. There's no reason to pretend otherwise."

Hermione sighed. "I feel like a pawn."

"In a way, we're all pawns," Thomas said dismally. "We follow your father's commands, hoping it'll maintain order and keep the peace within the wizarding world."

"And you doubt it?"

Thomas considered the question for a moment. "I know the future isn't promised," he said, patting her hand. "If someone had told me in my youth that I would lose both my leg and your grandmother within the same year, I would not have believed them."

"Do you miss her terribly?"

"How can I not?" he said softly. "The flowers in the garden haven't bloomed the same since her death. And throwing myself into my work only distanced me from my sons, but we all made peace with her death in our own way. I turned to inventing and created this."

Thomas handed her a silver pocket watch. The etchings on it were beautiful, and words were engraved on the back.

"Memento mori," Hermione read aloud.

She knew the Latin phrase's translation was *remember to die* but didn't understand why her grandfather would carry around such a morbid trinket.

"Open it," Thomas whispered.

Hermione opened the pocket watch and noticed it was rather different on the inside. A strange ocean-blue liquid was stored behind the glass face, swirling like a whirlpool, but there seemed to be a fractured image within it. Her eyes were drawn to it, and as she stared at it, it seemed to reassemble. She felt as though she were in some sort of fog.

Then her grandfather shut it, and Hermione blinked.

"What was that?" Hermione asked.

"A memory," Thomas told her.

She was confused. They had plenty of mirrors in the stores that would playback memories, some that you could even step into and watch them play out.

Thomas leaned in close to her and whispered. "It's a time trinket."

Hermione gaped.

"Time travel is illegal," Hermione whispered, shaking her head.

Thomas snorted. "I know that, Hermione. But I merely wanted to see—"

"Merlin's beard, Grandfather," Hermione said. "Please tell me you haven't been somewhere."

"Well, of course I have. There's no reason to make something you have no intention of using," Thomas said, rolling his eyes. "And unlike others, I haven't changed anything. But if *you* wanted to change something, you would have my full support."

Hermione's heart sank in her chest as she realized what he was implying. *Mordecai. He wants me to—no. I can't.*

She shook her head and came to her senses.

"You know I can't do that."

"Of course you can, it's more about being careful," Thomas said.

Hermione huffed out air. "Alright then, I *won't*," she told him. She couldn't do that to her father, though she had read many interesting stories about time travel. At the moment, she felt the risk outweighed the reward. "But where did you go?"

"Well, I visited myself in the hospital—"

"You're not supposed to come into contact with yourself," Hermione said, interrupting him.

Thomas scoffed. "I'm not daft, little girl. I was fast asleep and disguised myself as one of the doctors on the off chance that the other me woke up."

"What were you trying to do?"

"Well, I didn't succeed, if that's what you're asking," Thomas told her.

Hermione stared at him blankly.

"My leg," Thomas said, patting his left thigh. "I tried using the Forget Me Not spell on myself to see if it'd bring my leg back," he told her with a shrug. "Unfortunately, all it did was make me forget the portion of the duel where I lost it, and the other me fell flat on his face when he woke up. They don't exactly warn you about that in the spell book."

Hermione shook her head at her grandfather. The Forget Me Not spell was an advanced amnesia spell, it could erase memories from inanimate objects like images and people, but she would've never imagined trying to use it to heal herself. In truth, she wouldn't use it at all—she was at most a beginner in charms.

"But how did you do it?" Hermione asked.

"I used one of my memories to send me back," Thomas said. "But you know, I'm sure I left a trace somewhere, besides my newly missing memory. All time travelers leave traces."

"Who filled you in?" Hermione asked, trying to keep a smile from spreading on her face.

"Well, your father used a spell to bring my memories back," Thomas said. "I'm glad Malicent didn't do it. I couldn't imagine having no memory at all."

Hermione smiled at him. Then she stared at the pocket watch in her hands. It was beautiful but dangerous in the wrong hands. If the Magical Crime Unit learned about it, they would have reason to bring her grandfather in, and who knows what charges would be waiting for him there. They always only needed one thing to catch a member of a noble family, though she doubted her grandfather would break. Time travel had been illegal for centuries in the United States of America. After an infamous wizard used it to commit genocide, killing thousands and decimating entire non-magical populations. The Magical Crime Unit discovered them soon enough and prevented more bloodshed.

"It's been a joy talking to you, darling, but it seems our

time is up," Thomas said, and Hermione looked at him questioningly.

Thomas didn't look at her. He nodded to someone behind her. Hermione turned around and saw a group of six men standing by the hedges. One of which was her elder brother, accompanied by their father. Their father was dressed nicely in a suit jacket and stood beside a shorter, large man with a full beard. She could only assume it was the man her uncle Malicent frequently referred to as "Carmine," Joseph Carmine, Mordecai's father. To the left of Joseph were two well-dressed young men.

Hermione handed her grandfather back the pocket watch, and he cradled it in his hands.

"Thank you," she told Thomas, giving him a quick peck on the cheek before standing up.

Let's get this over with, she thought to herself.

Hermione walked with as much grace as she could muster, and it seemed as though all the eyes in the garden were watching her almost as immediately as she stood. But Hermione did her best to ignore them, keeping her eyes straight ahead and her head held high, trying to make it look effortless. And she'd almost made it over to them before she stumbled over her feet and nearly fell on her face.

Hermione cursed herself, wanting nothing more than to disappear. She was quite certain she heard one of the Barley sisters giggle before being chastised by their mother. In her daze, Hermione hardly noticed who'd caught her.

His hand was warm and strong, yet somehow managed to hold her's delicately. When she looked at him, she blushed. His face was stubbled with a brown beard that wrapped around a warm smile, which reached his catlike green eyes, though the smile wasn't mocking her. In fact, it was a rather charming smile.

"Are you alright?" he asked softly, maintaining his gaze.

He seemed to be waiting for a response, but Hermione had none.

"I apologize if I've overstepped. I know we haven't been properly acquainted," he told her.

Hermione wondered for a moment what he was referring to, then scolded herself. *The hand, you idiot*, she thought, staring at her hand in his own. Her breath caught in her throat as she broke his gaze to look at her father, Alfred, and brother Gianni. She saw Alfred nod, his dark hair neatly combed back, gray eyes noting the interaction between her and the young man, and beside him, with a strand of black hair dangling over his forehead, was a very serious-looking Gianni.

Hermione looked back at the young man holding her hand. "It's perfectly fine," Hermione told him as he offered her his other hand as well.

"At the risk of sounding too forward," he said, pausing to help her to her feet. "You look lovely, Hermione."

She took a deep breath, trying to regain her composure. "Thank you—um," she said, pulling her hands away and quickly dusting herself off.

"Mordecai," Joseph said, patting his son on the shoulder.

Hermione blinked a few times. She hadn't been completely sure that it was him—for a moment, she'd hoped— and in truth, his portrait didn't do him justice. Mordecai was taller than her brother, at least six feet three inches, and appeared to be a much more handsome version of his father. She could only assume that came from good breeding.

Joseph Carmine seemed to beam with pride at her surprise, though it dissipated when he looked to the second young man.

"And my second born, Peter Carmine," Joseph said.

Peter was tall and looked particularly thin standing beside Mordecai. He lacked the charm of his elder brother, appearing bored, from his dull gray eyes plastered on his long, narrow face that was only disturbed by a beak-like nose above the permanent frown that marked the corners of his lips. In fact, Hermione noted that his skin was the only thing that had any luster to it, as even Peter's suit was gray and bleak.

"As I was saying, Joseph. Unfortunately, Malicent couldn't attend this afternoon," Alfred told him. "One of his sons has fallen ill."

"Well, that's quite alright. Send them my best," Joseph said. "Gianni is more than a fine substitute for the day. But perhaps we could allow these two to get better acquainted with one another."

Hermione looked up at Mordecai, though he appeared more interested in the conversation than herself. But she did notice a small smirk on his lips.

"Yes, *but* she'll need a chaperone," Alfred said.

Hermione almost groaned aloud. She hadn't had a chaperone in nearly three years, and she'd partially hoped she wouldn't need one, considering they were engaged to be married. And at the moment, the most likely candidates for her chaperone were the least favorable in her opinion—namely, Rowan. And he'd be the first to volunteer.

But her preferred chaperones weren't available. Her mother was inside entertaining guests, so it couldn't be her. Her grandfather couldn't walk for long stretches of time.

Gianni would be with their father. Malicent wasn't here. And if it weren't one of them, she would rather be left to her own devices. She needed someone who would allow her to speak to Mordecai freely. She wanted to tell him about her interests in pursuing art, perhaps further schooling, and they could even decide on more structured and time-sensitive matters like children. But any traditional man would intervene in her carefully laid out plan. Though she knew having a chaperone was only proper, Hermione was growing more and more tired of propriety by the hour. What she needed was someone who, while they liked her, wouldn't care enough to disturb her plans.

She scanned the garden for her candidate, hoping they would appear, but couldn't find an ally. Then she saw Rowan walking toward them and just over his shoulder, her savior. She looked between Rowan and him twice.

"Christian!" Hermione called, smiling and waving him over.

Gianni raised an eyebrow, looking directly at her. He mouthed the word "no," his posture just as disapproving as his instruction, but Hermione ignored him. She turned her attention back to her other half brother, and relief flooded through her as Christian reached them at the same moment Rowan did.

"I think Christian would make an excellent chaperone," Hermione said to Alfred, hoping her suggestion would be considered.

"You do?" Gianni asked in disbelief.

She knew it was rhetorical and continued to look at her father.

"Really?" Alfred said. His gaze focused on Hermione as

though he were trying to read her mind. "Is this alright with you, Christian?"

Christian raised a brow at Hermione. Then he turned his attention to Mordecai and gave him a narrow-eyed appraisal, seeming to disapprove of his choice of attire. She assumed it was too stuffy for his taste, as Christian's suit was likely the less expensive of the two.

"Alfred, you can't possibly be considering this," Rowan said abruptly.

Alfred's eyes narrowed at Rowan. "And why wouldn't I, brother?" Alfred asked sternly. "Christian Carlisle is my blood, is he not? Are you implying that a son from our *shared* bloodline wouldn't be an appropriate escort for my daughter? Who could be better suited for chaperoning his sister?"

"Why—why—" Rowan stammered, his eyes darting between the Carmines and his fellow Mandrakes. "Why it may very well insult your guest," Rowan answered plainly.

A brief, awkward silence fell over the group.

Then Joseph spoke. "Eh, poppycock," he said. "Any son of Alfred Mandrake can well enough chaperone my boy. The means of Christian's birth are of no concern to me. It won't influence my opinion on any member of the Mandrake family."

Alfred nodded and exchanged a smile with Joseph. "Thank you, Joseph." His voice was calm and collected. But when he turned to Rowan, he shot a piercing glare at his younger brother. "Mind your tongue, Rowan."

"Forgive me, brother," Rowan said.

His fingers plucked nervously at his suit, straightening it. Then he turned on his heel and walked away.

Hermione took a deep breath. She wished she could

remind herself that Rowan's bark was worse than his bite, but she was quite sure the two were equal. Other than the slight disrespect her father had encountered, Alfred appeared calm and unperturbed. His gaze focused on his guests, and he nodded to himself.

"Now I'll show you the rest of the western grounds, where most of the statues reside," Alfred told Joseph. "Gianni, lead the way. Oh, and Christian—"

Christian turned to their father.

"Do keep them out of trouble," Alfred finished.

"Yes, Father," Christian said as they walked away. Christian's gaze focused on Hermione. "You're lucky I like you, kid," he joked. Then he looked at Mordecai. "Don't try anything funny I'm good at hexes, and I'm still her brother."

"Noted," Mordecai said.

"Perhaps we could walk to the pond," Hermione suggested. "The swans will be swimming about, and it's pleasant in the afternoons."

Mordecai agreed and allowed her to lead the way. They didn't speak a word to each other as they walked, and as she realized there were more people than she'd like at the pond, she wished she'd chosen elsewhere. The two couldn't sit together on the benches, as she didn't want to be stared at. And she had started to worry that she was offending him by remaining silent.

The pond was rather wide, and swans frequently bobbed their heads into it to fetch food. To the left of the pond, picnickers and couples chatted on the grass across the lawn area. The majority of the loyalists walking the perimeter of the pond belonged to the Augustine family, with their freckled pearly-white skin and thick black hair that bounced on their shoulders as they walked. Those that weren't walking were playfully sparring with members of the Barley family, willfully disheveling their dress shirts. Other members of the Barley family stretched out on the grass in pairs. The men and women ranged from brown to bronze skinned and mingled with others present. This didn't surprise Hermione as Selene Barley had agreed to marry William Augustine this past spring, and there was normally an intertwining of families afterward. After all, the marriages were meant to strengthen alliances and maintain a stronghold in the wizarding world; they weren't about love. Not even the affairs were about love.

Hermione was least happy to see that three of Oliver Graves's daughters were present; Eloise, Aurelia, and Christina—they were identical triplets, all with oval-shaped faces, almond-shaped gray eyes, and wavy golden hair. Each as much of a nuisance as the other.

"You've got to be shitting me," Christian muttered, apparently having noticed them as well.

Hermione glanced at him. She knew Christian rarely spoke to them but not that her disdain was shared. They were still his cousins, after all.

"Shall we sit in the grass then?" Mordecai asked.

"Well, perhaps—"

"Yes, let's sit as far away from my dreadful cousins as possible," Christian answered, interrupting Hermione and leading them away.

Hermione didn't know how long they could avoid an interaction with the Graves girls. She had the most disquieting sensation she was being watched as they sat on the grass. Christian didn't seem nearly as bothered by them, though he seemed to be searching for someone.

"Alright, I'll leave you two to it," Christian said to them. "I'll be over there."

He gestured toward two African American men sitting a few feet away. One of which Hermione recognized to be Tristan Barley, who smiled and waved when she looked over. She reciprocated the gesture, and just like that, Christian was gone.

"Well, alone at last," Mordecai said in jest.

"So, what would you like to talk about?" Hermione asked.

She knew where she wanted to begin, but she thought it best to ask him first, doing her best to remember her manners.

"Well, I suppose we could start with what your expectations are of me as a husband," Mordecai answered.

Hermione nodded and considered the question for a moment. It was similar enough to her own question.

"I would like to continue my studies," she started, trying to articulate her thoughts clearly. "And I would prefer to be with someone who is supportive of that."

"Yes," he said. "I wouldn't think of taking your studies from you. And I'd heard much about your art and couldn't imagine taking the opportunity to see it from the world."

Hermione shifted nervously. "Well . . . I'm sure that you want children, every Merlin man wants to carry on their legacy, no matter where they're from in Hampshire."

"I dare say you're right. I do want them. Others might not see me as tending to my duties or my position in my family if I didn't," he said softly. "The Graves would vocalize it, and the Van Dorens never miss a chance to start a rumor. The

Prices hate anyone that strays from tradition. But there's more to marriage, isn't there?"

"They would blame me, not you. My aunt sent me a letter about you being the most sought-after Carmine in ages."

"I wouldn't worry about it."

Hermione looked away from him and stared out at the pond. She could feel him staring at her.

"Well," Hermione started. "I suppose that—"

She stopped as his hand gripped her chin and gently turned her to face him.

"I'm in no rush," he said. "We'll have plenty of time to focus on those things *after* you've finished your studies."

He let go of her chin and lowered his hand.

After a moment, Mordecai said, "And I'm not sure what you've been told about me, but I promise you that I don't require much to be happy. The only traditional thing that will be involved in this marriage will be the manor I've inherited. All of our basic needs will be taken care of by staff. There are still many things I wish to do as well—travel, for instance. I would like to see more of the wizarding world. We are so limited in where we can go in Hampshire, and, in truth, I'd rather not travel by boat to leave it." He hesitated for a moment. "Your father's idea of joining Hampshire with the non-magical world is brilliant. It's an excellent campaign, and I hope he wins. I feel as though I've spent my entire life hiding from mundanes. Our new life together is the first glimmer of hope I've had in years."

"Me? Or my father's political campaign?"

"You, Hermione. Your father's political pursuits are what swayed me to continue with our marriage. I figured a man like that couldn't produce a close-minded child. The world is changing, and I want to be on the right side of history."

Hermione mulled over the thought. She knew he meant it as a compliment, but she hadn't expected their conversation to include politics. Her father's political run for senator of Hampshire in The Council was rarely at the forefront of her mind. She had been so focused on preparing for her first meeting with her betrothed that she hadn't given much thought to it.

She shook her head. "It's strange. I mean, strange to think we'll be getting married soon."

She looked up at the sky. It was clear and blue, empty except for the sun. Hermione imagined herself standing at the end of the aisle in the church, frozen, waiting, with nothing to hold her upright but her father's arm. She thought of marriage itself. The concept, but rather than marrying a man she loved, she would be growing to love a man she had barely just met. A Carmine, just like tradition dictated as fate would have it no other way.

"Yes," Mordecai said softly. "I suppose it is."

Death and Deceit

At dinner later, just after seven at night, Hermione sat down between her brothers, closer to the head of the table than she had ever been.

The chef had prepared a small feast, including a turkey, mashed potatoes, and green beans, which took up a significant portion of the center of the long wooden table. Most of the light in the room was coming from the golden chandeliers overhead. Last week, the living room had been repainted red, and the metallic scent still hung in the air, causing Hermione's nose to twitch. However, the smell didn't appear to be bothering anyone else at the table, though it was strange for her to see all eleven of her siblings at once.

In fact, she didn't think much could bother them tonight; they were all in such high spirits. And though her conversation with Mordecai had gone well, she couldn't help but think of all that awaited after they were married. She hoped for future stories of births, both of artistic and child-endowing measure; family dinners, with her husband, herself, and their own brood; but not the deaths that came with time or battles that she knew she couldn't predict. And though she hated to admit it, the thought of them welled up inside her and made her want to scream.

"Everything alright, Hermione?"

Hermione looked up, only now realizing she'd been staring blankly at her dinner plate.

"Yes, Ares," Hermione said, pushing down her thoughts. "How's Francine?"

Ares raised a brow as if he wasn't sure how to answer the question.

Ares Aristotle Mandrake was only seven years older than her, born in 1968 on the same day and month as Christian Carlisle. Though they differed in parentage. He more closely resembled his mother with pale skin, sapphire-blue eyes, and wavy brown hair. He was handsome and six feet tall with broad shoulders and attracted women with ease.

"Hmmm . . . she's quite well, *considering*," Ares said before drinking from his wine glass.

"Considering?" Hermione repeated.

"She's with child," Christian said as he shoveled another bite of food into his mouth.

Ares rolled his eyes at the contention in Christian's voice.

"I hardly see how that's your concern," Ares said sternly.

"Is it yours?" Hermione asked.

Christian scoffed. "Of course it's his, dear sister. Word on the street is that Ares has been making bastards nonstop. Tell me, brother, do you intend on taking a wife any time soon or simply continuing to make our father's life more difficult with every young woman you keep company with?"

"At least when people hear my children say the name of their father, they'll be held in better regard in civil company than your future children," Ares retorted. "I'm simply continuing to grow our house, *brother*."

Ares had spoken the word barely loud enough for them to hear, though harsh enough to ensure the insult was implied.

Ares, who constantly found himself walking the precarious line between acceptance and scrutiny on account of his birth, was born as the result of a clandestine affair between their father and his distant cousin, Alison, and was initially labeled as a bastard. However, after their father's first wife, Fonda Abbot, passed away during childbirth, Alfred became responsible for Gianni and their newborn twin sons, Alfred II and Elderic II. So in an act of love, or perhaps redemption, Alfred married Alison and publicly legitimized Ares as his son, silencing naysayers and seeking to provide Ares the status he deserved. Yet, within the wizarding community, opinions remained divided. While some embraced Alfred's efforts, others still clung to traditional beliefs, labeling Ares as a 'legitimized bastard.' The insult of bastardy was compounded by the discovery that his mother was the bastard daughter of Elderic Mandrake. Bastardy was a great shame to bear, especially if done alone. But unlike Christian Carlisle, Ares bore two Mandrake parents, and for loyalist families with traditionalist beliefs, that made him more worthy of their respect than Christian.

"I'm sure whatever woman you've drudged up won't be regarded with the same respect," Christian said.

Ares shrugged slightly and appeared to consider his words. "But my children will thrive."

"Enough." Their father's stern voice cut through the overlapping conversations, and the room fell silent.

Hermione bit her lip, nicking it, as she looked between Ares and Christian, concerned the two might come to blows. Their father was known for his even temper. Perhaps too lenient in light of her brothers' current squabble. But nevertheless, he rose from his chair. All eyes were on him as he raised his glass.

"I would like to make a toast," Alfred said, scanning the entire room before he continued. "First to Hermione—"

Hermione had to suppress a gasp. Her throat was dry, and she could hear her heartbeat in her skull, but she attempted to ignore it, forcing herself to put on a brave face when she felt anything but.

"Today, you've taken a step toward building a new life that strengthens our family as a whole and secures your future and those of your children." He smiled at Hermione, and she warmed. Then he turned back to the rest of the family. "And to family. It is so rare that I have all of you in one room together. Everyone that I love at one table. And I know you're all in different phases of your life, but I must tell you all that I stand here now, a proud father, husband, and brother. Though we may argue and find ourselves at odds with one another, we must always remain *united* against our true enemies. The same blood that pumps through all your veins is that of Merlin. A name that demands respect, but when all is said and done, we are all we have. Everyone you can trust is within this room. And though many have tried, we are the only ones that can truly bring our family to its knees."

Christian stared down at the table before raising his eyes

to look at Ares. Ares's face had reddened slightly, but neither spoke a word to the other.

"To family," she heard her mother repeat, raising her glass accordingly.

"To family," Gianni repeated, doing the same.

He glanced at Hermione and seemed to be suppressing a smile.

"To family," the rest of the table said in unison.

Hermione felt air push the word passed her lips and warm her heart.

On the morning of July fifth, she woke to a loud shout from the floor below and a pungent smell that stung her nose. *Smoke,* was her first thought. Either an elf in the kitchens had burned breakfast or her brothers, particularly the twins—Fillian or Fredrick—had left the iron on the other's shirt. This solemn morning had been disturbed by petty bickering erupting into riotous yelling. But, slowly, as Hermione descended the stairs, she caught wind of a charcoal-like smell, though what it was emanating from she could not see. She presumed it was on the dining table as a bevy of men stood around it, working on something meticulously, while the serving elves huddled in a corner, wide-eyed with blood stains on their aprons.

Hermione began to walk toward the kitchen, but Gianni stopped her.

"Gianni—"

"Stay back," Gianni said, grabbing her roughly by the arm and yanking her back.

Hermione hesitated. She wanted to argue but was still disoriented from the early hour. Her brain was in a fog, but she was quite certain the thing on the table was not an animal.

She looked up at Gianni as if she could read his thoughts. His eyes slid to the floor, his look weighted with sorrow and fatigue. She had never seen him so reserved, and she had begun to fear the worse. Hermione's heart lurched in her chest. She could think of few things that would give her brother such a look of stoic resignation.

A heavyset man in a gray wool trenchcoat walked over to them with a look that expressed the greatest sympathy.

"Dr. Thistle thinks it best to make him look—" The man hesitated. He glanced at Hermione and then turned his attention back to Gianni. "*Presentable*. And I do believe Malicent is on his way over," he said, continuing to speak, though Hermione wasn't sure her brother was hearing him. The man wore a necklace baring the medallion of the Saints, declaring his rank in the sect of Hampshire around his neck. "I know that all of this is quite difficult to digest right now— but be that as it may, Gianni, the Mandrake family is now entrusted to you."

Hermione's heart sank in her chest as she tried to look around the clergyman and past the bumping shoulders of Dr. Thistle and his rough assemblage of assistants. She soon realized, betwixt Eric Graves ordering two Augustine men about and a woman she recognized as Barbara Fauntleroy casting mending spells, that the charred remains of her father lay on the table.

Liars at a Funeral

Gianni's first proclamation of leadership was to postpone her wedding until October to allow their family a mourning period. Hermione wasn't opposed to this in the slightest. With a heavy heart and her father not yet buried, she could think of nothing she wanted to do less than attend a wedding dress fitting. Between her mother sobbing and her own sobbing, she was doing all she could not to become absorbed in her grief.

She cautiously descended the stairs the day of the funeral, dressed in the same black dress she'd worn to the garden party, with her curls voluminous and makeup minimal. Her mother was being consoled by the Graves women in the living room, and Gianni was in the kitchen, speaking to a few heir apparents and family heads with their uncle Malicent by his side. She was grateful that Gianni could manage his familial duties in his grief and even more grateful that she could slip out into the gardens without anyone noticing her.

Hermione sat on the same bench she'd sat on with her grandfather just days ago. The fountain was gurgling loudly behind her, and she was trying to focus on the sound to drown out her thoughts. But the more she tried, the harder she failed, and reality would sink in again, loudly proclaiming that now her father, grandfather, and hundreds of thousands of others were gone from a day that had since become infamous.

"Fortuna Bay Massacre."

Hermione jumped at the sound of her brother's voice. But he didn't seem to notice as he sat beside her.

"Can you believe this shit?" Christian said, holding up the day's newspaper. "The families of millions mourn the loss of the men, women, and children within the bay that day— but it doesn't quite cover the families that were entirely lost. Does it? I calculated at least twenty-four, and the number grows larger when you count smaller families without children."

He seemed entirely unaware of the fact that Hermione was only half-present in their conversation, while the other half was focusing on the cool metal of the time trinket in her pocket. A relic she had stumbled upon in the dining room, intending to return it to her grandfather when he arrived the morning of her wedding, unaware that fate would intervene. Now, it held the weight of a secret they had shared, forever reminding her of the profound loss she had endured.

She had replaced the watch fob with a silver rope chain so she could wear it around her neck when she wanted to keep her grandfather close.

"There were entire bloodlines lost, entire family histories

wiped out by dragonfire, and all these journalists can talk about is those lucky enough to have not been there."

But was it luck, she thought to herself. *Could they call it that?*

She traced the words engraved on the trinket with her thumb.

"The MCU is turning a blind eye to it. Of course, they're so easily bought off by the Dimitris after Father's death. Alfred Mandrake was well respected, but in the end, it meant nothing."

Memento mori, she thought to herself. *Remember to die.*

"And I hate to say it, but Ares is right," Christian said. "Yes, of course, there is a mole among the loyalists, but funneling all our resources into finding them isn't wise. Now would be the time to strike. They wouldn't see it coming. If Gianni keeps going this route, time won't be on our side when we do strike."

Time. Hermione's heart skipped a beat. *We need time,* she thought, and her heart began to beat faster.

She pulled out the trinket and held it in her hands. "Christian, you're a genius."

Christian cocked a brow. "Um . . . *thanks.* What did I say?"

"Don't you get it?" Hermione said to him. "Time! We need *time.*"

"Yes, I've just said that—"

"No, you said time isn't on our side, but it is!" she exclaimed, showing him the trinket.

Christian glanced at the trinket and then at her.

"*Okay,* a pocket watch," Christian said, his eyes filled

with a mixture of confusion and concern. "Perhaps we should go inside and have Dr. Thistle take a look at you."

Hermione rolled her eyes. "No, Christian, this isn't any ordinary pocket watch. Grandfather invented it. He'd left it on the dinner table last week before he went home."

"Well, I didn't know grandfather was such an avid collector of—" He paused for a moment. "What is it exactly?"

Hermione opened the pocket watch. Christian leaned in and looked into it.

"What is that?" he asked, leaning closer and closer until Hermione shut it.

Christian shook his head as though trying to pull himself out of a trance.

"It's a time trinket," Hermione whispered. "Grandfather invented one that uses memories. And all we need is one memory to save Father. We only need to go back a few days or maybe *months* before, and then we pop back like nothing ever happened."

"Merlin's beard, Hermione!" Christian said, barely raising his voice. "Do you know what would happen if the MCU knew we had one of these?"

"Yes, I do, but—"

"Then why in seven hells would you be carrying it around?"

"Don't you see?" Hermione said, urging him to listen. "We can use it to go back and save Father. Perhaps we could save everyone. We just—we just need—*Gianni.*"

Christian rolled his eyes.

"*Gianni?*" he repeated dubiously. "Were you not listening to me?"

"No—*Yes*, I was. That's the thing. You're both right. We

need to know who the mole is to save Father, but we also need to confront the Dimitris."

Hermione got to her feet and clasped the pocket watch around her neck. Christian stood and frantically shook his head.

"*We?* What on earth are you thinking?" Christian said. "You can't seriously be thinking of doing what I think you're suggesting."

"No, *we're* going to," Hermione told him.

Then she turned on her heel and began to walk toward the house.

"And what makes you think I'll go along with your little plan?" Christian asked as he followed her. "Hmmm?"

"Because you're curious how it works, because you don't want Dad dead any more than I do, because you're not going to let me go anywhere *alone* when the future of our house depends on me marrying Mordecai Carmine, and *because—*" Hermione paused, stopping in her tracks and looking up at him, waiting for him to finish her sentence.

Christian sighed and nodded his head. "I'm your brother, and quite frankly, you couldn't cast a memory charm to save your life."

Hermione kept her eyes forward, navigating through the crowd of people with Christian beside her, both nodding their heads at loyalists murmuring their condolences. She did note that she didn't see the Carmines anywhere among the sea of faces, which had started to worry her when they'd turned down a narrow hallway. They passed their father's office and stopped next to an enchanted portrait of their great-grandfather, Damon Mandrake. It had a nasty habit of blinking and an even nastier one of wailing if it was covered.

She suppressed a shiver at the sight of it. Christian ignored it entirely. He pressed a panel in the wall, and a hidden door creaked open. He stepped through first, and Hermione followed, shutting the door behind her. They made their way down a dimly lit stone staircase and heard whispering as they reached the bottom.

"I swear that's all I know," a male voice croaked out.

"All?" Malicent said sharply. "That couldn't possibly be *all* you know."

The man grunted and wheezed. "Please, Gianni—"

"You have no right to speak to him," another interrupted in a stern, velvety voice.

Hermione peered around the corner to get a look at the speaker. Eric Graves stood above a stranger on the ground, glaring down at him. The stranger's face was swollen and bruised, his hair clung to his head, and the clothes he wore were in tatters and stained with fresh blood. His feet were bare and dirty.

Gianni stood against a gray stone wall, staring at the ceiling, deep in thought. Mordecai stood beside him, speaking to him, and though Hermione couldn't read lips, she could tell he was comforting her brother. For a moment, relief flooded through her. Gianni may have been trying to bury his pain, but he wasn't alone. Their family still had allies, and they still had each other.

Her elation withered as Eric Graves's voice cut through her thoughts.

"Not after all you've done," Eric said. "Are you even ashamed of it?"

The stranger looked too afraid to answer.

"Yes? *No?* Nothing to say?" Eric said.

He flicked his wand, casting a hex at the stranger, causing them to writhe in pain on the ground. Eric waited for a few minutes before waving his wand again to stop the hex, and the stranger gasped for air.

"Come on now," Joseph said as the elder Carmine crossed the room. "Rowan, we know you're a good man, deep down . . . we just need you to answer the question."

Hermione blinked a few times. She forced herself to imagine the stranger without a swollen face and hair drenched in sweat—and found the familiar scowl of her uncle.

She watched as Joseph Carmine crouched down beside her uncle on the ground.

"And we need to know who it was that you told," Joseph said.

"Dimitri," Rowan said weakly.

As Hermione took a step closer, an unforeseen misstep betrayed her presence, causing her to stumble and emit a high-pitched squeak as she grabbed Christian's arm to steady herself. The sudden disruption drew Eric's attention, his keen senses zeroing in on the source of the sound. Startled, he turned toward Hermione, his eyes narrowing as he noticed her and Christian. His eyes scanned their faces as if trying to decipher how long they'd been standing there.

"Which Dimitri!" Malicent shouted at Rowan.

"*Malicent,*" Eric said in warning.

Malicent turned, and his eyes widened. Then all eyes were on Hermione and Christian.

Hermione gulped. "Um . . . sorry, I just—"

"Hermione," Rowan said weakly.

His words were just above a whisper, and Hermione felt a surge of anger. He was terrible. He had always been terrible to her, but to think that he had betrayed her father. His own brother.

Rowan moved to sit up but winced in pain and lay back down. She was angry but wasn't sure if he deserved to die. Though she was sure at least two of the men in this room wanted Rowan dead.

"You shouldn't be in here," Gianni said suddenly.

"Gianni, I—"

"Go back upstairs," Gianni said, interrupting her.

"But you don't understand—"

"*Now*," Gianni ordered.

But Hermione didn't move.

"And you—why on earth would you bring her down here?" Gianni said to Christian.

Christian hesitated for a moment, looking between Hermione and Gianni.

Then he sighed and said, "She wants to know who killed our father, and seeing as the cellars are where most meetings are held, I'd guessed you'd be here—and apparently, I was right. But I didn't know you'd be torturing our uncle." He shrugged at the statement and glanced at Rowan. "I know that Rowan isn't better than this, but you certainly are Gianni."

"Oh, come to lecture me?" Gianni asked. "Shall I guess what you're going to say? Plan stating that I, the long-standing heir apparent, the only one trained to handle these matters, don't know what to do? That I'm somehow incapable of performing the duties of my birthright."

Christian didn't answer.

"If you hadn't noticed, brother, we're at war," Gianni said. "Did you expect my handling of things to be pretty?"

Christian scoffed. "Do you think torturing him to death will get you an answer?"

Eric flicked another hex at Rowan. Rowan's body began to shake as he gnashed his teeth uncontrollably and boils rose on his skin. In between his strangled gasps, Rowan looked as though he were trying to form a word.

"Wait!" Hermione shouted, drawing the men's attention. "He's trying to say something."

Eric stopped the hex, and Rowan gasped.

He coughed and spluttered for a moment. "*Carmichael*," Rowan wheezed. "Carmichael Dimitri."

"The bastard," Joseph said, cocking a brow and looking to Eric.

"The bastard *and* his dragon," Eric corrected.

"Carmichael, really?" Mordecai said to the men. "Why would they trust him? He and Hermione are the same age, but I can't imagine he'd be Horace's first choice. If they'd sent him—"

"It wouldn't have been what we expected," Joseph said, interrupting his son. "That is why they would choose him. The boy's dragon would be of riding age but not large enough to draw attention in the skies. They wouldn't have known what hit them until it was too late."

"Well, if the journal was given to the boy, then it was given to the boy," Eric said matter-of-factly. He looked down at her uncle and tutted. *"Tsk. Tsk. Tsk.* All that matters now is that the enemy has declared war, and we must act."

Gianni nodded. He took a deep breath and turned to Mordecai.

"Mordecai," Gianni said, "gather the heads and their heirs in the garden. Tell them I'll be making an announcement at nightfall."

Mordecai gave a small bow and walked swiftly past Hermione, avoiding eye contact with her as he pushed past Christian and went up the stairs.

Gianni walked up to her and leaned close, his voice so low that only she could hear. "I'm sorry you had to see that." Then he stepped away from her. "I need you to go to your room. *Please.*"

"Gianni, you have to listen to me," Hermione said as Christian grabbed her arm.

"Let's go," Christian said.

"I have to tell you—"

"We'll talk later," Gianni said.

Hermione nodded and willingly followed Christian back up the stairs, trying to keep up with her brother as he pulled her along. She looked back over her shoulder, staring down the dimly lit staircase. Gianni was gone, and their voices had become whispers again. Then there was a flash of red light and a guttural cry. Her stomach seized as a familiar charcoal-like smell wafted by her nose, and she swallowed down vomit.

Bad Plan

July 12, 1996

Gianni never came to speak to her. She faintly remembered staring out her bedroom window into the garden last night. At some point, she must have fallen asleep waiting for him because, when she woke, her room was dark. Outside, not a single star shimmered in the night sky, but by the fountain, there was a roaring bonfire, and Gianni stood with his back to it. Twenty-eight men gathered around him in a crescent moon shape, their shadows dancing with the flame, their eyes on her half brother. The only sound was the strong male voice she'd grown accustomed to, spurring those men into action.

Hermione shook off the memory. It was a new day.

She straightened her coat and looked at herself in the foyer's mirror. She took a deep breath.

"And where are you off to?" Christian asked.

Hermione hesitated. She knew he would try to talk her out of it, but she also needed his help.

"I've been thinking about our next move," Hermione said, gesturing for him to follow her.

His brow furrowed, but he didn't ask any questions. Instead, he followed her out onto their front porch and shut the door behind him. The moment Hermione heard the door lock, she began to speak.

"The Dimitris are hosting a birthday party for their cousin today in Eighthgate," Hermione said. "I was going to find you and ask if you could *disguise* me as one of the Singleton twins so I could get into the party to steal Carmichael Dimitri's memory, then travel back in time and save our father."

Her brother sighed.

"Hermione—" Christian paused and shook his head. "Are you insane?"

"We can't just sit around waiting for the war to start," Hermione said defensively.

"I won't let you go alone! You could get caught or worse. It's too dangerous," Christian said.

Hermione didn't answer. Instead, she tried to ignore his concerns. Christian Carlisle was normally an optimist, and sometimes he was reckless, coming and going by way of magic around mundanes, and naysayers' scornful words rarely left a mark on him. Today, he was not that Christian. She needed *that* Christian.

She sighed and began to walk away. However, Christian wasn't far behind. They walked along the vaulted colonnade that stretched the length of the freshly mowed lawn to their home's front gate. Hermione often wondered which of their gaudier ancestors had deemed the structure necessary.

"You know it's a terrible idea, Hermione," Christian said

as they walked down the long gravel path leading to their front gate. "If you would take a moment to see reason—"

"No, Christian," Hermione said.

Christian groaned.

"But you're no good at the duplici charm—"

"And that's why I'm asking *you* to do it," Hermione said, interrupting him again.

Hermione knew that Christian was right; she had never cast a duplici charm successfully. She had managed to hide a blemish or two, even widen her eyes for a full hour, but never change her whole appearance. Someone with an advanced mastery of charms could cast a duplici charm that would change not only their physical appearance but their voice as well, effectively becoming a copy of another person for a time. Non-magiks typically called wizards and witches doing so "doppelgängers." But Hermione was a novice. Mastering charms took years of patience and practice. And the duplici charm wore off if the user told too many lies—but Hermione wasn't worried about lying. She was worried about getting out of the Dimitri mansion afterward.

"And you really don't think they would notice that two of their cousins aren't themselves?" Christian retorted.

Hermione rolled her eyes. "You're the one always saying that the Singleton twins were too prudish to even speak to their cousins."

"Yes, but they still *spoke* during school," Christian said. "They may have been awfully rude, but they certainly *spoke*. And like I said before, *it's too dangerous.*"

"Okay," Hermione said. "Then, by all means, come with me. No one will suspect a thing. We'll act *perfectly* dreadful to everyone we encounter at the party, perhaps make a snide remark or three each, find Carmichael, and steal his memory—"

"Which I'll have to do because you never mastered the Forget Me Not spell either," Christian said, stepping in front of her. "Bear in mind, I'd be taking the bigger risk here. If we're discovered—"

"But we *won't* be. Think about it. How would they know we're coming?" Hermione stated. "Everything went according to their plan. Father is dead, they control the Magical Crime Unit, they're probably only focused on celebrating little Susan—and their big win. It'll be easy. I promise, we'll pop in and pop out."

Christian shook his head and set his jaw.

"I don't like this, Hermione," Christian said.

He opened the metal gate, and it let out a shrill creak. Hermione shivered at the sound and followed Christian through it. He reapplied the protection barriers and warding spells before turning back to her.

"What if the Singletons show up?"

"Well, I can manage a freezing spell," Hermione said sternly.

Christian considered her answer for a moment and, when he'd decided it was satisfactory, gestured for her to follow him. She eagerly did, and before she knew it, they'd walked five blocks and turned into an alley.

"Alright, give me their pictures," Christian said.

Hermione pulled out last week's newspaper from her inner coat pocket. Her heart lurched as she flipped past the obituary section, glimpsing a sliver of her father's picture before she reached the engagement announcement section. In it, Alaina and Tanner Singleton stood beside their respective partners. Alaina was a pale woman with pin-straight black hair, sparse eyelashes, and heavily hooded eyes that appeared bored in the image. Her twin brother, Tanner, was equally pale but taller and bonier with sunken cheeks that gave his face an almost sickly appearance.

Christian pointed to the ground in front of him. "Stand here."

Hermione obeyed, positioning herself to face him.

Christian analyzed the image for a few moments and took a deep breath. Then he pulled out his wand and shut his eyes. He furrowed his brow and clenched his jaw as the seconds ticked by until the world felt eerily still.

Then his eyes snapped open, and Hermione nearly jumped.

"Geminus," Christian said, flourishing his wand.

A cool breeze brushed over her skin. Then her jaw seemed to stretch downward while the skin on her face pulled back tightly, and her hair straightened and flattened against her head. Her eyes burned, forcing her to blink back tears. As she took a deep breath, a wave of nausea overtook her, and she heaved onto the sidewalk. When she found her bearings again, staring into the puddle beside her vomit, she saw the pale face of Alaina Singleton.

When Hermione stood up straight and looked down at her hands, they were also pale, as if someone had washed away the brown in her skin.

"Wow, Christian," she began but stopped as she heard the unfamiliar voice that passed her lips.

Hermione shook her head at herself. *It's alright, Hermione,* she told herself. *It's just the spell.* And Christian had done a terrific job of it.

But when she turned to look at where her brother had been standing, she jumped. Her heart beat rapidly in her chest as she looked up at the slender, pale man in front of her. Hermione was certain that Tanner Singleton might be handsome if he didn't look like he was haunted by his own existence. She would almost be frightened if she didn't already know that it was Christian standing beside her.

"Stop looking at me like that," Christian groaned as he stretched. "You don't look too good yourself."

"Humph," Hermione said. Then she tightened her coat's belt so it fit snugly around her waist. She huffed out air, hoping to gather her senses; despite one phase of their plan being complete, they still had a long way to go. "Come on. We've got a lot of ground to cover if we're going to make it to the party in time."

Get the Memory. Use the Time Trinket. Return Home.

July 12, 1996

Fifteen minutes later, a quarter before two in the afternoon, they passed through a massive gate and continued down a narrow drive with rolling green lawns on both sides. Hermione carried a black box with a matching bow on top of it, hoping the dress would be to Susan Dimitri's liking, with Christian surveying their surroundings with interest.

On the lawn to their left, a group of older gentlemen were playing a croquet game, and he nodded at them as they passed.

To their right was a domed stone building with a glass roof and large oak doors, which Hermione would have mistaken for an aviary if it weren't for the size of the reptilian beast she saw entering it with a blond-haired man dressed in all black. Hermione had seen two dragons in a field at the Hampshire Zoo when she was six with her grandfather, and without him having explained that they'd come from eggs, she was sure she might have doubted that they'd grown from anything at all. She would have assumed they were once mountains beckoned from their slumber by the White Witch's witchcraft, and that was why Morgana and her descendants alone could raise and tame them. As such, the Dimitris were not only known for their dragons; they were feared for them. The Dimitris were the Mandrakes' only real rival, and they'd successfully weakened her family.

"Don't stare," Christian said, squeezing her arm.

Hermione looked at him, recognizing the seriousness in his tone.

"Remember, the Singletons have been here before," Christian told her.

Hermione nodded silently. *Focus, Hermione,* she chided herself. *Focus.*

"Alright there, Tanner?" one man shouted in a gruff voice.

A chill snaked up Hermione's spine.

Christian looked past her. "Quite fine, really," he responded calmly.

She turned in time to see the man nod his head, approving of the answer, while he scratched his gray beard. Hermione was certain she recognized the gray-haired man but couldn't place him.

"We'll have to pop some champagne to celebrate later," he said.

Christian forced a laugh in response. "I'd prefer whiskey, Uncle."

The man nodded slowly and smiled a ghoulish smile that made Hermione's insides turn.

"I look forward to it," the man said. "I'll see you inside, my boy."

Christian nodded his head and pulled Hermione along. Hermione felt a twinge of fear as her feet crunched over gravel, nearly tripping twice before they reached the front stairs, where they could see the crowds through the windows. The Dimitri mansion was certainly not a home to scoff at. It was the pride of Eighthgate, home to the Dimitri family and their dragons. But in Eighthgate, the neighborhoods were larger, with crowded rows of buildings, housing a multitude of lesser-known families that depended on the Dimitri's ten loyalists for survival.

"Where is your head?" Christian said sharply, pulling her in front of him.

"Who was that?" Hermione whispered, gesturing back at the men on the lawn.

"Nicholas Dimitri," Christian answered.

Hermione scoffed. "You mean the man that crippled our grandfather."

"Don't start," Christian said sternly. "Don't forget this was your idea. You were the one who wanted to come here. Who did you think you would see? There's not a single friendly face here. That's why we have to be careful." He held her shoulders, his expression serious, as he released a sigh that did nothing to soften his features. "Why do you think I made that stupid whiskey comment? You think I would ever want to share a drink with that man? *No*, but Tanner Singleton would."

"Nicholas Dimitri could have killed him," Hermione

retorted. "You can't expect me to just smile like nothing has happened. He —"

"Yes, I do," Christian said. "As long as we're the Singletons, he is your uncle and mine, and that means we have to show him respect. All we have to do is get the memory from Carmichael and leave. Right?"

"Right," Hermione replied.

"Then we'll figure out the rest later," Christian said. "For now, just breathe. We'll get through this—*somehow*."

Hermione took a deep breath and followed her brother up the stairs. Christian opened the door and looked inside the mansion, stopping to check that Hermione was following him. She was, of course, but she had the strangest feeling in the pit of her stomach that she should turn back. But then she remembered all that had been lost. Infiltrating the Dimitri mansion was far less frightening than the war that would come to pass if they did not save their father.

When Hermione stepped inside, she was almost instantly surrounded by tall women coming to regard the black box in her hands and congratulate her on Alaina's marriage. Christian walked away from her to speak with several men with gloomy expressions, gesturing toward Hermione as if to say he was going to blend into the crowd. Glancing around the room, Hermione's heart sank; Carmichael Dimitri was nowhere to be found in the sea of partygoers.

"Forgive me," one young woman said. "I was most impertinent when we last spoke."

She was a pale woman of small stature with dark brown hair that fell to her shoulders and dark green eyes. She didn't look much older than Hermione and wore a silver dragon necklace around her neck.

"Oh, well—" Hermione hesitated, considering how someone like Alaina might respond. "*Yes*, you were."

The young woman let out a nervous laugh. "Well, no matter. I hear poor Mordecai will be saddled with that Mandrake girl, and I wonder if he's regretting it now, considering—"

"Considering," Hermione repeated, interrupting her.

"*Considering* that her darling father won't be in attendance due to *circumstances*. That's all dear Helena is saying," a blond girl said, perking up in the circle of guests. "Here, let me just give this to Cheaves."

The blond girl took the black box from her hands and snapped her fingers at an elf. The elf hurried over, and she handed it off to them, grimacing as he left.

"Ugh . . . did it touch you, Lily?" Helena asked, her face contorted in disgust.

"No, luckily," the blond replied, dusting off her hands. "I swear they are getting more bold, but it's no matter. No need to talk about such unsettling matters when we should be celebrating."

Lily perked up and smiled at Hermione.

Hermione returned her grin. "I suppose we could sit in the parlor."

Lily and Helena quickly agreed with her idea, and Hermione followed them down a hall, passing a kitchen and a few closed doors. Partygoers greeted her as she passed with a smile and occasionally a hug, which she would reciprocate, hoping she appeared genuine.

As they sat down in the parlor, Hermione heard a muffled argument between two men. When she looked to the back doors that led to the garden, her heart skipped a beat.

Carmichael Dimitri stood outside arguing with Horace Dimitri, the head of the Dimitri family.

Horace Dimitri was tall with olive skin and short golden hair that matched his mutton chop beard. He was of pristine breeding, pure Morgana blood, and bore the proud features of the dragon line he was born into. He rode a green dragon named Laeros, the second-largest dragon in the magical world. The thought of taming such a large beast forced Hermione to suppress a shiver. The man was intimidating beyond comprehension, and at the moment, she was quite sure the look Horace was giving his bastard son could level cities.

Carmichael's eyes were downcast, and his ginger hair was slicked back. He appeared to mumble something, which didn't seem to lessen his father's fury.

"Oh, you didn't hear, did you, Alaina?" Helena said, drawing Hermione's attention. She leaned in closer to her until she was only a few inches away. "The great bastard was consorting with a Mandrake—that's how they got the journal."

"Journal?" Hermione said, feigning confusion.

"Yes, logs. They had every event Alfred Mandrake would attend all the way to September," Helena told her, appearing to revel in the fact that she wasn't aware.

Hermione's heart sank in her chest.

"All the way to September," Hermione repeated.

She felt as though she were trying to reconcile the thought in her mind, to sort through the confusing questions and muddled emotions in her heart. But the most important question was: *why now?*

Of course, they wanted us to look weak in front of the Carmines, Hermione chided herself.

Helena nodded eagerly and leaned back into the blue armchair she sat in with a look that made Hermione wonder what Helena and Alaina's relationship was like. She truly believed the two women may have made better enemies than family.

"I doubt my future father-in-law wants us consorting with the enemy," Lily said, plucking an invisible piece of lint off her clothing. "I mean obviously a Mandrake can't be trusted, and Abel told me that Carmichael hadn't consulted him about his plans beforehand," she stated matter-of-factly.

Helena gasped. "I can only imagine how displeased he is," she said, shaking her head. "And all while planning your wedding. He must be furious."

Hermione nodded silently, taking in the information. She had never seen Horace's ten sons, though she'd learned their names from birth, marriage, and death records that were upheld in the Church of Hampshire in Arok. The record book was thousands of pages and rivaled the size of the *Oxford English Dictionary,* but what she learned from it was gravely important to the future of her house when one considered knowing their enemies.

She knew Abel was the eldest son and heir apparent of the Dimitri family, and she'd concluded that he was newly engaged to Lily. Her uncle Malicent had disclosed to her that Abel was intelligent—and likely the best chance for a future treaty—and his right-hand man was Horace's second eldest son, Laertes, who was named for his father's dragon. Laertes rode the oldest and largest dragon in the magical world—Malthor, known as the

"Black Dread." A black dragon that hadn't been ridden since the end of the slave trade in 1808, whose prior rider was Vladimir Dimitri. She hoped neither Laertes nor Malthor was nearby.

"And to make matters worse, I think he might've tried to get your brother involved," Lily whispered to Hermione.

Hermione feigned shock. "I hadn't heard anything."

Helena and Lily exchanged a look.

"You must be positively relieved that your dear husband didn't get tangled up with Carmichael and them," Helena said, changing the subject. "Bjorn has always been a smart man. Imagine the chaos if he had. Count your blessings, I suppose. Is Bjorn enjoying his travels?"

"Oh, yes, of course," Hermione answered.

The instant she'd answered, she felt her face tighten, and her hand flew to her chin. It was just as she'd feared. Her chin had shrunk to its normal size.

You idiot, she chided herself.

If one lie could cause her chin to return to normal, what else could happen?

"Are you alright, Alaina?" Lily questioned. "You look flustered."

"It's just a lot to take in," she said.

Hermione held her breath, hoping it was a passable lie, and sighed in relief when nothing happened. She looked back out the windows and noticed that Horace and Carmichael were gone.

Damn, she thought. *Where did they go?*

She managed to regain her composure and smile for a few seconds, but as soon as she looked at her counterparts, neither woman looked convinced by her statement.

"Are you—" Lily started, then lowered her voice. "*Pregnant?*"

"What? No," Hermione said sharply.

The women looked relieved.

Helena wiped invisible sweat off her brow. "I'm glad, I was beginning to think that was why you'd been in such a rush to get married to Bjorn. I mean, he's *lovely*, but if you'd made a play for Mordecai—"

"We'd have the Carmines," Lily finished for her.

"Yes, well—" Hermione hesitated. She was beginning to feel very dizzy and was quite sure this was what these women considered polite conversation.

But as if the saints were smiling down on her, there was a terrific stir in the kitchen, crescendoing into an uproar. Her brother, still disguised as Tanner Singleton, bolted through the parlor and out the back doors with men chasing after him. Someone sent a red spell flying that made the windows in the room burst open, sending shards of glass everywhere and Hermione ducking behind the chair she sat in.

"After him!" a male voice shouted.

Without a second thought, Hermione got caught up in the crowd of angry partygoers rushing outdoors. The instant she was outside, she felt relieved. The summer air filled her lungs, and the sun beamed down on the hedge maze that made up half the garden.

"Split up!" the same man shouted, and Hermione leaped at the sight of the man. "Find him!" Horace commanded.

Hermione felt winded, and her thoughts seemed to keep bouncing from anxiety to terror and back again. But she forced herself to run into the hedge maze, hoping she would find her brother first. If the Dimitris found him first, what would happen then? The idea of losing Christian the same month as their father made her heart lurch in pain. She knew the only thing in life that was promised was death, but he was her brother, and she wouldn't let him die.

Her legs pumped underneath her as she made turn after turn, hoping there would be a break somewhere in the maze. She managed to keep running for a few minutes, but as soon as she reached a clearing, Hermione stopped to catch her breath.

In the center of the clearing was a fountain, and she had half a mind to dunk her head into it. When she checked her appearance in the water, she groaned and sank to the ground. She was getting tired of being Alaina Singleton. Somewhere in the distance, men were shouting as their feet beat the ground unforgivingly.

As the sun began to set, she finally caught her breath and went to stand, but when she turned around, her heart nearly stopped.

"Christian," she said, rushing to the other side of the fountain.

He looked like himself, though he had a small cut on his forehead, and his clothes were dirty.

"What happened?" Hermione asked.

Christian raised his hand, holding a vial with a glowing pale-blue liquid inside.

"Got into *fisticuffs* with Carmichael in the kitchen," Christian joked with a smirk.

His voice was weak as he sat up, wincing in pain and holding his left ribs.

"But before that," Christian said, using the fountain edge for leverage as he stood up, "I was with Horace in his office.

He gave me some champagne and showed me his trophy case —" He paused, having said the words "trophy case" with disgust.

For a moment, Hermione registered his grim expression, though she was relieved he was alive.

"Apparently, Horace steals precious memories from his targets before he kills them, and our dear uncle supplied him with one of our father's. So, I stole it back," Christian said, gesturing toward the liquid. "I placed a protection spell on the vial—only you or I can open it now—and I have no idea what the memory is, but we need to be careful not to get the two mixed up."

Christian pulled a separate vial from his coat and went to hand it to her. But somewhere in the back of her mind, she heard a faint crunch of leaves and shoved her elder brother, knocking him off his feet as she flung herself backward. The spell Carmichael had shot at them narrowly missed her head. Hermione tried to gather her senses but was finding it difficult as the pain in her shoulder was overwhelming.

"Over here," Carmichael shouted.

Christian shot a spell back, but Carmichael leaped out of the way. Hermione knew it would only be a matter of time before the men closed in on them, and she looked at the two vials on the ground. One was farther away, beside another opening in the maze; the one nearest was only a few inches away. Neither had cracked or opened, but she couldn't tell the difference between the two. Had the one in front of her been her father's memory or was it Carmichael's?

She ducked her head as a flash of green light came toward her and crashed into the maze, creating a large hole. Then as Christian and Carmichael's duel continued, Hermione heard the shouts growing louder and the pounding of feet getting closer.

Hermione grabbed the vial in front of her, pulling out the time trinket and opening it as she took the vial's cork off with her teeth. She carefully poured the vial's contents into the strange swirling liquid and watched as the liquid changed to a golden color. Then a loud ticking sound began to come from the trinket, though she could see no remnants of the pocket watch's clock.

She turned to see her brother get flung backward into a hedge by an invisible force. Hermione pulled out her wand and threw the first spell she could think of at Carmichael, causing him to become dizzy and then vomit blood. While the sight was unsettling, Hermione forced herself onto her feet and sprinted to her brother, throwing her arms around him as a loud gong rang out. She felt the ground disappear from beneath her feet, felt the air leave her lungs as her head connected with stone, and then there was silence and endless darkness.

When the Hell Are We?

Date Unknown

Without opening her eyes, Hermione smoothed her fingers over the rough, ice-cold texture of the wet concrete beneath them. The air was thick and filled with a pungent, urban, bready scent that assaulted her nostrils with every breath. She pushed herself up onto her hands and knees and gasped for air. For a few moments, all she could hear was the sound of her breathing, the hiss of steam releasing, and the faint chirp of scurrying mice. Hermione scanned her surroundings, and though her vision was blurry, she was able to make out a painted yellow line running the length of the concrete and, below that line, train tracks.

The subway, she thought. *Why are we in the subway?*

Hermione shook her head, trying to convince herself this was all just a dream, but the cool metal of the time trinket brushing against her chest reminded her that it was not. She looked to her left and was relieved to see her brother leaning against the white tiled walls just beneath a movie poster. They were certainly in the New York City subway in the non-magical world, she reasoned. Where on the subway line, she wasn't entirely sure. What year it was, was an even more worrying question. She kept hoping Carmichael would appear, but no one was inside the station besides her and Christian.

"Where the hell are we?" Christian asked, holding his head.

Hermione rubbed her shoulder. "I'm not sure," she said, pointing the tip of her wand at her arm and mumbling a mending spell. Her shoulder shifted and cracked, settling back into place. She sighed in relief. "Do you think Carmichael met Uncle Rowan here?"

"No, they met in an Italian restaurant in the city," Christian answered.

"How do you know that?" Hermione asked, looking around.

"I was in Carmichael's head for a while before I found the right memory," Christian said, pulling his hand from his head. He examined his fingers, perhaps searching for traces of blood. "Honestly, it felt wrong, like I was violating his privacy, trespassing into the deepest recesses of his mind. I saw every memory, heard every thought—it was unethical. That spell should be forbidden. But wherever we are now certainly isn't Carmichael's memory."

Shit, Hermione thought. *I picked the wrong memory. How the hell are we going to get back now?*

Hermione's face must've shown how she felt since her brother's expression softened.

Christian sighed. "It's alright," he reassured. "It's one of

Dad's good memories, remember—though I'd never taken him as a subway kind of guy. Clearly it can't be anything too bad. Really, what's the worst that can happen?"

She smiled at him. Hermione was weary and disoriented, but mostly she was confused. They weren't where they were supposed to be, and that was her fault. The time trinket, in all its mystery, hadn't given her even a hint of the time they were in, and her older brother was injured. What could she do now besides try again? And if they did try again and landed in the right moment in time, then what? She couldn't be sure her brother would make it. He was bruised externally, but that didn't tell her the extent of his internal injuries. Tears stung her eyes, and she wiped them away. She was furious with herself; she'd been such a fool.

Hermione took out the time trinket and opened it. The liquid inside wasn't moving, nor was it its usual bluish hue—it was disturbingly gray. She examined the outside of the trinket, finding nothing to explain what was wrong with it.

Oh, dear god, she thought. *Did I break it?* The thought made her anxious. It didn't have a single scratch on it.

A cool breeze brushed over her skin, and she was grateful she was still wearing her coat. She took a deep breath, thinking of a memory from her childhood, brought her wand to her temple, and pulled it out of her mind. The memory formed into an orb of glittering liquid. Golden in color, twisting and turning, she lowered it into the trinket, but the moment she released it, the trinket rejected the memory, and it splashed onto the ground beside them. Her heart lurched in pain.

Oh no, she thought. Her heartbeat quickened. *I did break it. How will we get back now?*

"What's wrong?" Christian asked as he let out a yawn and stretched.

"It's not working," Hermione answered, showing him the time trinket. "I tried putting one of my memories in, and it's not working."

Christian stared at it for a moment, then back at her.

"Did you already reset it?" Christian asked.

Hermione blushed. "Um . . ." She hesitated.

"Please tell me you know how to reset it."

She didn't answer.

Her brother stared at her blank expression and sighed.

"Come here," he said, and she moved to sit beside him.

He stretched out his legs and took the time trinket from her hands. He flipped it over and began examining it but sighed again when he couldn't find what he was looking for.

"Leave it to our grandfather to hide the reset switch," Christian said.

"There's a reset switch?" Hermione asked.

"Every time trinket has one. You learn about it in advanced charms," he explained, staring down at the trinket. "Some wizards make theirs automatic, but it appears our grandfather made this one manual—probably a wise decision. If he got caught with it, it'd be much harder to prove what it does."

"So we're stuck here," Hermione said bleakly.

They had mingled for hours in the Dimitri mansion in Eighthgate, trying to retrieve Carmichael's memory only to get stuck in the past. Time and time again, she regretted not paying attention in charms class, but this, by far, proved that it was the dumbest decision in her life.

Christian shook his head. "Not even close."

Hermione stared at him blankly, hoping he'd explain, but he didn't.

"How?"

"Well, wherever we are," Christian said, getting up off the ground, "our grandfather is alive and most likely our only hope of finding out how this thing works."

Christian offered her a hand, and she took it.

When Hermione got to her feet, she said, "But he hasn't invented it yet."

"It takes years to make a time trinket, Hermione," Christian told her. "I would even guess that it could've taken him decades. If nothing else, he might have a blueprint for it. Then he can show us how to reset it."

"Why would he do that for us?" Hermione said. "He won't know who we are, and saying we're from the future sounds crazy. So what will we do if he doesn't want to help us?"

"I don't know," Christian said with a shrug. "But he invented it. And he's the only one who would have the slightest clue on how to use it," Christian said, dusting himself off. "And the man has lived in the same mansion his entire life. So no matter what year it is, we'll be—"

In the distance, there was a sound like thunder cracking, but when Hermione looked up the stairwell to the street above, there was no rain.

"Chris—"

"Shh!" Christian shushed, moving in front of her.

His eyes were focused on something, but his shoulder was blocking her view. Instinctively, she grabbed Christian's arm with one hand and held her wand with the other, her heart racing, slowly turning her head to follow Christian's eyes to see what had drawn his attention. She looked to the other end of the platform, but there was nothing there. At least, nothing she could see.

Then someone mumbled something and searing white light filled the subway. Somewhere in the back of her mind, Hermione was sure she'd heard her brother whisper a spell, but in her confusion, she couldn't make it out. Tears burned her eyes as she began blinking, straining to see the caster, but then she was pulled from the spot, and her back was slammed into a wall. An ear-splitting, high-pitched ring pierced her ears and reverberated through her skull. When her vision cleared, the first thing she saw was Christian's arm in front of her protectively, holding her against the wall, and the second was the blood on her brother's temple.

"Don't worry, he can't see us now," Christian whispered. "I cast an illusion spell on the hallway."

Who? she thought but couldn't find the strength to speak.

She was disoriented but mostly frightened. Who would attack two strangers in the middle of the night? Christian's eyes focused on the hallway opening to the subway platform, watching and waiting for their assailant to appear. For a few minutes, all Hermione heard was passersby's voices coming from the streets above them, but somewhere on the platform, another sound slowly grew louder: the tap of footsteps.

Hermione blinked back tears as their assailant stopped in front of the hallway. He was young, but his dark hair was longer, and he wore a thick black coat with tailored pants. His wand was drawn as he strained to see inside the hallway, angling his head to look for any trace of them. He bore a striking resemblance to her half brother Christian.

Hermione could hardly believe what she was seeing. It

was their father, much younger, but it was him. And she was silently thanking the saints that he couldn't see them.

Then an explosive *boom* crashed beside him, destroying a trash bin and spewing its contents onto the platform. Alfred turned to the caster and sent a spell hurling back. For a moment, the crackle of spells being cast back and forth was the only sound echoing in her ears. She watched as spells erupted from Alfred's wand and he blocked those that came his way with an animated flourish.

As Alfred pressed forward, away from their hiding place, Christian gestured for Hermione to stand beside him, and the two moved closer to the opening, until they could see their father dueling.

Two men with painted faces dueled their father, three if she counted the man that appeared to be unconscious or dead near a staircase on the other end of the platform. Hermione had never seen her father duel before, but he was having no problem holding his own. Some spells collided with each other and burst on contact, leaving behind smoke. Christian and Hermione huddled together in shock and awe, staring as one man shrieked and keeled over onto the ground.

"Do you know what spell that was?" Hermione asked as she watched the man turn blue.

"Nothing I've ever seen," Christian answered, staring at the man in horror.

By the time the man was twitching on the ground, his eyes had swollen to the size of golf balls and their whites had turned a deep scarlet. Christian was white as a ghost and appeared to gag at the sight. Hermione was struggling to suppress her fear, so she shut her eyes. And for a few seconds, she listened to the sound of her heart beating in her ears, hoping it would soothe her. But then she heard another sound, a faint but cheerful humming. The song the stranger was humming was familiar.

Hermione opened her eyes, watching as a woman came down the subway stairs. Her dark hair was pinned back into a neat bun, and her warm brown skin reflected the light. The thick black coat she wore swallowed her small frame. A small purse swung on one arm as she walked, while her groceries were on the other.

Hermione gasped aloud, and Christian's hand flew to her mouth as the woman turned toward them. She stared down the hall for a few moments, then jumped as her bag of groceries exploded.

The woman looked down the platform at their father and went to run up the stairs but slipped as an invisible force grabbed her ankle.

"Leave the mundane out of this, Horace," Alfred demanded, and Hermione heard the crack of another spell.

The woman scrambled to her feet, clearly frightened, staring wide-eyed at the wizards. Her leg had been scraped, and her purse was damaged.

"Hermione, what is it?" Christian whispered, taking his hand away from her mouth.

Hermione stared blankly at the woman.

"We're in 1971," Hermione whispered.

"What?"

"That's my mother—we're in 1971," Hermione told him. "This is the day they met."

Christian looked taken aback as he stared at her mother. He scratched his head.

"Well, at least we know where we are now," Christian said, still wearing the same confused expression.

Hermione didn't know how to react. A younger version of her mother was staring blankly at the men dueling, lost and, all things considered, probably confused.

She wanted to reach out to her mother and pull her into the hallway for safety, but that wasn't how the story went. Hermione had listened to Isabel tell her about it time and time again. How her father came to her rescue, which meant at some point, she, Isabel Robins, would be in need of rescuing.

Hermione hesitated. She couldn't stop this from happening. This was the moment her mother learned about magic, and likely a moment in time that could have dire consequences if it was disturbed.

"Christian, we . . . Don't you think we should get out of here?" The desperation in her voice was evident. She shook her head, wanting to shake off the feeling, but a pit was slowly forming in her stomach. "We should go to Grandfather's mansion. I'm sure it'll take time to convince him."

Christian turned to face her. "You're right—"

A rough bark of laughter interrupted him, and they turned toward the sound.

Their father was pushing himself up off the ground, one hand flat against the concrete, his wand in the other, and blood snaking down the side of his face.

"You're a good man, Alfred, I'll give you that. I saw how you helped the Webb family. In truth, I wish I would've made that move first, but still, very *noble*." Horace said, smirking down at him.

Alfred glared at Horace. "What's wrong? Too afraid to face me on your own?"

Hermione was surprised he was asking for more. Fatigue tinged Alfred's voice, bruises had bloomed on his knuckles, and he seemed to wince at the slightest movement.

Horace raised his wand to Alfred's face and said, "Truth be told. I had thought killing you would be more of a challenge."

"Stop it!" a woman's voice shouted, and Hermione turned to look at her mother.

Isabel was still standing there, one hand clutching her purse. Her eyes were wide with fear, but she didn't budge.

"Forgive me, darling, I'd forgotten you were here," Horace said to her. He looked at the brutish-looking man beside him. "Didn't I say no witnesses, Bishop?"

Bishop smiled in a way that made Hermione's insides turn. She looked at her father, hoping he would find the strength to intervene. But Bishop walked by him without Alfred so much as attempting a grab at his foot, and the brute tucked away his wand. A tremor ran through her body as he drew closer to Isabel.

It didn't take long for Hermione to try to intervene, drawing her wand, ready to fight. Unfortunately, the moment she stepped forward, her legs weakened and she collapsed onto her hands and knees. She felt the cold, dark concrete beneath her fingers as the world around her seemed to shift and sway.

She could barely see Alfred struggling to stand, one hand holding his ribs.

No, this can't be happening to me, she thought as she blinked back tears. *What is happening to me?*

Hermione tried to think back on her grandfather's words, him telling her that time travel left traces, but she couldn't imagine what this was. What this meant. Then as the realization hit her, she felt the blood drain from her face. *I'm dying.*

It all seemed to be happening slowly. She could faintly hear her brother saying something.

"Hey!" Christian cried desperately.

Hermione tried to say something in return but found herself gasping for air. She could feel something enveloping her, felt friction against her skin, and then heard the blaring sound of a horn. Wind rushed at her face one moment, and then darkness filled the next. Each blink seemed to take away a moment in time, the darkness swallowing the world around her. Hermione desperately tried not to let it swallow her too.

Her cheek was against the concrete, her ragged breathing drowned out by a rumbling coming from below that caused pebbles to jump, and despite her valiant efforts, she couldn't stay awake.

The shriek of a subway train woke her, and its accompanying hiss seemed to fill her lungs with oxygen. The darkness was gone. Horace Dimitri and his cronies were gone. And Hermione found herself staring at Alfred as he helped Isabel up, only then faintly realizing that her elder brother was carrying her.

"Good, you're awake," Christian said as he stepped onto the train and sat her in a seat beside him. "We're taking the W to Pickering to The Faded Quill, then we'll walk to Grandfather's mansion."

Hermione looked up at the train map. It was the only subway train into Hampshire from the non-magical boroughs and was warded from being seen by humans. In all her confusion, she hadn't thought it'd be running. She took a deep breath, barely registering her brother paying the conductor for their tickets and assuring them she was tired.

Christian turned to her.

"What happened back there?" Hermione asked.

Christian scratched his head. "Well, I'd like to think you fainted, but I'm not sure."

"Do . . . do you think I was dying?" Hermione asked, weariness edging her voice.

Christian didn't answer. Instead, he looked down at his wand in his hand.

"Christian," she said.

He mumbled something.

"What?"

"I'm not sure," he repeated, looking her in the eyes. "But I called Dad, you know, by his first name. It felt weird, but he stopped. He and Horace were dueling again, and he just stopped." Her brother furrowed his brow in confusion. "He could've stopped Horace, but instead, he let Horace get away. Then he used a spell that sent ropes out of his wand like snakes, and the next moment, Bishop was on the ground, bound in ropes, slowly choking to death."

Hermione nodded. "Do you think that man was supposed to die today?"

Christian shrugged. "Does it really matter?" he asked. "Because the moment he was dead, *Alfred* helped your mother up and you were breathing again," he said, saying Alfred as though he couldn't reconcile the younger man with their father. "And I didn't care about much else in that moment."

"And Dad just let you leave?"

"He was too busy playing knight in shining armor with your mother," Christian answered with what almost sounded like disgust.

Hermione hesitated. Her head was spinning absorbing all this information. Knowing her father had not only killed one but two men tonight was a lot to digest. And she could hardly ever imagine her father killing anyone, yet he'd done it twice. Every time she'd heard the story of her parents, it had all been so romantic and dreamlike, but tonight, in reality, it was a nightmare.

"I always knew he would've been a different man, but what we just saw," Christian said. "I'd never imagined that."

We've Been Expecting You

Fall 1971

Within an hour, they'd arrived. They climbed the subway station stairs to exit at the intersection of Queens Road and Kitchener Boulevard. Outside, rain had clogged the gutters with branches and autumn leaves and honking motor traffic carried on block after block. By the time they'd walked five blocks, Hermione's hair clung to her face, and she found herself searching store windows for umbrellas. She couldn't remember the charm to create one, and the rain was only becoming more relentless. The magicks around them appeared less bothered by it. In fact, many New Yorkers moved as though they were fish navigating a fast-moving stream.

"How much farther do we have to walk?" Hermione asked her brother.

"Not much farther, now," Christian answered as they turned left at the corner.

Hermione groaned. She wished she had something to cover her head and was grateful when Christian pulled her into a bookstore.

It was a relatively small store with everything from cookbooks to spellbooks organized on bookshelves and herbology books stacked on tables. Hermione took particular interest in a leather-bound charms book that was the size, color, and weight of a red brick. The cashier behind the counter had brown skin and dark hair and was hunched over in a chair, reading a history book. He wore a dark green uniform with a name badge pinned to it that read Aleksander.

"Hello," Christian said to the cashier, drawing his attention. "We need to go to 702 Kitchener."

Aleksander gave Christian a narrow-eyed appraisal, seeming particularly unimpressed by the dirt on her brother's pants. Christian rolled his eyes before pulling out his wallet and taking out fifty Hampshirien dollars.

"Twenty-five for me and twenty-five for her," Christian said, holding out the money. "That should about cover it, right?"

Aleksander took the money and stared at it for a moment. Then he examined it in the light, checking if it was real. Once it met his approval, he nodded.

"This way," Aleksander said, gesturing for them to follow him.

Aleksander led them to the back of the store and down a dimly lit, narrow hallway that smelled like mildew and animal droppings. But when they arrived in the backroom, the lighting was brighter and warmer. It wasn't a particularly large room, and the white paint on the walls was peeling, revealing gray stone. But the room's northern wall had three doors made from dark brown oakwood with witches and wizards carved into the doorways.

"702 Kitchener?" Aleksander asked, directing his question to Christian.

Christian nodded. "Yes, we're visiting someone."

Aleksander yawned. "*Neat.*"

The man took out his wand and waved it in front of the second door. For a moment, the keyhole glowed, and then it returned to normal.

"I'm assuming it's not your first time using a door," Aleksander said.

"No, but it'll be her first using a *gateway*," Christian stated.

The cashier rolled his eyes.

"All you have to do is walk through," Aleksander said, opening the door and revealing a thick wall of black smoke. "Voilà."

Hermione had to suppress a shudder. She had hoped it was merely a dark room, but somewhere in the back of her mind, she'd registered that it was not. The smoke inside the door billowed like a cloud, but it was contained within it by an invisible force.

Hermione gulped. *I'm not going in there,* she told herself. *I can't.*

"There's no need to frighten her," Christian stated.

Aleksander cocked a brow. "Better to just rip the Band-Aid off."

Christian shook his head at the man's statement. He turned to Hermione and placed a hand on her shoulder.

"You have to take a deep breath before you step through," Christian instructed. "Gateways tend to make people feel a little dizzy. You might even feel a little bit jet-lagged tomorrow."

"You really want me to go in there?" Hermione said.

Christian sighed. "It's the fastest way. We don't have much time."

Hermione scoffed. "I beg to differ," she said, looking back at the door. "If I can get dizzy from stepping through a door—"

"It's *bewitched*," Christian said, interrupting her. "So, you may feel a little dizzy, and some people say they've even felt pulled by it, but not much else. There's nothing living in there," Christian explained. "I mean, you'll be crossing miles within a few seconds. Trust me, you'll feel something."

"Okay," Hermione said incredulously. She stared at the door. "But you're sure there's nothing living in there."

Christian nodded. "I'm sure."

Hermione hesitated. She preferred traveling by broom or even public transit over using a magic spell. In normal circumstances, she wouldn't walk through bewitched doors that would send her to any predesignated destination.

"Hurry it up," Aleksander demanded. "I haven't got all day!"

Christian glared at Aleksander.

Hermione stepped forward, inching toward the door cautiously before stopping in front of the threshold. She inhaled and took her first step through the door. As the cold air inched up her leg, something wrapped around her waist, wrenching her forward into howling winds and dizzying colors. When her vision cleared, Hermione's head slammed into the wet earth beneath her and blades of grass pricked her skin. She bolted upright and shivered, rubbing her arms furiously.

When she turned to look behind her, Christian stood there, and the dark gateway dissolved behind him. Christian helped Hermione up, and a few moments later, she felt the tip of his wand against her chest. He mumbled a spell, and warmth spread across her skin as her breathing returned to normal.

"What was that?" Hermione asked.

"I told you, you'd be traveling miles in an instant. There was bound to be some toll on your body," Christian answered.

Hermione scoffed and shoved him playfully. "Next time, we're buying brooms and flying them."

Christian laughed. "Honestly, Hermione. You just need to start using charms. This was so much cheaper than buying brooms," Christian said, looking down at his jeans. "Besides, grandfather's house is right down there, and we don't have to worry about parking our brooms somewhere."

"Seriously? Broom parking is what you're worried about at a time like this?" Hermione laughed.

"Hardly," Christian answered as he pointed his wand at his pants, and suddenly they were clean. "I'm thinking about how I'm going to explain how we got here to a man that's not met us—or at least met *you*."

∾

After their arrival in Kitchener Park, they followed a path that led them up to the nearby estates, passing homes with statues on their lawns, autumnal hedges, and glittering windows. The mansions stood tall amongst the trees, large enough that they were distinguishable from the townhouses of lower-class magicks a few miles away, yet not drowning out the greenery. The tree branches interlocked, braiding themselves together to shield the sidewalk from the moonlight.

When they finally reached the top of the slope, Hermione could see the full moon and, at the hill's peak, their grandfather's home.

It was strange to see the mansion so fresh and alive. Here the ivy that would climb the home's western exterior and consume windows and balconies was just beginning to grow. The angel statues in the front garden were upright and unbroken, no missing wings or shattered skulls. The dark wooden front doors looked freshly polished and seemed to reflect the light. As they drew closer, Hermione could see intricate carvings of slithering serpents, bitten apples, and tangled vines covering every inch of the wood.

Hermione heard Christian knock on the door but didn't quite register it until the door had already opened, and then she was staring at a silver-haired butler with pale skin standing in the doorway. Though Hermione was fairly confident she had never met him before.

"The lord of the manor wishes to speak with you," the butler said.

"I beg your pardon—" Christian started, hesitating for a moment. "But we—"

"He is expecting your arrival," the butler said, interrupting Christian. His eyes narrowed at Hermione. "It is rude to keep one's host waiting."

"He is?" Christian responded.

Hermione nudged Christian. "Well, of course he is," Hermione said to Christian. "If you can just point us in the right direction."

The butler stepped aside. "Through the corridor into the gathering room."

"Thank you," Hermione said, pulling her brother along.

She was half expecting Christian to break the facade, but luckily, he didn't.

The mansion was cold and, Hermione noted apprehensively, didn't have any family photos displayed. Instead, morbid busts of deceased relatives lined the hall, along with a painting of a grimacing old man impaled by an axe that still hadn't been removed. It was as if all the warmth had been drained from the place. When Hermione reached the parlor, she looked back at the front door, and the butler stood there, guarding it with a scowl.

The moment she stepped into the parlor, the heat nearly knocked her off her feet. Hermione shrugged her coat off her shoulders and draped it on a coatrack by the entryway. As her eyes scanned the room, she noted the roaring fireplace that was emitting the sweltering heat, two armchairs near it, a black velvet rug underneath them, and a sideboard cabinet on the opposite side of the room that had a scotch glass and a cane resting on it. To her left, bookshelves spanned the length of the wall, filled with leather-bound books that a gray-haired man was staring at intently. His back was to them, but she still recognized him.

He wore a black velvet robe and matching slippers. He

was standing eerily still, but it was their grandfather, standing there, with two feet planted on the ground and two legs attached to his person. Months before he lost one.

"She had predicted you would come."

Hermione nearly jumped out of her skin when their grandfather spoke.

"A *fortune teller* I presume?" Christian said with a bemused grin.

The man turned sharply with a scowl on his face. His piercing eyes focused on Christian.

"Don't mock me, boy," he said grimly, wiping the smirk off Christian's face. "I spoke to a *tarot reader*. And she'd told me those of my past would come back to haunt me as they've faced a great misfortune and desire my help."

"Well, I can assure you, Thomas. We aren't from your *past*," Christian told him. "My name is Christian, and this is Hermione, and . . . and well, we do need your help."

Hermione stared blankly at Christian. She knew they couldn't call Thomas their grandfather, at least not immediately, but it was admittedly jarring to hear her brother refer to him by his first name.

Thomas scoffed. "Ah yes, she told me already! You've come to steal my time and dwindle my riches," Thomas spat out. "And I'll have you know that I don't anticipate having much of either soon."

"Is that right?" Christian said. "Because I have good reason to believe that you will live for quite some time, Thomas."

"No," Thomas said.

Christian cocked a brow. "No?" Christian repeated. "And what makes you so sure that you will not?"

"She foretold a duel where I may die and rejoin my sweet Leigh," Thomas answered, striding across the room to the cabinet. "Or I may be wounded and be in need of this."

As Hermione looked closer, she wasn't sure her future grandfather was in good health. Thomas's skin was dull and taut over the rigid edges of his face. He stood tall, but his physique was swallowed by the coal-black robe he wore. And when the firelight touched his features, his weary eyes stared grimly at the cane he now held, one skeletal hand gripping the serpent head handcrafted by a wandmaker who served only the elite.

"I can tell you how the duel ends," Christian told Thomas.

Thomas looked intrigued by her brother's statement, then shifted his gaze to Hermione, as if trying to decipher the meaning behind Christian's words from her expression. She tried to force herself to look unmoved by their exchange, but she couldn't suppress her emotion. This was her grandfather. This man, speaking in a guttural voice that looked as though he'd fall over with the slightest breeze, who she knew was currently mourning their grandmother, Leigh Mandrake.

"She said the choice was mine," Thomas said weakly. "That I'm an old man, and I could just as easily throw the duel."

Hermione shifted uneasily beside her brother.

"No," she managed to say. "You can't."

"And there must be some reason, I dare say, that you need me alive, child?"

"Yes, there is," Hermione said, pausing as she refused to call him Thomas.

"Humph," Thomas said. Then he slowly approached

them, and Hermione fought the urge to back away as he came to a halt in front of her. His dark eyes locked with hers. "And what, pray tell, would that reason be, Hermione," he said grimly.

He paused and waited as though he expected her to back down.

Hermione lifted her chin stubbornly. "We aren't from your past, sir," she said. "We are from your future."

The Old Man and The Time Trinket

Fall 1971

The side of Thomas's mouth twitched as he stood there immeasurably pleased with himself. He examined the time trinket, flipping it over in his hands and back again. Hermione stared at her brother, who was so unbothered by the man's reaction that he'd requested wine from a servant to accompany his dinner. Thomas had taken the news surprisingly well. Hermione had come to realize that before the fall of 1971, their grandfather had never invented something as rare as a time trinket. Thus, he'd ordered the butler, Newman, to have the staff prepare a feast for his guests, and as this was cause for celebration, the food was to remain unpoisoned.

An order that, despite the heat of the parlor, caused Hermione to shiver. Then they transitioned to the dining room, where a long oak table accompanied cushioned seats. Moonlight poured in through five large windows evenly distributed throughout the length of the room, looking out on to the back garden. Each window's dark green drapes were gathered in brass curtain holdbacks that showcased a serpent's head.

Now, Hermione sat at a long oak table across from her brother Christian. A wide range of delicacies covered the table, including turkey and quail, steamed vegetables, gravies and sauces, and freshly washed fruits. Thomas sat at the head of the table, marveling at his future self's creation.

Hermione shot a look at Christian that did nothing to change his demeanor. He merely shrugged it off as if he expected her to solve this conundrum for him.

"It's truly marvelous, isn't it," Thomas said, holding the time trinket in the light and watching it shimmer. "I wish I could pick his brain on how he came to invent it. I mean, I've struggled to make trains that can fly, and yet, in the future, I create this, " he said as he admired it. "You can't begin to understand the possibilities. I remember drafting the blueprints, but for me to be so willing to bend the law to create it. What would drive me to do such a thing? Is it foolishness or daring to dream?"

Hermione smiled at him. She was glad to see the old man had abandoned his previously grim attitude, if only for the time being.

"But why—" Thomas said hesitantly, seemingly searching the pocket watch. "Why would I give such a thing to my grandchildren, unless . . . unless . . ." His expression changed as he stared at the words engraved into the time trinket. "How did it happen?"

"Dragonfire," Hermione began, and Thomas stared at her intently. "One of Horace Dimitri's descendants rode in on dragonback and reduced Fortuna Bay to ashes. You and our father—" Hermione stopped as she noticed Thomas wince.

"That's enough," Thomas said, holding up a hand as if he were waving away the words. "So why come here? Why not go back a few weeks before to prevent it?"

Hermione hesitated. She hardly wanted to admit that she wasn't any good at charms to him.

"Unfortunately, after I retrieved the memory from Horace's bastard son, Carmichael Dimitri, there was a mix-up between his memory and our father's—your son Alfred's—memory of Hermione's mother," Christian explained.

Thomas let out a dry bark of laughter. "Of course," he said, shaking his head. "Horace and his morbid fascination with others' memories. I hear he keeps a collection of them stored somewhere within his home, and I suspect you intended to return this memory to your father."

Christian nodded his head.

A small smile spread on Thomas's face. "An honorable decision," Thomas said, staring down at the trinket. "So what is it you two need me for?"

"We need to reset it," Hermione explained. "I never asked my grandfather—you—how to reset the time trinket. I suppose I was too busy scorning him for creating it."

A look flickered over Thomas's features, and Hermione recalled the shame she heard in his voice when he'd wondered how they'd come into possession of the time trinket. She watched as the old man shook his head. Perhaps at their actions or his own.

He looked back at the time trinket. "I have a few unfinished blueprints for my inventions, but from examining it now, I'm positive I intended its creation to be kept secret.

Looking at this, I believe it was the one I dreamed of the day of Leigh's death. It was a mistake to have created it. We are not meant to meddle in time. If Merlin knew of this foolishness . . . the damage that we may have done to the timeline, and I am the cause of it." He set the time trinket on the table. "I've spent my entire life inventing, seeking to create something greater than myself. This is proof of that, but if you change time, you must be prepared for the consequences."

"I am," Hermione said confidently.

She knew what her brother's reaction would be the moment the words had left her lips, and she could see Christian narrow his eyes skeptically, silently questioning the validity of the claim, out of the corner of her eye.

"The world isn't simple, Hermione. It isn't black-and-white. There is more to using the trinket than right or wrong. The problems of the world and their solutions are so much more complex. And if you follow this path, you may not like what you find."

The unknowns were a terrifying thought. "But if I don't, more people will die in a war led by our heir apparent. Gianni Matias is as much my brother as Christian. But with him as the head of our family, more people will die," Hermione stated matter-of-factly.

Christian and Hermione exchanged a look.

"The war between the Mandrakes and the Dimitris has been coming for a long time. You are aware that you are only prolonging the inevitable."

"If war is coming," Hermione stated, as she thought back to her father in the subway station, "then let my father be at the helm. Let the blood of those who would die for him stand beside him. Let that blood fall onto my father's hands."

Thomas nodded. "Very well then," he said, looking over at Newman in the entryway.

He walked over to the butler and whispered something to him. Then Newman strode off down the hall, and Thomas turned back to them.

"Newman will make arrangements for your stay here," Thomas told them. "Because, as you can imagine, we can't have you wandering around meddling with much else. I'm sure the pincers will be out looking for you."

Hermione had to repress a laugh. She was glad Thomas's nickname for the Magical Crime Unit's officers hadn't changed over the decades. Pincers were what he'd called the MCU's special task force, though their proper name was *dispellers*, and they were everywhere—tracking and hunting dark wizards or illegal uses of magic, especially time travel.

Christian rose from his seat. "Thank you for your hospitality, Thomas. I am very grateful, but I'm afraid I need to pick up a few things in town that I would prefer a servant didn't handle. It would only take me an hour or two."

Thomas huffed out air. "Very well then, Christian Carlisle," he said with notable exasperation. "Take some money, and retrieve what you need—but nothing else," Thomas warned, giving her older brother money from his wallet.

"No need to worry, I shouldn't take long," Christian assured.

Hermione rose to her feet, but before she could say anything, Thomas cleared his throat. "I believe it'd be best to continue this conversation in my workshop. We can look through my blueprints there. Two pairs of eyes are better than one."

Hermione nodded as she heard the front door shut, leaving her alone in an unfamiliar house with a man she hardly felt she knew.

When Hermione wasn't suffering in silence, wading through the disheveled stack of papers in Thomas Mandrake's study, she was sitting in an armchair by the fireplace. This time, she opted for a blanket to keep her legs warm. The study was quite small, and neat, despite his blueprints of half-finished or tossed-out inventions. Two bookshelves were filled with books on a multitude of magical subjects, speaking to his studious nature and endless interests. The room was bathed in light from an eclectic collection of mismatched lamps, the most peculiar of them rested on the old oak desk where Thomas was seated. Every time he moved, the leather chair would squeak.

"Any luck?" Thomas asked, leaning forward.

Hermione shook her head as she stared at the papers she'd left on the floor beside her: the anatomy of a dragon and blueprints for a ballista to slay it, and a page torn from a dark magic book about the cons of time travel.

"Nothing useful," Hermione said, grimacing at the page.

The first con detailed how time travel magic summons the essence of time in the air around the user and that navigation required a certain amount of skill to make it safely to their intended destination. Con two stated that the present became a set point in time, but the future was decided by a series of the user's decisions, who should consider each one carefully. And to be careful when using dark magic or "crude tools" to manipulate the past.

But Hermione was less sure of which decisions were important. The fundamental levels, or "know-how," of time travel were on an earlier page. *See page 98*, the italicized writing read, but only the author's name was written to lead her to its source, meaning she would have to scour the bookshelves for it. It would be easier to summon the book with a charm, but Hermione wasn't any good at those.

"What about the book this is from," Hermione said, holding up the page. "It's by Nikolai Verax—perhaps you were inspired by it. It warns—"

"Against using crude tools when traveling to the past," Thomas explained. "And I'd daresay that your presence has already likely changed some things. Can you think of anything that might've been changed, even by accident?"

Hermione never said a word about them running into their father. Her head started swimming with thoughts: the duel, her mother, her near-death experience. Her chest tightened as she remembered that moment, feeling like she was sinking into the ground, and would never come up for air again.

"I take it I am not the first person you've encountered today," Thomas said. "*Tsk Tsk Tsk* . . . your presence will have affected more futures than your own."

"It was a mistake—an accident. I chose the wrong bottle, that's all. I couldn't have known that our father—your *son* Alfred—would attack us," Hermione retorted.

Thomas shook his head. "Dear, I know it was an honest mistake, but you must remember that you do not exist here, and it's only a matter of time before your presence disrupts something."

"You don't think I know that!" Hermione snapped. "I nearly died, for crying out loud. That was never part of the plan. We were supposed to go back a few months at most—" She bit back her tears. "I can duel, but I've never been good at charms."

"Well, all things considered, Hermione—"

A knock came from the study's door, and Thomas turned toward it.

"Who is it?" Thomas asked.

"It's me!" a chipper muffled voice replied from the other side of the door. "Sorry it took us quite some time to get here. The car broke down near the library, so we had to walk in the rain."

Thomas looked shocked. "You walked? You could catch pneumonia," Thomas said. "I would've sent Newman to get you."

"Oh, I just didn't want to be a burden," the woman replied. "Sebastian was getting a little fussy in the car, and Christian was just so excited to see you."

"We've brought back sweeties!" a child's voice called. "And I saw a hippogriff when we were on our way over!"

Thomas glanced back at Hermione and then stared up at the ceiling as if he were calling on his ancestors for help.

"I'm sure you have, dear boy," Thomas said as he scratched his neck. "Christian. I'll tell you what, you get ready for bed, and we'll talk all about the hippogriff before you go to sleep."

The sound of small shuffling feet came from behind the door, and then the child answered, "Okay!"

Hermione's heart sank in her chest. She felt flushed and her mind was whirring. Though she had never heard the woman's voice before, Hermione knew exactly who she was. Kassandra Graves, the younger sister of Eric Graves, was rumored to have been used as a pawn to excel her family's rank in a plan that succeeded after she'd given birth to Hermione's brother Christian Carlisle. Alfred had a second son with Kassandra, but he was murdered alongside his mother in November 1971.

The longer Hermione stood there, the more she could hear her heart beating in her chest.

"Just make yourself at home, Kassandra," Thomas said. "I'll be out in a moment."

"Thank you so much again, Mr. Mandrake," Kassandra said. "Go on, Christian, upstairs to your room."

Hermione could feel her heart pounding in her chest.

Thomas gave Hermione a stern look. "I'll be back in a moment. I'd forgotten they were visiting today," he explained. "Try to make yourself comfortable."

Hermione knew his statement was meant to be reassuring, but she couldn't suppress her shock. She was in the house with a young woman who was practically a ghost.

Nikolai Verax's Temporal Tempest
Theory

Fall 1971

After Hermione shuffled her way to the guest room and fell into bed, she stared blankly at the ceiling. As time passed, she found the mural of three snakes constricting an owl less comforting.

Newman had found *Inethical Magic* by Nikolai Verax for Hermione after she explained her poor charms skills to him. Unfortunately, every time she started reading the book, the reality that there was a soon-to-be-dead woman just a few doors down broke her concentration, making it impossible to focus. It wasn't long after her sixth attempt that Christian entered the room wearing a solemn expression.

Hermione sat up to speak to him but wasn't sure where to begin, so she sighed and settled for the first thing that came to mind. "Did you know your mother would be here?"

"Do you remember everything from when you were three?" Christian said with a yawn. "Besides, we've got more pressing concerns."

"More pressing?" Hermione shook her head at him. "You don't think that we should do something?"

"Like what exactly?" Christian questioned, taking a seat at the small desk in the bedroom's room right corner.

Hermione hesitated. "Well, I don't know—"

"Exactly," Christian said. "We can't tell her that she's going to die any more than we can do anything else . . .if we interfere with something here, we could very well not be able to save Dad."

"I know that, it's just—"

"Just what? You think I wanted her dead? She is *my* mother, Hermione, but I don't want her dead any more than I want you dead, which, need I remind you, *nearly* happened," Christian stated.

Hermione stared at him in disbelief and found that she couldn't help but be a little concerned. She then noticed that Christian wouldn't meet her eyes.

"What is it, Christian?" Hermione asked, analyzing his grim expression. "What's happened?"

Christian sighed and leaned back in the chair. "We were followed."

Every muscle in Hermione's body tensed. "How is that possible?"

"Hell if I know," Christian said as he rubbed a hand over his face. "I just had this feeling we were being watched before we went into The Faded Quill, so I went back to the station and checked it out. But like Grandfather said, *time travel leaves traces,* and I found someone else's aura lingering around."

"Did you recognize it at all?"

Christian shook his head, still wearing the same strained expression.

Hermione didn't know what to think. Christian knew his way around charms. He was by far a skilled wizard, and with everything else that had already come to pass, though she wanted to deny it, she knew he was right. Someone had followed them, and that someone was likely a Dimitri from their time. It took all her strength not to heave in that moment.

"Christian, I . . . What should we do?" she squeaked out. She hated that she sounded like a helpless little kid. "If it's one of the Dimitris, then they couldn't have gone far."

And, of course, her older brother was smart enough to take precautions to make sure they weren't followed to their grandfather's mansion in Kitchener.

She was grateful she'd brought him along. After so many days of suffering and dreading their father's funeral, she was almost glad they were stuck in the past. She wished they'd landed in the right year but was mostly glad she wasn't alone.

"What about the time trinket?" Christian asked. "Did you find anything out?"

It had taken him longer to ask than she'd expected, but she didn't feel the need to make a joke right now. She didn't want him to think she was taking matters lightly.

"I couldn't find any blueprints, but . . . *Thomas* said he'd continue searching while I got a good night's rest," Hermione explained to Christian. "He sent some maids to fetch us some clothes, and I put mine away—oh, and I set yours over there." Hermione pointed to the dresser with an assortment of shopping bags, many of which were stores she'd never heard of and assumed had gone out of business in her time. But the clothing within them would help them blend in.

Christian sighed. Then he got up, went over to the bags, and looked at what had been bought for him.

Hermione could sense his disappointment, but then remembered something that would lift his spirits.

She flipped open the book and nearly shouted. "But I did find this."

Her brother turned in shock. He moved closer to her, abandoning the shopping bags to sit beside her on the bed.

"Temporal tempest theory," Christian read, and then he paused a moment. "I think I remember reading about this in school. Verax believed that if enough ripples were made in the time stream, one timeline could completely destroy another. Some mundane scientists called him insane—but a criminal from England backed him up. You know, the guy who tried to erase Lincoln from history?"

"I never understood why he'd chosen a mundane to erase in the first place," Hermione said.

Christian shrugged. "Why do people choose anything?"

Hermione stared at her brother, waiting for his answer.

"Money," Christian said. "That's all it takes."

"But do you really think one timeline could destroy another?"

Christian rubbed his chin. His eyes narrowed at the text as if he were struggling to make sense of it.

"It says if two timelines are close enough to each other, it's entirely possible but potentially *necessary*," Christian said.

"What do you mean?"

Christian hesitated. "Well, think about it, Hermione," he

said, his expression hardening. "What happens to our timeline if we save Dad? Another version of us would take our place, so—"

"We would no longer exist," Hermione said, finishing his sentence.

Christian nodded. "We have to sacrifice our timeline. It needs to be completely severed from the tapestry of realities to save our father, *ourselves*, and thousands of others." He took a deep breath. His voice trembled with a mixture of urgency and remorse. "I understand the gravity of what I'm asking, but I don't see any other way, Hermione."

"So, what are our options?" Hermione asked. "We either cause a temporal tempest and destroy another timeline or we —what? Cease to exist?"

"Exactly."

"And you're okay with that?"

"Well, it's either we do this and live or save our father and, as you've already pointed out, *cease to exist*," Christian answered matter-of-factly. "There's no reason to feel guilty about it. To create a temporal tempest, we would have to disturb the timeline six times within a month—"

"A month?"

"Temporal tempests are time sensitive. Besides, that shouldn't be too hard. After all, we've already disturbed the timeline twice—"

"Once."

Christian shook his head. "Twice. We brought a Dimitri here with us. They'll likely do some damage here too. It's more a matter of figuring out how much they've done."

"And how do you plan on figuring that out?" Hermione asked.

"Simple," Christian said, standing up and gathering the shopping bags. "After we see if Thomas has found anything in the morning, you're going to figure out how we get back while I figure out which Dimitri followed us."

"What?"

Christian smiled wickedly. "Oh yes. You got us here, and you'll get us back."

Before Hermione could argue, he gave her another devilish grin and slipped out the door. Her heart dropped. He somehow expected her to figure out time travel with Thomas Mandrake, a man who, until their arrival, was unsure of his own future.

The moment the door closed behind Christian, Hermione undressed, tossed her clothes on the desk chair, then set her shoes beside the door and carefully placed her wand underneath her pillow. She pulled on a nightdress a maid had brought up for her, hoping to find some respite, but immediately after lying down, she grabbed her wand and held it protectively over her chest. It was an instinct she thought had gone away during her days in the girls' dormitory at boarding school.

She pulled the covers snugly around her, maintaining a firm grip on her wand. And though this mansion was familiar, she felt like a stranger here. Thomas had easily accepted his future and, in turn, them as his grandchildren, and Hermione couldn't help but think of how easily she had come to accept the life laid out for her.

Hermione squeezed her eyes shut, trying to force herself to relax. Soon she was able to block out her thoughts and focus on the buzzing sound of the lamp in the corner, and then, creaky floorboards, the pitter-patter of small feet, and a child's voice calling goodnight to their grandfather.

Hermione groaned as her breakfast plate was placed in front of her. She had spent most of the night tossing and turning, trying to make herself comfortable to no avail, and now, she felt utterly exhausted. Last night, Hermione had hoped she would wake to discover it had all been a dream, that her father was still alive and Gianni wasn't waging war, that they weren't in the year 1971, that she hadn't nearly died, or rather ceased to exist. Perhaps Hermione was actually having an anxiety-induced nightmare—or wedding jitters—and she would wake to her maid upset that she'd overslept in bed, safe at their home, her wedding just hours away. And she could laugh about it, probably with Christian, and he would question her sanity, but they would laugh.

But no such luck. She was in 1971, and so was Christian, and despite the terrors of yesterday, she found herself famished.

"Any progress on the—" Hermione hesitated as she noticed the little boy across from her staring at her intently. "*Project*," she finished.

"What project?" he asked, curiosity filling his large doe eyes.

Hermione stared at him blankly. No matter how hard she tried to shake off the feeling, she was having trouble reconciling that the doe-eyed child with a head full of bushy brown waves that had informed Thomas he was only eating yellow foods, with the exception of mangos, would grow up to be her half brother Christian. Internally she had begun to refer to him as Tiny, to make matters less jarring. But she was still having some trouble, and the child craned his head curiously at her, as though he were wondering if she'd understood his question or if this fell under the secret language of adults who were hiding something from a child his age.

"Do you and Grandfather work together on his inventions?" Tiny asked.

"Um . . . well," Hermione started. "I suppose we might be *this* time."

Tiny smiled.

"Right. Right," Tiny said, nodding. "So he's hired you to help with the flying car? Grandfather said I'm not big enough to work on the car, b-but I get to watch from the side some times. He and Newman nearly got it off the ground last time. Didn't you, Grandfather?"

Thomas nodded but continued to squint at a newspaper. His glasses were on the table, but he refused to put them on.

"So, where do you come from?" Kassandra asked softly.

The woman's voice oozed kindness. Not the type of kindness Hermione had become accustomed to receiving from the Graves women of the future—arrogant, pretentious, and even somehow managing to sound opportunistic. She sounded genuine, and Hermione's heart panged with guilt, knowing she couldn't tell Kassandra about her impending demise.

"We've come a great distance to visit Thomas," Christian explained to Kassandra, coming to Hermione's rescue.

She wasn't doing well with articulating her thoughts this morning.

Kassandra smiled sweetly. "Oh, you're from the old country?" She stated, "Funny—"

"Funny how?" Christian said, feigning offense.

"Well, funnily enough, you and Alfred look a lot alike. I'd almost assume you were brothers if I didn't know any better, and I've met all the Mandrake men in Hampshire," Kassandra dutifully informed them, examining his face with her eyes. "You've got the same face, well, except for the hair—but I'm assuming that must come from your mother's side of the family."

Christian opened his mouth to respond, but he shut it again. Then it seemed as though all the blood had drained from his face.

"They're Alfred's distant cousins," Thomas said, taking his seat at the head of the table. "And they were quite late on their arrival. I'd been expecting them for quite some time."

"Is she a Barley?" Tiny piped up.

"Christian," Kassandra chastised, and Tiny bowed his head in shame.

His face twisted with sadness, cheeks reddening, and doe eyes staring at the floor.

"Do forgive him," Kassandra said with a sweet smile. "I'm sure you're of proper birth."

Hermione noticed her half brother wince at the phrase *proper birth*. Tiny reacted much of the same way, looking more ashamed than he had beforehand.

Hermione understood what the child was implying, as her skin more closely resembled the Barleys, whose long African American lineage created skin tones that ranged from a light golden brown to deeper and darker bronze. She knew Tiny would only lack exposure for a few more years, likely less as he'd eventually meet her mother, Isabel. Kassandra was only twenty at the moment, according to the date on Thomas's paper, as it was October 1971, Tiny was newly three. This woman's birthday was near Christmas, but she wouldn't make it to her birthday. And no matter how hard Hermione tried, all these redundant facts wouldn't stop turning over and over in her head.

"Um . . . Thomas," Hermione said, drawing the man's attention. "How long do you think we will need to complete our . . . *project?*"

Thomas took a swig of his coffee and then thought for a moment. "A year or two at worst, six months at best, and a week or two if we're lucky."

"What?" Hermione squeaked out.

"I'd say there's still plenty to work out in our research," he said. "If we conduct ourselves in an orderly fashion—"

Oh sweet Merlin, she thought, *we're stuck here. I got us stuck here.*

His words became muddled and far away. Her thoughts began to race, and suddenly Hermione swayed. Caught in a daze of some sort, she faintly registered her brother's concerned expression, then the next thing she knew, the floor rose to meet her, and the world was unbearably dark.

Afternoon at Pleasant Manor

October 1971

A grandfather clock tolled somewhere inside the bowels of Pleasant Manor, and Hermione winced at the sound. There were about 8760 hours in a year, which meant she might still have 8735 hours before Thomas reached a solution, and from the confused expression on his face, she was betting on more. Thomas, was leaning against the sideboard cabinet, blueprints in hand and a look of intense focus on his face.

A day had passed since the disheartening news, making Hermione distraught and turning Christian Carlisle into an avid reader. Thomas marveled at her brother's studious nature, though Hermione knew what her brother was planning. Christian was researching everything he could about creating a temporal tempest. It was one in the afternoon on a Saturday, and she was certain that he was awake upstairs, flipping through old books, while she sat in the parlor, sweating by the fireplace in an armchair that was probably older than her.

She spent most of the morning reassuring herself by considering all the ways their circumstances could be worse—including the possibility of fainting again and being unconscious for another ten hours. But as she considered sleeping the day away, a door near the front of the house creaked open.

Thomas jumped and spilled his tea on his blueprints, causing her heart to sink in her chest.

We're never going to get back, Hermione thought as she stared at the blueprints in horror.

But Thomas waved his wand over them and pulled the liquid from the pages, restoring them to their former glory. Then he spun on his heel, and a grimace settled on his face. Hermione followed his gaze to the hall, where a man who looked exactly like her father stood. And, of course, it was her father—not that this much younger Alfred knew that. Nor did he bear any of the warmth her father did. In fact, his expression shared an uncanny resemblance to a bust on the mantelpiece in the living room, beside two equally discomforting busts of her grandfather and uncle Malicent.

"Alfred?" Thomas stated pointedly.

Alfred didn't respond; instead, he stared tentatively at Hermione with a puzzled expression spreading across his face. "And this is . . ." He trailed off. "Don't I know you from somewhere?"

Hermione stared at him blankly. Her chest tightened. He didn't remember her. While she was relieved that he didn't, a lingering fear gnawed at her, that he might eventually place her. She still hadn't told Thomas that they'd run into him earlier.

"She's your cousin—Hermione," Thomas answered for her, now staring down at his blueprints. "And what brings you here so early in the morning?"

Alfred walked over to the armchair across from Hermione and took a seat, his eyes still on her. "I couldn't sleep," he said. "I figured I'd get some fresh air. Then Malicent told me you had guests, and as two of my sons and their mother are here, I thought I'd pop in for a visit."

Thomas chuckled dryly. "While I appreciate your concern, your cousins hardly pose a threat to you or anyone else in our *family*. In fact, as I recall, it was my suggestion for Kassandra, Christian, and Sebastian to relocate within the first half of the month, but you wouldn't have it."

Hermione's head reeled at the emphasis on the word *family*. Their heritage, their birthright, all of it would be lost if they couldn't make it back. And the mere mention of Kassandra traveling made Hermione nauseous. She knew Thomas was purposefully changing the subject but wished their conversation didn't have to revolve around Kassandra.

"We need to at least consider the dangers of them traveling at the moment," Thomas said. "You may be the head of our family now, you may even go by Lord Mandrake, but you are still my son, and I beg you to see reason." Thomas took a deep breath. "They shouldn't travel now. There is war in the air—"

Alfred's gaze turned pensive. "There's always war in the air."

Hermione suppressed a shudder. He sounded like Gianni had, and it frightened her. Her father would never be so curt, especially with her grandfather. The Alfred Mandrake she knew was diplomatic, he listened to his advisors, and he . . . he had spent decades preventing war in Hampshire. And this young man was a skilled wizard, but the longer the argument dragged on between the two, the more young and naive he sounded. And perhaps she was harsh to believe so, having thrown together a half-hazard plan herself to save him—or the much older, more mature, and more reasonable version of Alfred Mandrake.

There was nothing about dealing with her mid-twenties father in any of those theory books. At the moment, all they had was Nikolai Verax, a French wizard and infamously famous philosopher who had written numerous manuscripts condemning the usage of dark magic. And the books were undeniably clear on the fact that a temporal tempest caused two timelines to collide, resulting in the destruction of either one or both: *"The violent fluctuations of a temporal tempest resemble that of a hurricane, obliterating all in its path without weakness or remorse. A collision of two realities, holding similarities but grappling with incomprehensible differences. The mutual shift in time will be an uneasy battle for both realities. In the end, one will reign, as there can be no other—and to destroy a world that is not your own, in my humble opion, would be criminal."*

The moment she woke from her fainting spell, Hermione sought a solution. She took the first opportunity to finish reading the book, but the more she read, the worse she felt. She couldn't understand how, in all his wisdom, Nikolai Verax hadn't theorized a solution to save both worlds.

"The dominant reality will be altered by the other. These changes are unpredictable. They are no more understood than

the most fearsome creatures of the magic world. A reality disturbed will have repercussions for all that live within the dominant. All magic is not without cost, and even if the greatest good occurs from the tempest, dark magic always comes to collect."

"Enough!" Hermione shouted.

The two men turned to look at her, appearing to have forgotten that she was in the room.

"I hardly think now is the time for a father-son squabble," Hermione said. "Do you?"

Alfred scoffed at her words.

Thomas shot him a look of warning but then returned his focus to her. "Hermione, have you considered getting some rest?"

Hermione was taken aback by his suggestion.

"Of course she hasn't. She's been helping you sort through your collection of absurd contraptions," Alfred sneered.

Thomas narrowed his eyes at Alfred, then quickly he regained his composure. "I'm merely concerned about your well-being."

"But never mind Kassandra, Christian, and Sebastian," Alfred interjected pointedly. "What could you be working on that's so important . . . Hermione?"

Hermione's face flushed, and she balled her hands into fists. She wanted to yell at him. *Stopping Gianni from starting a war in your name. Saving your life. Saving my reality—my future,* she thought, staring at Alfred. But his expression remained unchanged. He wasn't threatened by her. In fact, he looked bored. And for a moment, she felt he was testing her.

So Hermione took a deep breath to compose herself and answered as politely as she could muster. "We're working on something that will change lives."

"Really?" Alfred said skeptically.

"Yes . . . it's going to save countless lives . . . you just don't know it yet."

"So Father has 'sold' yet another soul on another *world-changing* idea," Alfred said mockingly. "Darling, unless you're a seer, you can't truly know the future."

Hermione smirked. It was hard not to laugh.

For a moment, she wanted to tell him she was a time traveler and knock that ridiculous smirk off his face, but she chose not to. This wasn't the time or place to reveal that information.

Alfred cocked his head to the side and then slowly began to nod.

"You were at the subway station," Alfred said, and Hermione's heart dropped.

She wanted to respond, but her mind had gone blank. She couldn't do anything but stare at him.

Alfred chuckled. "Yeah, that's it." He nodded, relishing in his discovery. "That spell your friend shot at me nearly knocked me off my feet. I was impressed. We could do with more fighters down here like him. In fact, they should've sent him down when we called for aid. What's your relation to him? Cousin? Wife?"

"He's my brother," Hermione answered. "And I doubt he'll have any interest in *your* war."

"It's not *my* war," Alfred corrected sharply. "I'm only fighting it to keep the peace."

"Funny way to keep the peace," Hermione retorted. "You

nearly killed me!"

Alfred's face contorted, and Hermione's heartbeat quickened.

"When?" Alfred asked. He studied her coolly, maintaining a composed, penetrating gaze.

Hermione scoffed. "At the station," she said.

His detached facade briefly cracked as a flicker of surprise momentarily crossed his face. But just as quickly as it appeared, his expression resettled into a mask of calm indifference, concealing any hint of emotion.

"I only shot disarming spells in your *brother's* direction," Alfred said, eyeing her strangely. "The only spell that could've potentially hurt someone was the one Horace made ricochet back toward the mundane that was present, but I don't recall seeing you or your brother at the time. Besides, that spell wouldn't have killed you."

Hermione chewed her lip. "Well, um . . . what about the human?" she said, hoping to change the subject.

"What about her?" Alfred responded, easing back into the armchair.

He took the bait, she thought, and her shoulders relaxed.

"What happened to her?"

Alfred scoffed. "Well, I didn't hurt her if that's what you're thinking," he said, though he didn't seem at all interested in elaborating further. "But she certainly wasn't in as much emotional distress as you were by a rogue spell."

Hermione gritted her teeth, and she was prepared to administer a severe tongue lashing, but Thomas interjected before she could do so.

"Perhaps the stress of the situation caused a panic attack," Thomas offered sincerely. "Which is why I think it'd be best for you to rest for a few hours. You've clearly had a rough couple days—*travel* can take a toll on the body and especially the mind when you've come such a long way."

Hermione took a deep breath. She could feel the weariness in her body as he spoke of it. Her legs ached from running, and she was sure that bags were developing beneath her eyes. Travel did take a physical toll on her, so she could only imagine what the effects of time travel had done to her physically. And when Hermione thought back on it, she had never fainted in all her life, though she had never landed nearly thirty years in the past before either.

Alfred stared at Hermione, observing her as if he was attempting to decipher her intentions, based solely on her expression and attire. And when he reached a consensus, he said, "We can finish talking later, at dinner, and perhaps you and your brother can join me and my friends for a parlor game at Castle Mandrake."

Hermione wanted to argue but found all her earlier qualms and anger giving away to exhaustion. So instead, she simply said, "Okay."

An Evening at Castle Mandrake

October 1971

Three hours later, they stood on a porch in front of an important-looking wooden door carved with intricate designs of snakes. Hermione faintly recalled it being exchanged for a less elaborate door when she was six. They waited for Alfred, who had taken it upon himself to leave Pleasant Manor early to ensure his servants prepared his home for extra guests, thus leaving them to fend for themselves. And to Hermione's surprise, Christian also accepted the invitation and even implied it was a better option than sulking around the manor.

Hermione turned her back to the door, closed her eyes, and took a deep breath in and out. *We just have to make it through the evening,* she told herself. *Thomas will find a solution.* She was hoping to convince herself of that. She repeated the action several times, feeling calmer with every breath, but before she could release the ninth breath, she heard a loud *crack!*

Her eyes snapped open. She meticulously scanned the front yard until she noticed a stream of residual smoke in the air that led down to a group of ten people walking toward them.

"Recognize any of them?" Christian asked lowly.

"No, why would I?" Hermione answered.

Christian gestured toward them as though it would make them more familiar.

"From the walk alone, I'd guess the blond is Eric Graves, and beside him, Martha Harrington, his soon-to-be wife. The Graves sisters, Fey and Yelena, then, of course, your fiancé's father, and—"

The door opened behind them, and Christian bit his tongue.

A thin, dark-haired male teenager with round glasses and black attire stood in the doorway, staring at them, as though he were trying to intimidate them. Hermione felt her lips quiver as she tried to suppress a laugh, but Christian didn't do as much to hide his amusement.

"Christian," he said with a smile, holding out his hand to the teen.

The teen met it with his own, but his eyes narrowed at Christian. "Malicent," he said, not letting the handshake go on for too long. "So, you two are our cousins."

"I'm afraid so," Christian said jokingly.

Malicent didn't crack a smile.

Hermione finally did. She had never been less intimidated by her uncle. Of course, he would become a skilled wizard and her father's right hand, but this version of him was neither of those things.

"I'm Hermione," Hermione said, introducing herself.

Malicent's eyes flicked over to her. "Yes, Alfred mentioned that you seemed rather perturbed by your present circumstances—whatever those may be," he said, and from his expression alone, Hermione wondered what Alfred had said about her. He shook his head, ruffling his wavy hair, and shifted his pointed gaze behind her. "Took you long enough, Eric."

"Merlin, are you starting already?" Eric said, looking him over. "Martha might begin to think I'm marrying you come summer. And who might you be?"

Hermione blushed; she hadn't expected his question to land on her. She had hardly thought of how she was dressed when she left but couldn't help thinking of it under his critical eye. Eric Graves was easily the most princely-looking man she'd ever seen. Though it wasn't his golden hair or his catlike gray eyes that caused this effect, nor his flawless pale skin smoothing over his perfect angular features. It wasn't the casual black suit he wore either, but perhaps it was the quiet confidence sternly contradicting an underlying haughtiness.

"Hermione," Martha answered for her. She wore a cream-colored dress and a cheery expression. "Alfred had mentioned that you may need some company, and I hope that Eric's sisters and I will do."

Martha gave Hermione a warm smile before climbing up the stairs to better introduce herself.

"I'm Martha," she said sweetly, darting a glare back at Eric, who scoffed in response. "Well, shall we take this party inside, Malicent?"

Malicent stepped aside to let them in, leading them into the foyer, where everyone quickly shed their coats as if they were a second skin. Fey and Yelena were also wearing cream-colored dresses—and Hermione felt as though she'd missed the memo. She wore a satin dress that was a deep green color —one of her family's colors.

"This way," Malicent said. "Don't dawdle. I don't want anyone to get lost."

Hermione smiled understandingly—certain the latter comment had been directed at her and Christian. Christian didn't seem to notice—or, more likely, care. Instead, his eyes wandered around the halls as the group walked. She kept pace with him but felt slightly annoyed. Christian hadn't given her any implication of his intentions for coming to Castle Mandrake or if she could be any help in whatever plan he'd concocted. But at the moment, he was too busy taking in the differences between this and their home in 1996. She had immediately noticed oil paintings lining the walls of the long hall they were being led down, each paired with a bust, portraying a Mandrake man bearing an expression ranging from melancholia to arrogance. But none of them looked as though they were delighted with having their portrait painted. The lights in this hall were gold and made every painted face look brighter, even if their expressions were grim.

In time, they passed another hall that was crowded with statues, where serving elves were dusting, wearing cloth masks over their face to avoid breathing in the debris. But no matter how far they walked, and no matter how high or low she searched, she had not seen one clock. Not anywhere hidden amongst the paintings, or standing on a table, or hidden behind a tapestry—there wasn't a clock anywhere. It was strange but mostly unsettling.

In the absence of a clock, time seemed to waver,

unbroken by its rhythmic tick. Each hall held its breath as if trapped between past and future, caught in a haunting limbo where actions and their reverberations intertwined.

By the time they'd reached the living room, Hermione felt as though they had walked miles, and perhaps they had; she didn't care. When she saw the black and emerald-green button-tufted leather sofas, she was more than happy to take a seat. But the moment she sat down, someone cleared their throat. When she turned to where the sound originated, she was unsurprised to see their host.

Alfred's lustrous black hair fell to his shoulders, and he wore an expensive-looking green suit with a serpent broach. His wand was in a holster on his belt, and he had a solemn expression on his face. Eric was the first to step forward to greet him, clapping him on the back, which made Alfred crack a smile. And as he greeted his guests, for a moment, Hermione thought he looked handsome, in a way that made him a factual imitation of Cupid. It was no wonder her mother had fallen for him.

Despite his arrogance, he wasn't hard to look at.

"If you'll excuse us for a moment, we need to fetch the game. Christian, mind helping?" Alfred said, and Christian nodded.

Alfred led Christian and the other men away, leaving Hermione with the women.

"Glad we're rid of him for a while," Yelena said with a small smile.

"Yes, Eric has been—" Fey agreed. Then she signaled a serving elf and turned to Hermione. "Rather difficult, I'm afraid. Your arrival is very untimely."

Martha sighed, darting a glare at Fey, though the apple-cheeked woman rolled her eyes at her soon-to-be sister-in-law.

"It's hardly Eric's fault. Kassandra was never any good at seduction," Martha stated as two serving elves arrived to serve them tea and biscuits.

Yelena giggled as if enjoying a private joke. "And if he would've just asked me to do it, we would already be married," Yelena said, pride in her voice, as she took a long sip of her tea. "Mmmm, it's been a while since I've had cinnamon tea," she said, looking at Hermione, acting as though Hermione hadn't been present during the exchange.

"Well, if Kassandra wasn't his type, neither are you," Fey said curtly. "The two of you could easily be mistaken for twins—well, except for the hair."

"Excuse you—"

"Not to break up this—" Hermione said, interrupting Yelena. She hesitated as everyone in the room turned toward her. "Riveting discussion. But aren't you wondering what's taking them so long?"

The three women exchanged a look and then began to laugh at some private joke she hadn't been a part of.

Hermione raised her eyebrows. "What's so funny?" she asked.

"Well, you don't really believe that Alfred trusts you, do you?" Yelena asked smugly. She uncrossed her legs and leaned forward. "Just because you share the Mandrake family name, it doesn't mean anything," she said, shaking her head as if Hermione were a child. "I mean, you could be the new one, for crying out loud, and he's had quite enough of them."

"Yelena," Martha said sharply.

"New what?" Hermione asked.

Fey furrowed her brow, clearly confused by her question. "Alison is dead. Isn't that why you're here? You're the proposed replacement?"

Alison . . . Alison . . . where have I seen that name before? Hermione thought, puzzling over it. All this fuss over a woman named Alison, that they thought she would replace. Then she knew where she'd seen it and her heart dropped.

Alison Mandrake, mother of Ares Aristotle and Achilles, her father's second wife and the only one he'd divorced, who had died giving birth to Achilles.

When she was able to gather some semblance of thought, Hermione said, "Oh no! I'm not here for that." She paused to let a wave of nausea pass. "We've just come a long way to visit Hampshire."

It had occurred to Hermione that Alfred's suspicions about her hadn't been put to rest, but never had it crossed her mind that his suspicions entailed her being offered as his new wife. Hermione had to stifle a gag. She would never, and hopefully, she would have the time to clear that up.

The women appeared less concerned and, Hermione noted apprehensively, changed subjects to Alfred's upcoming birthday party and its dress code. She waited for a few moments for someone to acknowledge the change. When no one did, a disquieting sensation took hold of her.

Fey gave Hermione a pitying look as if she noticed Hermione was having trouble keeping up the charade. "Hermione, are you alright? You're looking rather ill."

"Yes, I'm—" Hermione started to say, but a faint ringing in her ears had begun to grow louder.

She shifted uncomfortably as she scanned the living room

for the source of the sound. "I just . . . I need a moment," she mumbled as the ringing grew even louder, drowning out the gossiping women around her.

Her throat tightened as if a snake had coiled itself around it. White light flooded into the room, bright, all-consuming light, then the air was sharp. Each breath she took was ragged, desperate, the tiled floor beneath her rising and falling. A voice, calm, methodical, and melodic, called to her in the vast emptiness.

Hermione's fingers smoothed over the cool tile beneath them—had she fallen? She didn't remember falling. She pushed herself up, wavering as she stood.

When she steadied herself, she realized Martha was holding her up, bearing some of her weight. Martha was asking something, the words forming on her lips as she spoke, but Hermione couldn't understand them. She dizzily pulled away from Martha, and suddenly the bright light faded and Hermione was back in the living room. Though the earth shifted beneath her, she swayed side to side, trying to find her footing, refusing to fall. Then someone called her, but she refused to turn back.

And the farther she walked, the quieter their voice became. Hermione's heart raged inside her chest, beating so hard she thought her ribs might break. By the time she'd entered another room, the ringing had become unbearable, and no matter how far she walked, she couldn't escape it. It was everywhere. She hoped that counting the specks of dust on her dress would distract her, but when that didn't work, she found herself navigating around a kitchen island until she stopped in front of a sink.

Cornered by the piercing ring, she swore that at any

moment, she would vomit up something vile—perhaps a New York rat or whatever was violently gnawing her insides, causing her to make such a scene. But as the ringing quieted, somewhere in the distance, she heard a warm voice, deep and concerned, and it faintly registered that it belonged to her brother—Christian Carlisle.

A few moments later, he wasn't so far away from her—in fact, he was standing beside her. She was keeled over, holding onto the edge of the sink in a mostly unfamiliar room, suffocating on dry air.

Hermione tried to gather her senses, trying to think of what could've caused this. *Poison,* she thought to herself. But she doubted that any of Thomas's staff would've done so. A hex? No, she would've felt that. Even if she was god-awful at charms, she was still a witch.

Metal, sink, tile, window, she thought, listing everything in the room, hoping to pull herself back to reality. There was one window in the room, and it was right in front of her, looking out into the backyard, directly at the statue of her great-grandfather Damon Mandrake. Then she realized that she was being studied and that there was a weight on her right shoulder.

Christian, she thought. She looked toward her brother, whose hand was on her shoulder and whose eyes stared into her own.

He told her to breathe, and she obeyed, believing that the suggestion was in her best interest. And slowly, her heart rate settled, the air dampened, and breathing became easier as the weight baring down on her and the gravity of the past few days slipped away.

"She's okay," Christian told someone behind him.

Hermione didn't dare follow his eyes because she knew who it was. She could faintly see him in her peripheral vision. How tall he stood reminded her of him, even though what she saw was only at a distance. It was him.

"You're sure?" he asked.

And she began to wonder how they had known she was in distress.

Had she passed them when she had left the living room? Had Martha rushed to tell them what was happening—or had happened? She took another deep breath, wondering what could have possibly come over her and how much time had gotten away from her.

"I'm not—" Hermione said. "I'm not—I want—" She was stammering. Stumbling over such simple words. She hated hearing herself stammer.

"Come on, deep breaths," Christian instructed.

Hermione took a deep breath in, and when she exhaled, the weight on her chest lightened. "I want to go home," she said and immediately regretted it. She sounded weak and childlike, but it was the truth.

What had she done? Sweet Merlin, what had she done?

Good Plan

Her skin prickled with embarrassment as she realized what she had said, and Christian suddenly turned away from her. "Can you give us a moment alone? We just need to talk. When everything is settled, we'll meet you in the garden. There's no need to worry."

Hermione brought a hand up to her chest, feeling her heartbeat settle. "You really don't need to worry. I promise. I'm sorry for making such a fuss."

"No need to apologize. When you feel able, do join us in the garden," Alfred responded. Then he turned on his heel and left.

For a moment, she saw her father, much older, and heard his voice, much deeper. *When you feel able, do join us in the garden.* It was warm, familiar, and made her begin to feel safe. She'd thought she would be able to hold onto that feeling for a few seconds longer. But then Christian pulled out his wand and cast a spell on the room. He walked over to a small table against the wall and sat down.

He tossed a pile of papers on the table and began reading through them. When he found what he was looking for, he smiled.

"Hermione," he said. "Come here. I need to show you something." He gestured to a chair at the table.

She sighed but joined him.

Hermione sat down and tried to get a glimpse of what he was looking at. Her brother looked at her, mischief in his eyes, and she waited for him to say something.

"Do you see it?"

She cleared her throat. "See what?" Hermione croaked.

"Really?" he asked and frowned slightly. "I thought it was evident, but—" He paused and shook off the emotion. "I cast a silencing charm on the room. No one can hear us."

"It's a newspaper," Hermione said.

"I know that. Look."

She nodded.

"Do you see it?"

Hermione looked harder. She checked the column by Christian's thumb and suddenly understood. She remembered the Singletons' marriage announcements but hadn't noticed the obituary section. Among the older magicks that had died was a photo of her father, and his birth and death dates and obituary should have been beneath it. But both his death date and obituary were gone, and even the photo seemed to be fading. Something that would only happen in an aging newspaper.

"That's a good thing, isn't it?" Hermione asked.

"It'd be better if it were completely gone," Christian said softly. "But *yes*, we can take it as a good thing."

"When did it happen? What do you think it means?"

"If I had to wager a guess, it was when I spoke to Alfred earlier," Christian said softly, sifting through the pile of papers until he found one. "We were talking about magical artifacts that the Mandrake family has. You know, Achilles's armor, the crown of immortality, Morgana's spell book, that sort of thing. And there was one I thought he was lying about . . ." He shrugged, trailing off as he finally stopped on a piece of paper. "But then we went to the north wing, and he showed it to me in the museum."

Christian passed her the page, and Hermione stared down at it. There was an image of a man holding a wooden relic. And other, more detailed hand-drawn images of it with descriptions: *taken from lignum vitae, an unyielding wood capable of holding strange power. Light as air to its proper wielder, a weighty beast to the unworthy. Centuries held within its bones . . .*

"Amada's staff?" Hermione said in disbelief. "They still have her staff?"

Amada Torneau was a powerful witch and the wife of Damon Mandrake. History depicted her as a force to be reckoned with when she was alive, and her staff had been a gift from Death himself that had stayed in Castle Mandrake's museum for generations—though it was stolen by robbers in 1980. And how they'd managed to navigate around the wards was a mystery to her.

"It hasn't been stolen yet," Christian told her, staring down at it. "And perhaps it never will."

Hermione grabbed his wrist as she realized what he was suggesting. "No."

"We have to."

"Do we really *have* to?"

"We need a third disturbance."

Hermione met her brother's gaze. His eyes were dark, without even the slightest hint of mischief in them. She drew in a sharp breath.

Did they really not have another option? Then she remembered that Nikolai Verax had made it perfectly clear in his book that there needed to be six. And for a man that didn't want magicks using dark magic, he had a bad habit of giving step-by-step instructions on how to use it.

"How are we doing it?" she asked.

"Well, last I checked there were warding spells on the display case, but there weren't any on the staff itself, so it should be relatively easy to burn—"

"Burn?" She was finding it hard to believe. As a child, Hermione would have been excited just to see it, but *burning* a family relic?

"Yes, *burn*. It'd be the fastest way to get the job done."

"Yes, but," Hermione said hesitantly, "it's still in a case, and you don't know what spells could be protecting it. I mean, it's valuable, Christian. They didn't just leave it out in the open."

"No, they didn't. The wards on the display case might take some time to remove, that's why I'll need your help," he explained, then he shrugged. "Alfred thought it would be nice to invite us to a dinner party he's throwing."

She blinked, trying to make sense of what he was saying. "And you're mentioning this now because?"

"Because it provides us with the perfect opportunity to destroy the staff," Christian explained. He scratched his chin, deep in thought, as he considered the statement. "Eric volunteered to take a shift at the museum, but even if you do distract Eric long enough for me to get to the staff, it'll take both of us to destroy it. Unprotected or not, Amada's staff is powerful, and it might try to defend itself."

Hermione nodded slowly, faintly registering that Christian had mentioned Eric Graves but deciding she'd figure that out later.

"I can contain it," Hermione said honestly. "The staff. I mean, I might not be the best at charms, but I know how to use a shielding charm."

"Hermione, I don't doubt your gifts, but I think that sometimes you do," Christian mused.

Then he waved his wand in the air, and the sounds of serving elves cleaning passed through the kitchen. He smiled and gave Hermione a hug.

"I'm sorry I haven't been there for you, Hermione."

"You have," Hermione said, tears welling in her eyes. "It's just been hard, and I'm scared, Christian."

"Everything's going to be okay. As long as we've got each other," Christian told her, hugging her tighter and giving her a kiss on the forehead.

Hermione buried her head in his chest and began to feel safe again. A moment later, she heard the sound of the back door opening.

~

Even the gardens looked different. Rose bushes adorned the perimeter, and there were several new statues, leaving Hermione to wonder if they'd been removed or destroyed nearly thirty years from now. Most of the garden had brick paths that reached all the way to the fountain where the bench sat, where many years from now, she would sit with her grandfather. And yet the back of Castle Mandrake looked almost familiar, all the glass windows perfectly shined, giving glimpses of serving elves busying themselves with their work. At the moment, that brought her some peace. Although, however unfortunate it was, there was a Dimitri somewhere out there, likely propositioning others with money to help them track her and her brother down, perhaps to kill them and put them on display back home as a warning to future foes. But for now, she was here.

And what was most on display was the fine velvet coat Eric Graves had parted with and tossed unceremoniously on the grass, shedding all manner of earlier finery to duel Alfred Mandrake, who had done the same. Malicent stood by, monitoring the fight and ensuring everything was done fairly.

"You want a sparring partner?" a male voice said.

Hermione turned to him. He was pale with dark eyes and thick red-brown hair that was neatly cut. He was more rugged looking than his brothers, with a less charming personality and a stockier build. He wasn't ugly, but he was her Uncle Rowan, and he was smirking at her.

Hermione had to stifle a gag as she realized he was flirting with her.

"No, thank you, I'm quite fine," Hermione said, giving him a tight smile.

Malicent scoffed. "Stop making our cousin uncomfortable, Rowan."

Rowan rolled his eyes. "Oh, pipe down, pipsqueak! I'm just letting her know other options are available," Rowan said, grinning proudly. "After all, seeing as she has no interest in Alfred, I don't see why not. It's rare a woman her age isn't already spoken for."

Hermione darted a glare at Rowan. If she hadn't been sure whether her uncle had always been rude, she was now.

"No need to be rude," Yelena said. "I suppose certain lifestyles aren't of interest to everyone."

"It isn't rude to state facts," Rowan retorted. "I mean, she's only got a few good years left in her before she has no use to anyone."

"That's enough," Alfred said, barely raising his voice, and everyone looked to him.

When Hermione looked back at the makeshift dueling rectangle, Eric was dusting himself off and had a few scrapes, which Martha appeared to be attentively healing. Alfred was the clear winner.

"I've hardly said anything," Rowan snapped.

"Did I stutter?" Alfred said sharply. "No matter what your concerns are brother, she's our cousin and you needn't press her situation."

Hermione stared at Alfred. She wasn't sure which man she was angrier with, but she'd heard enough for one day.

"Don't speak for me," Hermione said, getting to her feet. "I can defend myself!"

She hadn't realized she had shouted at him until Alfred's expression changed—he was furious. It took her a second to realize what she'd done—she'd spoken out of turn and openly challenged the lord of their house in front of his inner circle. Hermione watched him warily. He towered over her, his eyes meeting her own, watching, waiting for her to back down. And it took all her nerve not to.

"You are on thin ice as it is," Alfred told her and then leaned down to whisper in her ear. "You and your brother may not be here to proposition me, but you are lying about something, and you are in my domain. Eventually, I'll find out. Maybe not today, maybe not next week, but I *always* find out."

Always, she thought, the word echoing in her skull.

He stood back up to his full height and looked her up and down. "Take out your wand," he demanded as he began walking to the other end of the dueling rectangle. "Take out your wand," he repeated.

"Is this really necessary?" Malicent asked, directing his question at Alfred.

Alfred glowered at him. "It is," he said, gesturing toward Hermione.

Hermione took out her wand and was having a difficult time concentrating. Malicent hesitated for a moment but then shook his head and gave the signal to start.

She managed to dodge Alfred's first spell, gasping at the sight of it, but her mind was muddled, and she was hit with the second. The spell struck her in her left arm, sending shooting pain through her shoulder, causing the nerves in her hand to twitch. It was a spell she couldn't identify.

As she tried to shake it off, Alfred pressed forward, and with a flourish of his wand, another spell came flying at her chest. But by some miracle, she blocked the spell and parried right, throwing a disarming spell back at him. Alfred not only blocked the spell but managed to send it back to her.

Her mind was a mess, but her newfound adrenaline numbed her shoulder. The two met blow for blow, but eventually, Hermione slipped on her feet and had to catch herself. She stood back up and took a few deep breaths.

She was slower than he was, and that put her at a severe disadvantage. To make matters worse, this young man would still become her father, and she couldn't very well do anything to hurt him without potentially messing with their future—and creating an unplanned third disturbance, which could have even greater repercussions on *her* future. But there was only so much she could do with disarming spells.

As he approached her, she raised her wand and cast a spell that she hoped would throw him off balance. But he deflected it and again tossed it back at her, sending her soaring through the air until she slammed into the grass, far away from the dueling rectangle. All the air left her body for a moment, and she gasped.

"Alfred!" Malicent shouted, but Hermione couldn't imagine trying to sit up to look at them. "A Merlin knows when to stop. What the hell is the matter with you?"

Faintly, Hermione was aware of someone running toward her, of her brother crouching down beside her and saying something.

But she couldn't manage to say anything, so what came out sounded more like a squeak. She lay there, breathing raggedly, until she slowly slipped into the darkness.

After

October 1971

Hermione woke with a start. She shielded her eyes from the bright lights above her. *Skylights,* she thought. *Why on earth are there skylights?* She sat up. Her ribs still a little sore, but she was glad to be alive. When her vision cleared, she spotted Christian at the other end of the room reading a book.

"You missed quite the spectacle," Christian mused, pulling a chair up to the daybed she was on. "I've never seen Grandfather so angry. He chewed out Alfred like he was a little kid. But he did make some good points. As Lord Mandrake, Alfred controls forty percent of Hampshire, so he can't go around dueling every person that slightly challenges his authority—it makes him look weak." Christian leaned back in the chair. "But I thought you held your own. A few broken ribs, but I mended them."

Serves him right, Hermione thought. But when she

thought of herself lying on her back in the grass, her cheeks flushed with embarrassment.

"And where are we?" Hermione asked, looking around the room for something familiar.

"Oh, come on," Christian said with an amused look. "At least take a guess."

Hermione rolled her eyes. Then she took a moment to think about it. The room certainly wasn't a suitable bedroom —this daybed was built for napping, perhaps, as the mattress was lumpy, but it certainly wasn't made for an overnight guest.

Scanning the room, she noticed wooden tables bearing tools and springs, half-finished gadgets, and a pile of papers that had fallen onto the floor. On the wall nearest to her was a torn blueprint of what appeared to be plans for a flying machine, and the word FAILURE written beside it in bold red capital letters—and then it clicked.

From her surroundings, she guessed it was Thomas's old workshop. She could imagine him tinkering, trying to make each invention work, but each invention, every new discovery, amounted to nothing. And after the death of his loving wife, eventually, he gave up the title of Lord and passed it down to his son before returning to his childhood home.

"Why'd you bring me to Grandfather's workshop?" Hermione asked.

"Well, the entire room is protected by a silencing charm," Christian said. "So it seems as good a place to talk as any."

"Sheesh, how hard did I bump my head?" Hermione said, wincing as she touched her head.

Christian considered her question. "I mean, I had to close

up a small cut, but other than that, your head seemed fine. You might feel a little out of sorts for a bit. One hell of a duel though."

Hermione thought of Alfred towering over her, the fury in his eyes, and the sound of his voice when he'd whispered his suspicions into her ear. She swallowed down bile. Their small victory of discovering Amada's staff was short lived and overshadowed by the fact that they had overstayed their welcome.

"What's wrong?" Christian said. "You look like you've seen a ghost."

"Alfred suspects we're up to something and—"

"Of course he does," Christian said. "I'd be disappointed if he didn't."

Hermione rolled her eyes. "And what, pray tell, do you think we should do about it?"

"Nothing."

Hermione sat up in the daybed and stared at him. Had he not heard what she said about the young Lord Alfred Mandrake? Had he forgotten how badly the same lord had injured her in a duel?

Christian sat motionless, holding two maps with locations covered in Xs. The maps were of the mundane and magical worlds, and they appeared to be mended together by glue at the intersection of the train station. Under any other circumstances, Hermione would have swatted them out of his hands, forcing her half brother to acknowledge the problem at hand. Instead, she stared at Christian while cradling her head, relieved she was still alive.

Her father was the last person she would ever suspect to

nearly kill her—albeit this was a younger, rasher version of him. Christian looked up from the map, his eyes glittering as though he'd made a discovery.

"I just—I don't think that's important. But I think I'm getting close," he said. "You know, to finding out which Dimitri followed us." He gestured to the maps, spreading them out in front of her.

Hermione was hesitant to look at them. But she forced herself to shake off the feeling and inspected them.

She couldn't make sense of any of the endless Xs marked on the page. Though, she guessed that he'd ruled out their grandfather's childhood home as an area of interest.

"I think they'd avoid the obvious places," Christian said.

Hermione swallowed dryly and immediately wished she had water. "How do you know? They may not be some clever conjurer."

"Yes, but I've also checked. Here, here, and here," Christian explained, pointing to various points on the map. "There weren't any magical traces of them near Pleasant Manor or anywhere within a five-mile radius."

She cleared her throat. Christian pulled out his wand and summoned a glass, filled it with water, and handed it to her. Then he carried on as if she had never interrupted.

"I did find traces of them around local Dimitri hangouts," Christian said. "I didn't stick around too long though— couldn't pass as a Dimitri, and I haven't found any pictures of their loyalists that aren't dead. So without anyone to mimic, the closest thing I can predict is—"

"They're looking for help and looking for us," Hermione said.

Christian nodded, but he was smiling slightly.

"What?"

"It almost felt like we took a step forward in managing this whole debacle."

There was a long silence between them, and then he added, "Right. We've got a dinner party to attend and a time-line to corrupt."

By the time Castle Mandrake's serving elves had washed Hermione's hair and scrubbed her skin raw, it was nearly nightfall, but the Graves women insisted on finding her a dress in Fonda Abbot's old dressing room. Yelena and Fey debated over which Lady Alfred Mandrake had better style when she was alive; Fey relied heavily on the fact that all the dresses within the room were worn at one time or another by the first lady, Fonda, but Yelena retorted with how Alison was not a looker, nor did she have an extensive wardrobe; however, she did add a few of the more regal dresses, which stayed preserved in the castle's museum. Hermione had no opinion on either.

"You should wear this one," Martha said, handing Hermione a green gown with snakes embroidered on the bodice. "I'll lace you up."

Hermione didn't get a chance to reply before Martha shoved her behind a dressing screen. Though if Hermione were honest with herself, she didn't resist as she would be more than happy to remove her mud-riddled and torn green satin dress.

"But what about Laoghire?" Fey mused. "Now there's a scandal."

"Laoghire?" Hermione asked as she tossed the dirty dress over the screen.

She thought about peeking out but didn't want to appear overeager.

"Fey, you know we're not meant to mention her," Yelena said, sounding almost playful.

Hermione peeked from around the dressing screen and noticed Yelena was snickering.

"Oh, I liked Laoghire," Martha murmured sadly as she sewed pearls back onto the hem of the blue gown she intended to wear.

"What happened to her?" Hermione asked, pulling the other gown on and inspecting herself in the mirror.

Her hair looked nice, though she rarely wore dresses like this to anything short of a ball, and Hermione couldn't remember the last time she'd attended one. But she was surprised at how much it complimented her and would likely look even better once it was laced up. And strangely, Hermione found herself wishing that she could attend more balls.

Maybe I could ask for one before the wedding when I get back, Hermione thought. Then she chided herself. *Focus, Hermione, focus!*

Hermione shook off the thought. She still had to distract Eric and get into the museum without being noticed. They still needed to destroy Amada's staff—because what if they never got another chance? She couldn't risk getting distracted by dinner parties, balls, or her wedding.

"Little miss Laoghire Laney Mandrake was Alfred's other mistress when he was married to Fonda," Yelena said coyly. "But I can never remember if he started seeing her or Penelope Price first."

Hermione coughed but didn't comment. Though she already knew the answer. Her immediate distress was caused by how tightly Martha was lacing the dress.

"It wasn't Penelope first. Laoghire was Fonda's handmaid remember? Handmaid at seventeen, mistress at nineteen," Fey corrected.

Yelena rolled her eyes. "As though it made a difference. He was still bedding Kassandra and Penelope," Yelena said. "I swear, he was putting out bastards as though it was going out of style."

Martha scoffed. "As if you aren't eager to marry him all the same," she said sharply. Then she turned her attention to Hermione and loosened the strings. "Sorry, you don't go out often, do you?"

Hermione gasped for air as the garment loosened, and Martha properly fitted it.

"Our marriage would be different," Yelena stated matter-of-factly. "Our children would be of proper birth and hold greater claim to the house. After all, blood may reign supreme, but bastards are beneath true-borns *always*," Yelena said, admiring herself in the mirror. "A bastard could never be head of the Mandrake family—do you have any idea how many families would defect?"

"Do you think so?" Martha asked. "What if they were all that was left?"

Yelena and Fey exchanged a look, and both grimaced at Martha's proposal. Fey made a fake vomiting sound and held her chest as though the thought overwhelmed her. Hermione had to stop herself from rolling her eyes, but the Graves family was known for their traditional values. True-born children were born within wedlock. Bastard-born children were born without any of those protections. True-borns were passed titles. Bastard-borns couldn't receive them unless they were legitimized—but Hermione knew her family would never have to deal with any of that. Even with the younger Alfred's frequent seed-spreading, her eldest brother Gianni was alive and well. He was heir apparent, and he'd succeed their father when his time came.

"You're ever the progressive, Martha. And I suppose . . . it's *admirable*," Yelena remarked.

"But perhaps those ideas are best kept to yourself," Fey added. "We wouldn't want to unnerve Hermione with such talk."

"What ever do you mean?" Hermione said sweetly, and as she saw Fey's expression shift, she knew that she was beginning to dig a hole for herself.

"I'm sure you know what I mean."

"Not in the slightest," Hermione said, checking herself in the mirror. "I find Martha's thoughts quite refreshing."

Yelena's grimace caught Hermione's eye in the mirror, and she had to suppress a laugh. She hadn't thought the Graves woman would be so easily bothered by her opinion. Though the silence between them became too long for Fey, so she interrupted it by mentioning accessories to wear with their gowns seeing as the late Fonda Abbot had the most abundant collection—and the latter comment started another hefty debate. This time Hermione surrendered and took part, actively discussing how often columnists discussed Fonda's many, many luxury jewelry pieces that could rival and surpass any royal mundane's collection and gossiping about the mysterious Alfred Mandrake of Merlin county and bickering over notorious nobles—actively participating in two activities she would have never predicted herself to enjoy.

A Night in the West Wing

October 1971

From where she stood on the balcony, Hermione saw lights moving across the front lawn toward Castle Mandrake. They were bobbing along with guests flooding in through the gates in a steady stream, their voices faint from where she was. She had managed to escape the Graves women by excusing herself to the bathroom, though she'd taken a detour and reached the west wing quickly enough. Or as quickly as can be believed in a large castle. But in that time, she'd managed to spy an unattended guest list that was at least several pages long. And she couldn't help but think to herself. Could they possibly be so lucky? Had Alfred truly somehow invited over two hundred people to this dinner party and they'd all RSVP'd? Or was it just her imagination? Silently, she waited, thoughts racing, until all she could hear was the rhythmic thump of her heart, and the raindrops on the balcony railing, and the toll of the grandfather clock.

Finally, ten o'clock.

She spun on her heel, determined to make her way to the museum without being seen, and her heart leaped to her throat as she saw Eric crossing the nearby hallway, only a few feet away from her. She was thankful he didn't stop until he had rounded a corner at the other end of the hall. For a moment, she wanted to turn around and sprint in the opposite direction, but instead, she forced herself to follow Eric at a normal pace and a safe distance.

Once near the library, she risked peeking at him from behind a broken statue. He wasn't looking at her. In fact, he didn't seem to notice her at all. He was sitting in a chair near the museum entryway, one hand covering his yawning mouth.

Hermione hesitated. *What was it Christian had said?* She faintly recalled him telling her Amada's staff was located in a central exhibit beside her taxidermized pet, Fluffs, a white Persian cat. There were warding spells around the staff itself. She was sure Christian would be removing them by now.

Years ago, when Christian had explored the museum as a teen, he stumbled upon a hidden alcove. The passage, concealed behind a painting, demanded a mastery of magic Hermione had yet to acquire—a complex charm that was the key and allowed entry to the user. A twinge of frustration grated Hermione's nerves. Christian's discovery in adolescence became his advantage. Thus, while he effortlessly entered the museum, Hermione had to seek an alternative route.

Every moment she stood there was another moment wasted.

She stepped out into the light and waited for her heartbeat to return to normal. It took longer than expected, but when she was calm, she walked up to Eric at a surprisingly normal pace and smiled at him.

Eric looked at her and cocked a brow.

"Hi," Hermione said.

"Humph . . ." was the barely audible noise that passed Eric's lips. "Are you lost or something? "

"No." Hermione laughed nervously.

"Then what do you want," he asked in a disinterested tone. "The party's downstairs."

He pulled a book from his inner breast pocket, flipped it open, and began to read.

Hermione stared at him blankly. She assumed that was Eric's way of ending the conversation, but she couldn't allow that.

In a snap judgment, she pulled out her wand and said, "Immerbus Amare."

She watched as a tangled silver surge of waves leaped from her wand and swam up Eric's nose. And suddenly, she had his full attention. He stood up and stared down at her, his eyes fixed on her.

She would have scorned herself if the charm hadn't worked so well. Of course, Hermione knew it was dark magic. Nikolai Verax had written about it; the "love drunk" spell made victims deeply infatuated with the caster. It was quicker than seduction, and the fact that it was considered dark magic was neither here nor there.

"Now, Eric, I need you to help me," Hermione said.

He leaned close to her. " Whatever you need."

She took a step away from him.

"I need you to take down the barrier so I can get through,

and I need you to show me where Amada's staff is. Can you do that for me?" Hermione said softly. He looked at her and then at the entryway. For a moment, he hesitated.

Then Hermione spoke again. "I really need you to take down the barrier."

Eric nodded slowly and took out his wand. His hand began to shake slightly, but it steadied. And with a flick of his wrist, a line of white particles shot out and the barrier fell.

Then the museum lights flickered on, illuminating the gray tile floors and revealing a vast collection of magical artifacts, including the crown of immortality. The crown was encased in a glass tube at the center of the exhibit, suspended in the air by its own magical properties. But before Hermione could take it all in, Eric groaned beside her. With a wave of dread, she saw him clutching his forehead.

Damn it, she thought.

She'd gotten too cocky; the spell was already wearing off. Eric shook his head furiously, keeling over.

"What's happened?" he slurred.

He looked at Hermione and then into the museum. His eyes met hers, and recognition spread across his face. Her heart skipped a beat. And even though she knew she had done the spell properly, obviously, it was no longer working on Eric.

"What did you . . ." he started.

She lifted her wand. "Tranquitis," she said quickly.

Eric paled and stiffened and fell onto the floor. Hermione's heart pounded in her chest.

Well, there goes that idea.

She'd stunned him, but it was only temporary. Sure, she was no good at charms, but she was good at hexes. Sure, she no longer had a guide to Amada's staff. She would probably struggle without his help, but struggling was better than being caught. So she grabbed Eric by his feet, deciding to pull him into a nearby closet and shut him inside. Afterward, she conjured a latch and padlock, locking it quietly.

She briefly felt a surge of guilt as she stared at the door. Then she thought of her father and Gianni and all the people that had died because of the Dimitris, and her guilt faded away.

Suddenly, she heard shouting, and when she turned around, she saw shadows on the wall headed toward her.

Panic got the best of her, and she rushed inside, moving as fast as she dared, but she lost her footing and fell onto her hands and knees, sending her wand clattering across the floor until it reached the crown of immortality's case. Behind her, heavy footfalls rushed through the hallway. She wanted to grab her wand, but she forced herself to hide against a display case holding Merlin's robes, hoping the garment would obscure the uninvited guests' view of her.

"Eric!" a voice called out from behind her.

Looking over her shoulder, she saw a young Rowan teetering on his feet, searching for the other wizard. He looked both ways and perhaps toward Hermione when he looked into the museum. She waited a few moments, afraid that she had been seen. Then, in the silence, she heard footsteps.

"Guess he's gone to the bathroom or something," Rowan told someone.

They sighed. "Of course," said a familiar voice. "He's never where he's supposed to be."

"No need to be so harsh, Malicent," Rowan said. "I'm sure he'll be back any moment now."

"I doubt it," Malicent said. "Hmmm . . . why is the barrier down?"

There was silence between the two of them.

"Oh, you're imagining things," Rowan said. "I'm sure whoever took it down just forgot to put it back up. It's only us and a couple of friends tha know how, after all."

"Eric!" Malicent called, and Hermione gulped. He sounded angry. "Eric!" he called again.

Hermione peered at the entryway and watched in horror as Malicent stepped inside. He looked around silently and pulled out his wand.

She pressed her back against the glass and, for a moment, swore her heart stopped. She quieted her breathing and hoped that would be enough to avoid detection.

"Eric!" Malicent shouted.

Rowan groaned. "Honestly, Mal, you're being dramatic!" he said. " Just reset the barrier, and we can return to the party. I'm sure Eric will be back any second."

"But—" Malicent started.

"Tell me, what could Eric possibly be doing that could be so concerning? It's Eric, after all. At most, he's showing some woman a good time before he's bound to Martha for the rest of his life. It's hardly our concern."

"It's just—"

"I've heard enough, Mal," Rowan said, interrupting his younger brother again. "We could be downstairs at the party, but instead, we're up here calling a man who clearly doesn't want to be found at the moment. So we should go back down and enjoy ourselves, as Eric already is."

Hermione waited silently. She stared at her wand against the glass display case, undoubtedly too far for her to reach. There were two of them, and she had no way of explaining why she was there. And they would be hard-pressed for an explanation. If she moved, she risked giving away her position, but if she didn't, it would only be a matter of time before Christian came looking for her.

Her heart began to race as she waited for Malicent's decision. Then, after a few moments, he sighed.

"Yes, I suppose you're right," he said. "Perhaps I'm overreacting. I'll reset the barrier, and we can rejoin the others."

"I know I'm right," Rowan said cockily.

Hermione couldn't help but roll her eyes. But at the same time, she was thankful. Thankful that Malicent was young and unsure of himself. Thankful that this younger version of him lacked experience with war and didn't trust his instincts yet. And she was even thankful that Rowan was cocky.

"Atta boy, Malicent," Rowan said. "Now that we're all set, we can get back to the party."

Hermione peered around the corner of the display case and saw Malicent take one last look into the museum before following his older brother. But she didn't move until their footsteps were so faint she could hardly hear them.

Slowly, she got up and walked toward the crown of immortality's display case. Her muscles relaxed once her wand was back in her hand, and in that same moment, she spotted a hallway lined with display cases of wands and portraits of their deceased owners.

She admired them as she walked through it. But she'd been so focused on the wands that she skidded to a stop when she saw Damon Mandrake's name engraved on a plaque beneath a black wand with runes carved into the hilt. His portrait was different from the rest. And though it took her a moment to realize the difference between them, she knew what it was. The eyes were looking at something. She followed its gaze, sure she must be hallucinating.

Hermione gaped when she emerged out of the hallway. Damon's gaze landed on a portrait of Amada at the other end of a wider exhibit of the women in her family. Beside it was a display case with the backside of a white cat.

She sighed softly. Relief washed over her as she walked past the women's exhibit to the taxidermied cat and smiled when she saw Christian. He was crouched beside a large display case, wand in his mouth, slowly plucking the glass off.

He said something, but it was muffled.

"What?" Hermione asked.

He let the wand fall out of his mouth and said, "Give me a hand."

Hermione earnestly nodded. She grabbed one end of the glass as her brother grabbed the other, easing it off and setting it down on the floor. When she looked at the staff, she noticed how the pale bark wistfully twisted around itself, like three snakes forever bound together in a warm embrace. The thought came to her to touch it, and somewhere inside her, she felt a pang of guilt. She was frightened, but she knew what they needed to do for the greater good of their world. Their future.

Hermione opened her mouth to speak, but Christian held up his hand, signaling her to stop. He stood up, then gestured for her to do the same and stepped back from the staff. She drew herself up onto her feet and waited, doing her best not to make a sound.

Her brother grabbed his wand off the floor, then he waved it, and the staff began to float.

He stood there for a moment in silent contemplation, but she understood. It was easier to think about destroying it than to actually carry out the act.

"Ready," Christian said, aiming his wand at it.

Hermione aimed her wand at the staff as well.

For a moment, she couldn't believe it. If someone had told her a few months ago, she would be nearly thirty years in the past, staring down Amada's staff, about to burn it, she would have called them insane. Yet here she was. Silently telling herself that at any moment, she would be on the ground, keeled over in pain from a rebounded spell, begging for death because the staff could make a move to defend itself.

"Ready," she said nervously.

But what choice did she have?

"We'll go on three," Christian told her.

She took a deep breath to calm her nerves.

"One."

Her chest tightened, and she tried to shake it off.

"Two."

She glanced at her brother. A bead of sweat streamed down his face, the determination in his eyes was nearly contagious, and she hoped she might find some of her own.

Christian took a deep breath, and as he exhaled, he shouted, "Three!"

Incindie, she thought, flicking her wrist. Fire spouted from her wand in a controlled stream, and Hermione cringed as it reached the staff.

To her surprise, the spell didn't rebound. The flame consumed the staff until it was swallowed whole, and her brother glanced toward her. Then she nodded, realizing it was a signal.

She cast a containment spell, creating a field around it. Then the staff began to spark, flinging light particles within the barrier, each one like a small firework—until nothing was left.

Hermione lowered her wand, and the spell dropped.

"That's it?" Hermione asked, feeling slightly underwhelmed. "All that, and—"

A horrible inhuman wail filled the air, and a burst of blinding light turned the world white. Air swept her off her feet, sending her backward until her back crashed into something solid. Hermione faintly registered the pain as she plugged her ears in a futile attempt to block out the banshee-like shriek. Suddenly air rushed all around her, the blistering winds biting at her skin as she fell forward and her head connected with the ground, and then the world was silent.

The Price of Change

Hermione groaned softly. Her body ached with a dull, persistent throb, a painful reminder that she had endured something beyond her comprehension. Memories of a haunting ordeal danced at the edge of her consciousness, just out of reach like fragments of a nightmare.

Her eyes fluttered open, and for a moment, she couldn't place where she was. The world around her was a murky haze of dimly lit shadows where a chilling hiss slithered through the air, sending shivers down her spine. Panic gripped her, and she scanned her surroundings, her heart pounding in her chest.

As her vision cleared, she saw it--smoke curled lazily from the remnants of Amada's staff, its once-mighty form reduced to ashes and embers.

"Don't move."

Christian, she thought. She shut her eyes for a moment,

feeling relieved she wasn't alone, and then turned her head so she could see him.

"I'm almost finished," he said without looking at her. "I just have to mend a few more wounds, but I can't promise you won't have some scarring."

Hermione nodded. She was too weak to argue. She was just grateful to be alive.

"What was that?" Hermione asked, but Christian didn't answer.

She felt stiff but was slowly regaining feeling in her legs and was trying to ignore the throbbing in her lower back.

What happened?

All she knew was that one moment she was standing, and the next, she was waking up on the ground. Her brother knelt over her, healing her wounds, and she was at a loss for words. Christian was working meticulously on her back, and she could feel her muscles twitching. She stared at the ash again, and relief washed over her.

We did it, she thought. *Somehow, we destroyed it.* But at what cost? Memories of the staff came rushing back to her: the sudden burst of light, the air rushing around them, and that sound. What could make a sound like that?

Hermione pushed herself up, pleasantly surprised her brother didn't stop her.

"Easy," Christian said, helping her the rest of the way.

Hermione knelt on shaky knees and coughed.

"What was that?" Hermione asked again.

"The disturbance," Christian answered. He looked around and shrugged. "I don't know what I was expecting it to be like, but it wasn't that."

"Do you think it'll be like that every time?" Hermione asked.

"Well, according to Nikolai's notes, each disturbance will be more intense than the last," Christian explained. He cleared his throat. "We'll just have to be careful."

He looked around as though he was searching for something.

Hermione opened her mouth to speak but stopped as Christian put his finger to his lips in warning. Christian crept close to the ground, stopping at the base of a broken display case and peering around it. He gestured for her to stay and made his way into the women's exhibit. Hermione sat there in silence, listening to the sizzling ashes of the staff.

After a few minutes had gone by, Hermione hurried after Christian. Each step was more painful than the last. Though the wounds were gone, her back still ached, and when she caught sight of her back in an ancestor's magic mirror, she surveyed the damage. She didn't care that her dress had been torn. But, unfortunately, there were small scars peppered over her back, some flat and others rigid and raised. She couldn't imagine how much pain she would have been in if Christian hadn't healed them. They may be difficult to explain when she got back home, but she could worry about that later.

When she finally found Christian, he was hiding inside a display case, with the door cracked ajar, looking at something in the wand hallway.

The moment he saw her, he looked annoyed and pointed at the hallway. Hermione leaned to get a better view, and her heart nearly stopped. Young Alfred was staring at the portrait of Damon Mandrake as if he were trying to gather some of his wisdom or perhaps his strength.

Thankfully, Alfred hadn't seen her yet, but she was worried he would find Christian at any moment, and she couldn't imagine it ending well. At first, she wasn't sure what to do, but then she got an idea—a bad idea, but an idea all the same.

Hermione walked over to Alfred calmly, acting as though she had no reason to worry. Thinking that if Malicent and Rowan had returned to the party, they might've brought their thoughts on Eric's whereabouts to Alfred, which would be the perfect excuse as to why she was here.

"Lost, cousin?" Alfred said, never looking away from Damon's portrait.

"No," Hermione said with a small smile. "I was just looking around and lost track of time."

Alfred turned to her. "Was Eric with you?"

"No, I haven't seen him," she lied. "I've just been looking around the museum. Why?"

He sighed and rubbed a hand over his face. "He was supposed to be guarding the entrance, but Malicent told me Eric took down the barrier for some reason, so I decided to come and check on him," he said, looking deathly serious. "But since you're here, I'd like to apologize for my behavior earlier. I shouldn't have lashed out at you like I did. There's no excuse for it, and I hope we can make amends one day."

For the first time since she'd arrived, Hermione saw the smallest glimpse of her father. Back home, Eric was her father's closest friend and confidant, so she could imagine that whatever reason he needed to speak to him was important, but, unfortunately, he wouldn't find him tonight, and it was her fault.

"Are you alright?"

He shook his head. "But you needn't worry," he trailed off, seemingly trying to end the conversation.

Hermione knew it, but when she glanced over at Christian, he signaled for her to distract him. She nodded.

"Um . . . I'd been told something rather interesting," Hermione said.

"Oh, and what's that?" Alfred asked.

"About your children."

Alfred's piercing gray eyes narrowed, and she had to suppress a shudder as she remembered the last time he had that look on his face. She had lost that duel and could have lost her life. It took all of Hermione's nerve to keep talking.

"That they have different mothers—"

"You mean that they're bastards."

Hermione was taken aback by Alfred interrupting her.

"There's no need to mince words. I know what they all say about them," Alfred said, staring more intently at Damon Mandrake's wand. "I legitimized them."

"Well, I'm sure they'll thank you for it. They'll have a father to their name. They won't be outcasts, and I'm sure Laoghire and the others were glad."

"But I'm sure you've heard the talk from the rest of our family—perhaps even from your father—that there shouldn't have been others to begin with."

"My father believes in giving others grace for their indiscretions. Especially those that we've already held ourselves accountable for."

Alfred studied her for a long moment. "Do you ever wonder what it would be like without all these rules, Hermione? I did. Or at least I did with Laoghire. I knew they wouldn't let me marry Kassandra, but even if they did, I wouldn't have my other sons. Guess I don't think I would have. It's just—there's no ordinary life in this world. Sometimes the weight of our name is too heavy."

"Much too heavy for one person to bear," Hermione said with dawning understanding. "You wanted to marry Kassandra."

"I saw a future with her at one point, but my advisers thought otherwise. They guessed it was the Graves family making a power play," he said, his eyes suddenly fixed on the portrait. "Perhaps they were."

Hermione felt her heart sink. She wanted to reach out to him, hug him, but was afraid she'd overstep some unspoken boundary. Or come across as plotting something. But mostly, she was afraid he'd stop talking. Though she now realized that Christian was long gone.

"You know, I've heard of places in the wizarding world where ice blooms like flowers from the sea, and the wind smells of honey, and the more I think of them, the more I know I'll never see them."

"Well, there's still time," Hermione said softly.

Alfred sighed.

"I'm not so sure there is. My advisers think I should marry again," he said, looking at her. "Of course, you know what my suspicions were." Hermione nodded in response. "But my father has brought it to my attention that it's yet to be decided—but I don't think I can do another arranged marriage."

Hermione was relieved to hear it but wanted to play a

convincing part as the Mandrake cousin from out of town that was also of pure Merlin blood.

So she said, "Why not?"

Alfred let out a bark of dry laughter. "Well, Fonda and I hated each other. We only shared a bed when we were required to. She was more after the money than the title. Alison was cold, but she could be warm at times. We came to a mutual agreement to do our duty and produce a few heirs. Then our lovers could entertain us. Which offered me some reprieve from everyday life. Some days I would hideaway in my father's workshop, rest on the daybed, look over his inventions, but after her death. I don't know. I couldn't sleep, I could hardly eat. I felt lost for a while. But every day since then, I've tried to undo the damage I did to our family name. I want more for my children." He turned to her then, ignoring the portrait of Damon Mandrake, his expression serious. "I've spent my life playing by their rules. But now I think I want something different."

"Like what?"

"I'm not sure you remember her. But there was a mundane in the station that night. I took her home and healed the scrape on her knee. She asked me to come see her the next day. Because she wanted to understand what had happened. So I did. And we spent hours just talking—I thought it'd be a shame to erase her memory. And I told myself I'd do it another day. Every time I would see her out on the streets, I'd tell myself next time . . . next time, I'll do it but—"

"You can't," Hermione finished for him.

An expression flashed across his face. It looked like sadness or maybe confusion. Hermione looked up at the portrait and wondered what their noble ancestor would think of it. She imagined, given the time he lived, that Damon would have adhered to traditional values, cold, calculated values that had protected the Merlin bloodline for centuries. She thought of her father. He had chosen his third wife, a mundane, the very same one who this young man was talking about now. And she wondered what Eric Graves had told him when they'd had this conversation.

"Could you see yourself marrying her?" she asked before she could lose her nerve.

He nodded. "I can. But how am I supposed to do that? Some loyalists may defect."

"Then are they really loyal?" Hermione said with a shrug. "If they believe in Merlin's lineage and your right to the power you've inherited, a mundane shouldn't change any of that."

He glanced at her and then back at the portrait. "You're a good cousin, Hermione," he said quietly. "I wish I could help you."

"Help me?"

"You look lost," he said matter-of-factly. "And you may not believe it, but if you're in need of help, you can tell me. We are family, after all."

Hermione stood there, dumbfounded. And though she was hesitant to give anything away, she went against her better instincts.

"When you were in your father's workshop, you didn't happen to see an old pocket watch?" Hermione said, hoping she didn't sound as though she was begging. "Might've appeared slightly criminal."

"Slightly criminal," Alfred repeated with a bemused grin.

But he did think about it for a moment. "Well, if it had anything criminal in nature that would've led to my father's arrest, I'm sure it would've been hidden—out of sight, out of mind," he said, giving her a look, as though hinting at something. Before Hermione could question him further, he said, "And I hope we can keep this between us. I wouldn't want anyone getting the wrong idea regarding either of our fantasies."

Then without another word, he gave her a small bow and walked away from her.

Hermione watched him disappear around the corner but decided to follow him, hoping to catch him before he left the museum entirely. She had no such luck and sighed as she stared at his back.

Hermione groaned, then heard a "*psst . . .*" a few feet away from her.

She turned and jumped, seeing Christian's floating head. He chuckled and took off a cloak that had been draped around his shoulders. She assumed either dried blood or dirt stained the fabric, which made her particularly uneasy.

"Where did you go? And what is that?" Hermione asked.

Christian laughed again and said, "Cloak of concealment —I think this one belonged to King Arthur, but I'm not sure."

Hermione rolled her eyes. "How old are you?"

"That's funny, coming from someone who hasn't even been born yet," Christian said with a smirk.

Hermione suppressed a smile, and for a brief moment, she felt like everything would be okay.

The Morning Time Stood Still

October 1971

Hermione sank into the chair, staring blankly at the blueprints in her hand, eyes tracing the lines of the drawing on the sheets of paper, hastily examining the notes. She sank deeper into the armchair in front of the fireplace, thinking only of the thin papers in her hands. Then Thomas cleared his throat. She looked at him, and he leaned in toward her, hunching over and resting his elbows on his knees.

"Where did you find them?" Thomas asked, gesturing toward the blueprints.

Hermione stared at him blankly for a few seconds. She could faintly remember thinking it—how uncomfortable that daybed had been. And if she didn't act, she'd always wonder if her hunch was right. Her mind raced to remember the spell to reveal hidden objects. Then there they were, right beneath the mattress. *Out of sight, out of mind.* Alfred had said it with such confidence, hinting at something. She was certain of it. And now these were the proof.

"Alfred told me," she said, handing the blueprints over to Thomas.

Thomas eyed her curiously. "He what?"

Hermione shook her head. "No, no, no. He merely hinted at it," she explained, and the older man calmed. But she could barely remember where the proverb had been used. Then it hit her. "My father used to tell me this story about wizards, two notorious criminals that have to hide their treasure so that no mundane can find it. But they use a spell to hide it from prying eyes, and it isn't discovered for two hundred years . . ." Hermione trailed off, as she couldn't help but remember how her father's voice would take on a low, secretive tone as he reveled in the wizards' daring escapades, recounting every time they'd outwitted the Magical Crime Unit time and time again. The details of the bedtime story had faded over the years, but the feeling of her father's arms wrapped around her and the wonder and excitement it had ignited remained strong. "I'm sorry," Hermione said, realizing she'd stopped talking. "I'm afraid I can't remember the rest."

"No matter, dear girl," Thomas said, patting her knee. "With these, I can certainly reset it. Why, the switch is just here," he told her, pointing one boney finger at a portion of the blueprints, and she nodded.

Hermione wasn't sure what she was looking at. The time trinket's inner mechanisms were somehow more interesting than those visible to the naked eye, but she couldn't make heads or tails of them. A normal pocket watch's anatomy was already complicated, different, especially those beloved by mundanes. But the time trinket had a near-living presence, its pieces folded into one another, with unicorn hair and golden strings pulled from fairy's blood bearing an uncanny resemblance to veins, all sheathed in a protective casing. If the gray liquid was its beating heart, the reset switch was its defibrillator.

"So you can fix it?" Hermione asked.

Thomas chuckled to himself. "Yes, why, I'm quite sure of it."

A wave of relief washed over her. This nightmare was almost over. If everything went well, they could extract one of their memories to get them to the right time and place. Then they'd stop their uncle, stop the war, save their father and the future. Hermione was eager to get it done. Thomas could reset the time trinket. She and her brother would be on their way. It would all be over soon.

The rain started around midnight, pelting the mansion's windows and roof in a way that made a shiver run down her spine. Trees swayed with the night's unforgiving winds, the younger trees bending, their branches torn from their bark bodies, while their older counterparts stood against the test of time. Lightning burst across the sky in blinding flashes, casting an eerie glow over the city below it. Hermione nearly jumped the last time the thunder struck, each time rumbling like a growl from a giant beast, shaking the floorboards beneath her feet. It was a primal sound, echoing through the dining room like the beating of a battle drum.

Hermione stood alone, anxiously awaiting her brother's arrival, with only a dim lamp to comfort her. The foyer was just outside the dining room. She hoped to catch Christian on arrival—surprise him with the good news. But she didn't know where to begin Then someone kicked open the front door, and she nearly jumped out of her skin.

"Quickly!" she heard a deep male voice say. "Get him into the dining room! Carry him if you must."

It took a moment for Hermione to register it was Thomas.

But as she stepped forward and all the lights in the living room flickered on, Hermione's senses were overwhelmed by the acrid stench of ash and burned flesh. She winced at the sight of Christian as they set him on the table. His dark hair was disheveled, and his coat was blackened with soot.

"What happened?" Hermione asked, staring down at her brother in horror. "Christian! Christian!" she called, trying to get him to open his eyes.

Thomas ignored her and turned his attention to Christian, who had begun thrashing.

"Hold him down!" Thomas ordered, and Newman obeyed.

Christian resisted at first, then went slack. Hermione's first instinct was to stop them, but then she realized Thomas was pointing his wand at Christian's forearm. She gasped at the sight of it.

The skin was blackened and charred, blood was draining from an unknown vein, and the white slivers of exposed bone made her stomach churn. Then she returned her attention to her brother's face. His eyes were closed, and his face was twisting and contorting in pain. Then Thomas began mumbling a spell she couldn't quite hear. And Hermione watched in shock as her brother's wound began to knit back together, the charred flesh slowly regenerating before her eyes. It was a feat of magic she had never witnessed before, a testament to her grandfather's power and skill. As the spell traveled the length of his forearm, Hermione watched as the layers of skin reformed, the bone disappearing beneath the renewed tissue. Christian's face began to relax until his brows unknitted and his eyes opened. She let out a sigh of relief.

"What happened?" Hermione repeated.

Thomas spoke first. "From what I've heard, he was attacked on the street by some of the Dimitris' goons," he explained. He turned to Newman. "Grab some bandages from the cupboard and wrap his arm. I need to be sure the spell sets."

"How many were there?" Hermione asked.

"Too many," Thomas answered as he watched Newman leave the room. "But it seemed like your brother knew one of them. Kept mumbling a name—"

Christian gasped weakly, his eyes filled with confusion and uncertainty. He mouthed a word, but Hermione couldn't tell what.

"Mikel, I believe he said," Thomas told her.

Hermione furrowed her brow as she struggled to make sense of the name. She stared at her brother's lips as he mouthed it again.

"Carmichael?" she asked to clarify.

"Yes," Christian whispered weakly from the table.

She moved toward Christian, and he began to cough. Then Newman returned with a roll of bandages, which Thomas took and then dismissed the man. Thomas looked at her as if waiting for her to explain that "Mikel" was actually "Carmichael."

Hermione sighed. Keeping him in the dark wouldn't do them any good, but she didn't want to reveal too much about their future. Thomas may not have all her grandfather's wisdom, but he was smart and skilled enough to create the pocket watch, which meant he was smart enough to realize they were creating a tempest. And the last thing she wanted was for their plan to be found out.

"Someone followed us here," Hermione explained. "I'm not sure how it's possible, but he did, and his name is Carmichael Dimitri. He's one of Horace Dimitri's bastards, and this is the second time he's attacked my brother."

Thomas nodded and seemed to think over his response. "I think it's quite clear that he has it out for your brother," he said as he securely wrapped Christian's forearm with the bandages. "I take it that this Carmichael has done far worse."

"I'm afraid so," Hermione answered, looking at her brother's bandaged arm. "What spell did you use?"

"It was a charm," Thomas said. "Do you not know charms?"

Hermione's cheeks grew hot from embarrassment.

"I do—I'm just—I'm not good at them," Hermione answered.

"Then allow me to teach you."

"I hardly think now is the time!"

"There's no better time than the present," Thomas stated sharply. "Look at your brother. If anything's clear to me now, it's that one of you needs to know the deflection charm. I've taught it to all my boys—how my son never managed to teach it to you is beyond me. But it'd be best to remedy that now, lest something like this happen again."

Hermione's cheeks burned, and she thought about hexing Thomas and petrifying him, if only for a few minutes.

"Thousands of Merlins in the world, and you're the one they overlooked, miserable and unable to produce a charm. What exactly were they training you to do?"

He was right, of course. She knew in her heart that she hadn't been trained like her brothers. But she wasn't about to tell Thomas that. She could already imagine the response, and the clear disdain on his face only made matters worse.

"Fine," Hermione stated. "I'll let you train me, but first, you have to get Christian to a bed, this is hardly an appropriate place for him to rest."

"You have my word," he told her, his voice stern. "Mackenzie!" he called into the hall, stopping a servant. "See to it that young Christian is taken to bed and looked after."

"Yes, your lordship," the servant mumbled, curtseying and then rushing away.

Hermione had thought that Thomas would be more difficult, but deep down, some part of her had hoped he wouldn't be. Some part of her had wished for someone to take the time to help her with her inability to do charms. Or, at the very least, useful charms. She was trained to meet graduation requirements but not for combat. Not for war. Her duties had been so wrapped up in her arranged marriage that her studies hadn't taken priority. She had skirted by without mastering charms, and here she was with some magical skill, but not enough to heal the way her grandfather did. Tonight she had found the blueprints, she had succeeded, and Christian had been attacked in the streets. Maybe she no longer had a choice.

The thought of learning a charm filled her with hope, hope that had so easily slipped away before, for their future, for her magic to grow stronger, for the war they would end before it could ever begin.

Potential

October 1971

As Thomas led her down a narrow flight of stairs, shadows seemed to materialize around them, concealing any trace of stairs ahead. The only thing illuminating their path was a ball of light floating at the tip of Thomas's wand. The pungent aroma of damp stone and dust filled her nose as they went deeper and deeper into the depths of the unknown.

Finally, they arrived at a metal door that shrieked as Thomas pushed it open. Inside, the room was spacious, with a low domed ceiling and walls made of rough stone. The room was well lit but cluttered with magical artifacts and bookshelves. Along one wall was a bookshelf filled with ancient tomes with faded spines. On another, dusty jars were filled with colorful powders and elixirs.

Thomas walked to the center of the room, where a large rectangle had been etched into the stone floor. The moment Hermione stepped inside, the door shut behind her.

She took a deep breath to calm her nerves, taking in the sharp smell of stone. Hermione assumed this was a training room and noticed a casting circle in the square.

Hermione watched as Thomas closed his eyes and brought his wand to his face. Then, he muttered an incantation under his breath.

A wave of energy escaped his wand, rippling through the room like a shock wave, and the air hummed with magic. Suddenly, a pungent smell burned her nostrils. It was a potent mix of sulfur and smoke, with a hint of sweetness that made her stomach churn. It was unlike anything she had ever smelled.

"What is that?" Hermione asked him.

Thomas opened his eyes. "Dragonfire."

Hermione's heart sank in her chest. She could only imagine the horrors those people faced that day at Fortuna Bay—that her father faced that day. But from the look in her grandfather's eyes, he knew them all too well.

"Do you know how your uncle Adrian died?" Thomas asked.

As she stared at him blankly, her mind raced, trying to remember the man. But she was quite certain she'd never met him. She waited so long that the air was still and quiet, but in her mind, it dawned on her. Her father's twin brother—the original heir apparent.

"Can't say that I'm surprised," Thomas said. "I suppose Alfred chose to forget him—but it's no matter—too painful a memory. But I thought I'd make you understand what you could be facing in your future. If the war carries on."

"The smell of dragonfire?" she said slowly.

She stared at him in silence, trying to understand his

point. But she couldn't.

He snorted. "That is the smell of worlds being torn apart by flames of a creature beyond mundane or wizard-kind's comprehension," he said, his expression becoming hard. "The dragon's roar is the worst of it, but then there's the crackle of burning buildings crumbling down, the chaos, the bodies piled up, that overwhelming sense of helplessness you feel when you realize you can do nothing."

"So it's—"

"It's a reminder of what will happen if you should fail," Thomas told her. "In your future, your father is dead and a war is brewing."

"From the looks of things, the war never stopped," Hermione retorted.

Thomas let out a bark of dry laughter. When he finished, he said. "I suppose you're right."

"Then what am I supposed to gain—"

"What are you supposed to gain?" he repeated. Thomas scoffed and shook his head. "Spoken like a true Mandrake, but I suppose something had to last all these years. And I'm not surprised it was our arrogance."

Hermione bristled at the wizard's condescending tone. "Look, I know I'm probably not your ideal student," Hermione snapped. "I'm sure you'd much rather be teaching this to my brother. But I know what's at stake," she shot back. "And I'm willing to do whatever it takes—"

Thomas snorted. "Really, whatever it takes? You have no idea what you're getting yourself into—both you and your brother are completely reckless. You're just children playing with magic. You don't have the wisdom or the skill to make a difference."

Hermione clenched her fists, refusing to back down. "I may be young, but I'm not stupid," she said firmly. "I know I have a lot to learn, but I'm willing to put in the work. I won't let you or anyone else stand in my way."

"It's not just about action. It's about strategy, power, precision, and control. You don't have what it takes."

But Hermione refused to be deterred. She knew the consequences of failure could be catastrophic. That was why she'd decided to go along with her brother's idea. Perhaps she was arrogant for believing she could prevent her father's death, perhaps selfish for wanting to reap the benefits afterward by eliminating a different version of herself, but she couldn't just give up. The air around her seemed to thicken as if the weight of her expectations were bearing down on her.

Thomas stared at Hermione for a long moment, his expression unreadable. Finally, he nodded curtly. "Fine," he said. "If you're serious about it, I'll teach you the charm. But don't say I didn't warn you."

Hermione nodded, took a deep breath, and took out her wand.

"This particular deflection charm is dark magic," he said. "You may have seen Nikolai Verax's warnings about it. But it is, in fact, the most powerful—and the most useful."

The wizard then mumbled a few words under his breath, and a previously unnoticed seam in the stone wall opened up, revealing a pitch-black passageway. Hermione heard the unmistakable sound of footsteps and the thud of wood before a wooden dummy stepped out of the passage. It stopped in the dueling rectangle, its limbs twisted, one wooden hand holding a wand, and its carved features bearing a grotesque grin. It stood at approximately three feet tall, and its glassy eyes, though disturbingly humanlike, held an uncanny quality. The pupils were unnaturally dilated, engulfing the irises in an eerie darkness that seemed to devour all light. Hermione's heart jumped when the dummy moved, its limbs jerking until its head turned toward her as if it had a mind of its own.

"Now watch closely," Thomas said, seemingly ignoring the wooden creature's movements. He held up his wand and waited.

Suddenly, the dummy lunged at her with surprising speed, flourishing its wooden arm and sending a jet of purple light hurtling toward her.

Hermione began to move, but Thomas stepped in front of her, shouting, "Icio!" The wizard's voice echoed throughout the room. A beam of dark energy shot from his wand and collided with the dummy's spell, causing a loud explosion. But instead of dissipating, the dark energy curved and arced back toward the dummy, hitting it squarely in the chest with a resounding boom.

The impact threw it backward, its limbs flailing about as it spun. When it finally skidded to a stop, it wheeled itself back into position, as if wishing to duel further, unwilling to lose to its opponent.

"The key is to time it right," Thomas said, lowering his wand to his side.

Hermione stared at him, then at the dummy, then back at him. She couldn't believe what he was saying to her. He wanted her to fight that?

It looked so lifelike, yet inhuman, as if it were waiting for her to make the first move. She couldn't shake off the eerie feeling that it was watching her, waiting to pounce. The wizard's insistence on her dueling it only added to her discomfort. She had come here to learn, to become stronger, but the thought of fighting it frightened her. She had seen it move, its limbs jerking and twitching as if it were alive.

As she raised her wand, she couldn't help but wonder what kind of dark magic had brought the dummy to life. Its chest bore a burn mark from the impact of Thomas's spell, and yet it longed for more, glassy eyes boring into her. Hermione braced herself for the worst, the cold sweat on her skin making her fingers slick on the wand. The air was thick with the scent of burned wood and a strange, acrid magic.

Hermione's heart rate quickened as she tried to remember the incantation and the precise wand movements.

"Remember," Thomas said. "You have to time it just right. The moment the spell leaves Sir Reginald's wand, you must strike."

Sir Reginald, Hermione thought, looking at Thomas as if he were deranged. Then she looked back at the dummy.

Her eyes widened in horror as she stared at the wooden dummy before her, realizing it was her grandfather's old foe— Sir Reginald, the notorious dark wizard. Suddenly, everything clicked into place—the way the dummy moved, the wand it possessed, the strange energy that seemed to emanate from it. It was said that Sir Reginald had been responsible for countless atrocities and had no mercy for his victims, and now, here he was, a wooden dummy in her grandfather's basement. It took a moment for her to process it.

She had heard stories of her grandfather's past, rumors of dark deeds and fallen foes, but she had never thought he had ever resorted to such twisted magic. Thomas had been known for stopping Sir Reginald, but no one had ever known the dark wizard's whereabouts afterward. In truth, Hermione had believed he'd died during the final duel between the two wizards. The realization made her shiver as she remembered the stories of Sir Reginald's cruelty. The fact that her grandfather had turned him into a wooden dummy and that it had hardly immobilized him was a testament to the evil that Sir Reginald had possessed. Her mind raced with horror and disbelief as she slowly turned to face Thomas.

"You turned Sir Reginald into a wooden dummy," she whispered.

The wizard's expression was unreadable, but Hermione could feel the weight of his gaze on her. "Yes," he replied. "And now he serves a different purpose."

The dummy's movements became more erratic, jerking back and forth as if ready to strike. A wave of nausea washed over Hermione as she wondered if she was truly ready to face an opponent that had once been such a powerful and feared wizard.

"He can't strike until you're ready," Thomas told her.

Hermione was convinced she would never be ready. But still she nodded, her eyes fixed on Sir Reginald's wand.

Suddenly, a bolt of red light shot toward her. She reacted quickly, shouting, "Icio!" and slashing her wand through the air, but her spell missed, and she was hit. She stumbled and landed hard on her back. Hermione felt a pang of frustration and disappointment, and the dummy tilted its head as if trying to get a better look at her.

She imagined the wizard watching her with a cold gaze, his lips twisted in a cruel smile, and Hermione scrambled to her feet.

She pointed her wand at the dummy and started to

mutter an incantation. But the dummy was quick, and it retaliated with a blast of its own. Hermione attempted the spell again, giving a weak "icio." Her wand sparked, but it missed, and Hermione narrowly dodged Reginald's attack.

"Focus," Thomas ordered from the sidelines. "Remember what I told you."

Strategy, power, precision, Hermione thought, recalling his words. *And, Merlin, what else?*

She stared at the dummy, and she swore it almost looked entertained.

Control. Sir Reginald had lacked control. The charm Thomas had promised to teach her came from the kind of magic that couldn't be easily controlled. It was a force that could consume even the most powerful and leave them as empty vessels, like the wooden dummy—once man—now attacking her.

Again and again, Sir Reginald cast spells at her, and each time, she failed to counter them. Hermione's confidence waned, and she began to doubt herself. But she wouldn't give up. She kept practicing, standing up every time she fell, even as sweat dripped down her face and her arms grew heavy. And finally, after what felt like an eternity, she saw her chance.

The dummy cast a powerful spell at her, and Hermione waited, poised and ready. At the last possible moment, she swung her wand in a sharp, decisive arc. A surge of power flowed through her like she'd never felt, and dark tendrils of energy sprang from her wand. A burst of black energy exploded on the point of contact, and the dummy's spell reversed and was sent hurtling back at him. When it reached him, swirling ribbons of pure light wrapped around the dummy's arms and legs and pulled them taut. The dummy struggled against the light, its wooden joints creaking and groaning. Hermione gritted her teeth, watching as the demonic creature struggled against the spell. After what seemed like an eternity, the dummy's squirming finally ceased, and it slumped to the ground, inert once more.

Thomas's voice filled the silence as Hermione stood there, panting and staring in disbelief at the motionless dummy. "Well done, Hermione," he said. "Well done!"

A wave of horror washed over Hermione as the wizard approached her. "I know you may not understand now, Hermione. But sometimes difficult decisions must be made, sometimes sacrifices must be made for the greater good."

"And Sir Reginald—"

"Was a dangerous man," Thomas said, placing a hand on her shoulder. "Death would've been too easy for him. So I stopped him the only way I knew how, but he'll never mutter a word or lead another army again."

Hermione nodded and looked back at the dummy, feeling a mix of horror and pity. She knew Thomas was right. He had done the right thing. But she couldn't wrap her head around the idea of a living person being turned into an inanimate object.

Thomas put a comforting hand on her back. "Come, let's leave this place. I think we've done enough for today."

She watched as Thomas muttered a few words under his breath, and the stone wall opened up. He flicked his wand toward the dummy, and it slid back into the opening, and the seam sealed shut once more.

Parting Words

October 23, 1971

As Hermione stood at the bottom of the stairs, every parry and strike still echoed in her ears. She had just finished another grueling training session with Thomas, and her muscles ached. It had been a week since her brother's attack; he had been placed in an enchantment-induced coma under Thomas's orders. Now he was awake, and somehow, she needed to tell him about the dummy.

She didn't know where to begin, but her guilt was inescapable. Every day she managed to defeat the dummy, and every day was another reminder that Thomas was a different man than the grandfather she knew. This was the secret he'd kept hidden all those years, and she couldn't help but wonder, in the future, was Sir Reginald still down there?

As she climbed the stairs, a dull ache passed through her body that caused her chest to tighten, serving as an unwelcome reminder of the panic attack that had gripped her not so long ago. Her hand instinctively clutched the banister, seeking support as her mind replayed fragments of it—Castle Mandrake, the gossiping women, and the fear that had threatened to swallow her whole.

Shadows of doubt lurked in the corners of her mind, whispering cruel words and gnawing at her confidence.

What if I'm too weak? she thought. *What if I can't do this?*

As she made her way up the stairs, each step seemed to mock her, shrieking at her, a chilling reminder that even in victory, the battle against her inner demons was far from over.

Her body trembled with residual tension as she reached the bedroom door. Hermione knocked softly.

"Come in," a weak male voice called from the other side.

She swallowed dryly and opened the door.

Her heart ached as she looked at Christian resting under the blankets. The dark circles under his eyes were prominent. She thought of her brother's pain, but she approached the bed and pulled up a chair to sit beside him.

"Well, how was it?" Christian asked weakly, his eyes barely open.

"How was what?" Hermione asked.

Christian eased himself up in the bed and set his bandaged forearm on a pillow. "Training with Thomas. I heard from Mackenzie that you've been working on the deflection charm."

Hermione nodded, remembering how she'd struggled and when the power finally coursed through her body, how good she'd felt, but her blood immediately ran cold at the thought of the dummy.

"Um . . . it was fine," Hermione said hurriedly. "More or less," she added quietly.

Christian cocked a brow. "What's wrong?" he asked.

She considered reassuring him and telling him that nothing was wrong, but she didn't see the point in lying to him.

Hermione stared at the floor and kneaded her hands. "I . . . I feel like I've made a terrible mistake," she said softly, her voice heavy with guilt. "The magic Thomas taught me . . . it was dark magic, Christian. Our grandfather defeated a dark wizard with dark magic."

"Whoa, slow down," Christian said, putting a hand on her shoulder. "Start over."

Hermione took a deep breath. "When Thomas offered to train me, I was a little upset but also very excited! I wanted to do well. I wanted to master at least one charm. But when he'd told me it was dark magic, I didn't even hesitate," Hermione told him. "And yes, of course, I learned how to do it, but not before learning that our grandfather turned Sir Reginald Fitzgerald, the dark wizard, and I dueled him. I know he wasn't a good man, but dark magic? And why didn't I hesitate, Christian? Wouldn't a better person have hesitated?"

Her brother's eyes widened. "Sir Reginald Fitzgerald? You faced off with him and lived? I thought he was dead."

Hermione shook her head, trying to organize her thoughts.

"No, that's the problem! Our grandfather turned him into a wooden dummy and has been using him for my training . . . and possibly other training—"

"He turned him into a dummy," Christian said with a bemused grin.

"It's not funny! And that's not the point! The point is, Thomas used dark magic to turn him into a dummy," Hermione stated. "And I just can't shake the feeling that there's more to their final battle than we know."

Christian laughed. "Hermione, our grandfather is not a dark wizard. The man started a social club centered around cleaning up and restoring damaged areas of Hampshire. He's not some evil genius."

Hermione shook her head, and Christian squeezed her hand reassuringly. She looked into his eyes.

"Everyone has their secrets, Hermione."

"So we should what? Chalk it up to future good behavior?" Hermione asked.

"No," Christian answered. "I'm not saying we ignore it. But we can't change the past, only try to learn from it. And just because you've learned a charm that happens to be dark magic doesn't mean you're a bad person."

"But Christian—"

"Shhh . . . when we get back, we can ask Grandfather all about it," Christian said. "But for now, let's focus on the present, no pun intended, and look on the bright side."

"Bright side?" Hermione asked.

"Yeah, that little duel between Carmichael and I created another disturbance. That's what caused the damage," Christian said, gesturing toward his bandaged arm. "Horace's henchman got the worst of it." He shrugged and then smiled. "Four down, one to go."

Hermione nodded, feeling the weight lift off her shoulders. She knew her brother was right, but the guilt still lingered. But she couldn't exactly explain it. What more could she say? How much she'd liked the feeling of the power flowing through her? No, she couldn't tell him that.

She took a deep breath and felt a renewed sense of purpose.

"You're right," she said. "We need to focus, keep a low profile and stay out of trouble until Thomas can reset the time trinket. We'll just enjoy the rest of the time we have here and then return to the future."

Christian nodded. "I'm glad that's settled. I guess that means we'll be attending Alfred's birthday party in a few hours," Christian said, smiling weakly. "You should get some rest before we go. You look like you've been hit by a griffin."

"Look who's talking," Hermione said playfully.

She stood from the chair and walked to the door, trying to shove down the sense of dread filling the pit of her stomach. She sighed and grabbed the doorknob but couldn't move.

You should tell him, she thought. *He'll make you feel better.*

But then she found her nerve and forced the feeling down, replacing it with a sense of determination. She and Christian had come this far and faced so much. She wasn't going to let anything stop them now—not even a dummy.

Hermione was trying to keep up with her brother, shuffling behind him with both hands holding onto her dress skirt. The gown she wore hugged her tightly; the bodice was accented with intricate beading that added a touch of glamour and allowed for some breathing room. The skirt flared into a gentle A-line, swishing elegantly as she walked. Its emerald-green color shimmered under the lights of the ballroom, making her stand out amongst a sea of black suits and scarlet-red gowns. Her hair hung about her shoulders, tightly coiled, cascading down her back in a dark curtain. Luckily, this meant she was able to relax, despite the bruises on her legs from an earlier fall facing Sir Reginald.

When they had first entered, she couldn't help but be awestruck by the sheer opulence of it all. Clearly, her father had always been one to throw a great party. Chandeliers hung in the entrance hall, practically glittering, and the walls had been adorned with gold accents that gleamed under the soft light.

"They'll wear off by the end of the night," Christian told her, gesturing at the gold accents. "But they're pretty good, all things considered."

Hermione rolled her eyes. Whether they were created by magic or not, magic itself never ceased to amaze her.

Other guests, dressed in fine attire, mingled with one another, sipping champagne and nibbling on hors d'oeuvres. As they made their way through the crowd, they caught snippets of conversations about the latest newlyweds, the newest of magical technologies, and rumors about the wizarding world. But Hermione never saw their host and was beginning to wonder where he was.

They soon found themselves in the ballroom, where a live orchestra was playing music, and the Graves family was surprisingly all in attendance. The room was decorated with emerald green and gold, with white floral arrangements that seemed to glow. Hermione greeted Martha first, who was adamant about giving her a hug, which she happily accepted.

"I'm so glad you're okay," Martha said after they'd separated. "I'd heard that something had happened to Christian, and I'd thought the worst."

"No, luckily, she wasn't there," Christian said with a smirk.

Martha flushed red. "Oh, sorry, I'm glad you've recovered," she said softly. "How long will you not have use of your arm?"

"Thank you, and I don't imagine it will be too long now," Christian told her. "It was some minor damage."

Hermione looked at him in disbelief.

Minor damage, she thought. *He could have died.*

"Yes, and at least it isn't your wand hand," Martha noted, pointing at his other hand.

Christian nodded, and Martha appeared to be getting more flustered by the moment. Then Hermione noticed a man in navy-blue attire approaching them. Seeing the badge on his waist belt, she swallowed hard.

Sweet Merlin, not right now, she thought.

Martha nearly jumped once he stood beside them. "Forgive me, this is my father, Marshal Harrington. He's the chief of the Magical Crime Unit," she said, gesturing toward the man.

Marshal Fergus Harrington, Hermione knew his history well. He was a member of the Bane family, but he'd taken his wife's surname to start anew. He was wearing his uniform. The jacket was tailored to perfection, with gold buttons running down the front and a crisp collar. His badge glinted proudly on the breast pocket, displaying the emblem of the Magical Crime Unit. His trousers were a matching shade of blue and cut in a sharp, straight line. His black shoes completed the ensemble, gleaming brightly, giving him an air of authority and elegance. Despite being at a party, he hadn't seemed to have let his guard down.

"No need to worry, I'm one of the good guys," Marshal Harrington said with a laugh. "Besides, I'm off duty, unless Alfred needs some extra security, which I'm sure he won't. After all, you Mandrakes take care of your own."

"Yes, yes, we do," Christian said with a nod. "Now, if you'll excuse us, we're looking for our host."

Christian slipped further into the crowd, and Hermione hurried after him. She exchanged pleasantries with a few people as they passed and thank yous with those who complimented her dress or hair, but she struggled to keep up with her brother. So much so that she was grateful when he finally stopped at the bar to order a drink from the barman, a male elf in a black uniform with two earrings in each pointed ear.

"Are you alright?" Hermione asked.

"Not particularly," Christian grumbled, gesturing toward his arm. "The damn potion wore off, and the crowds aren't helping."

"Well, we just have to find Alfred and say goodbye, then we can leave," Hermione told him.

"I think I'll just head to the coatroom and back to Pleasant Manor," Christian responded. "I can imagine I'm bad company at the moment."

"I understand," Hermione said softly. "You know this really isn't my thing either, but we can't just leave without saying goodbye. It would be rude, after all."

"You can stay, but I'll head back," he said.

Hermione's ears perked up at that comment. Stay? She could hardly imagine staying without him, and she'd at least want to be sure he made it home safely. And that he wouldn't do anything reckless.

Hermione looked up at him. "You aren't thinking of doing something stupid, are you?"

"Like what?"

"Finding Carmichael? You're hardly a threat in your state, and before we confront Carmichael, we need an actual plan," Hermione stated.

Christian hesitated for a moment before finally nodding in agreement. "Alright, I know. You don't need to lecture me. But just make it quick. I want to get back to the house. And wish him happy birthday from me too."

"Just wait by the coatroom. I'll be right back," Hermione promised.

Hermione re-entered the crowd of partygoers, weaving her way through the throngs of people until she reached Eric Graves, who was flanked by Rowan and Malicent.

"Have you seen Alfred?" Hermione asked him.

Eric cocked a brow at her. "Why? Planning on hexing him?"

"What?" Hermione retorted.

"The last thing I remember before I fell asleep in front of the museum was seeing you," Eric said. "So you must've hexed me."

"Or you were just tired," Hermione corrected.

"I wasn't tired," Eric snapped.

Rowan laughed. "Oh, you're making a big deal out of nothing, Eric. I doubt little Hermione had anything to do with you sleepwalking again. I told you to cut back on your drinking."

"The last time I sleepwalked, I was six, Rowan," Eric said harshly. "I know she hexed me. I know she did it!"

Malicent rolled his eyes. "Calm down, Eric," Malicent said before turning his attention to Hermione. "Alfred is upstairs. Last I checked, he was reading books in our father's old workshop."

"Thank you, Malicent," Hermione said with a smile.

It took Hermione longer than she would've liked to get up the stairs. Mainly due to her underestimating the weight of her dress skirt as she carried it. As Hermione approached the workshop, she couldn't help but feel a twinge of guilt knowing her brother was waiting for her, but she had to at least say goodbye to Alfred before they left. But then she stopped when she caught sight of Alfred with a young woman dancing by a window. The young woman was dressed in a simple yet elegant yellow gown that complimented her brown skin, with her brown hair in a curly bob. The host was wearing a dark suit, and if she wasn't mistaken, the two were laughing.

Alfred caught Hermione's eye and broke away from the woman to greet her. "Hermione, so glad you could make it," Alfred said, greeting her with a hug.

She returned the hug, though she was shocked to be receiving one.

"Allow me to introduce you to Isabel," he said, taking the woman's hand. "Isabel, this is Hermione, she's my cousin."

"It's nice to meet you, Hermione," Isabel said with a warm smile.

Hermione's breath caught in her throat. "The pleasure is all mine," she finally managed to say. "You look stunning."

Isabel laughed nervously. "Thank you. I'm afraid it's all I had."

"Don't sell yourself short," Alfred said softly. "You're by far the most beautiful woman I've ever seen."

Hermione couldn't help but notice the way he looked at Isabel.

He's always looked at her that way, Hermione thought, her chest tightening.

She hadn't realized how much she missed her mother until that moment, and seeing them together now, young and alive—their whole lives to look forward to—gave her hope. This was what she was fighting for—her family.

It was clear Alfred was smitten with her, and Hermione couldn't blame him. Isabel was naturally charming, intelligent, and beautiful. If Hermione managed to become anything close to the exceptional woman that her mother was, she would be lucky.

"Well, I'll leave you two alone," Hermione said. "Christian and I just wanted to wish you a happy birthday and say that we've really enjoyed the party."

Alfred turned to her, a smile on his face. "Thank you, Hermione. I'm glad you and Christian could make it. Speaking of Christian, I don't believe I've seen him."

Hermione smiled politely. "Oh, I'm afraid he's just not feeling well at the moment. We're probably going to head back to Pleasant Manor. I'm so sorry we couldn't stay longer."

Alfred nodded understandingly. "Of course, of course. Thank you for coming, Hermione. It means a lot to me."

Hermione smiled and nodded, then turned to leave. As she made her way back to the staircase, she stopped and looked back to see Alfred and Isabel appearing to be lost in each other's company. She couldn't help but feel a twinge of sadness for herself, wondering if she would ever find love and happiness with her betrothed as her parents had. But she also felt a glimmer of hope, knowing that even in the midst of chaos and danger, there was still something worth fighting for.

Midnight at Willowsby Avenue

October 24, 1971

Hermione weaved through the halls, her heels clicking against the marble floor and echoing through the vast space. When she made her way to Castle Mandrake's entrance, she stopped and scanned the foyer. Her eyes darted to every corner of the room, even checking a small sitting area where two serving elves were cleaning, but her brother was nowhere to be found.

Maybe he stepped out to get some air, Hermione thought.

Taking a deep breath, Hermione pushed open the heavy double doors to step out into the cool night air. She walked down the front steps, trying to ignore the shadow the building cast down on her. As she searched the lawns, she noticed a group of partygoers mingling out front. Young men sparring in finely-tailored suits and young women in elegant gowns sitting on the grass, their laughter ringing through the crisp night air.

Hermione walked the length of the pathway, her ball-gown swishing around her ankles as she passed groups of wizards and witches, hoping to spot her brother. She caught snippets of conversations about politics, the brewing war, and magical artifacts in the mansion's museum, but there was not one whisper of her brother. As she neared the front gates, she spotted a man leaning against a pillar, smoking a cigar.

Against her better instincts, she approached him, noticing a strong earthy scent of tobacco mixed poorly with the sweet aroma of the white roses surrounding him. He was tall and muscular, with a chiseled jaw and dark, intense eyes. His hair was dark brown and slicked back, and he wore a black tuxedo that hugged his broad shoulders.

"Excuse me," she said, "I was wondering if you'd seen my brother. He's about your height with dark hair and an injured arm."

The man took a long drag of his cigar, blowing out a cloud of smoke. Then he nodded slowly. "Yeah, he headed out the gates about half an hour ago, but I'd be careful if I were you. I heard there was some trouble in town between the Dimitris and the Banes."

"Trouble?" Hermione asked. "What kind of trouble?"

"You know, the usual," the man said. Then he shrugged as if wanting her to leave him alone.

Hermione thanked him and turned to leave.

"I wouldn't do that if I were you!" the man shouted after her. "There's war in the air!"

A sense of unease washed over her, and with a final glance over her shoulder, Hermione pushed open the gate and began her trek toward town, hoping to find her brother before something bad could happen.

Hermione's heart pounded as she raced through the streets. Her walk for the first few blocks was fine, but began to panic the moment the smell of smoke with a hint of a sickly sweet stench wafted past her nose. The closer she came to Willowsby Avenue, the greater the chaos and destruction.

Cars were overturned and ablaze, shops were smashed and looted, and injured witches and wizards lay scattered about, moaning in pain. And that smell was everywhere.

Dragon, Hermione thought, slowing herself to a walk.

She stopped in the middle of the street, craning her neck upward to search for the dragon in the sky. The sun had set hours ago, casting the town in a dim, hazy light. As the acrid stench of burning flesh assaulted her nose, Hermione could feel her eyes burning as she tried to spot the beast.

Hermione wiped the tears from her eyes and shook her head. She tried to breathe.

He would've gone inside, Hermione told herself. *He wouldn't have interfered.* She stepped around broken glass and debris, her eyes scanning the area frantically for any sign of her brother. *Or maybe he was never here. Maybe he called Thomas and he'd gotten a car. Maybe—*

Hermione's heart skipped a beat as she saw the Magical Crime Unit arriving on the scene, their wands drawn and at the ready. Her stomach churned, and though she knew they weren't searching for her, she had the urge to try and blend in with the magicks that were still standing.

She approached a burly witch holding a grocery bag, her face lined with worry.

"Excuse me, ma'am, what's going on?" Hermione asked, her voice barely above a whisper.

The woman's face twisted into a grimace. "The Dimitris and the Banes were at it again," she said, her voice heavy with anger and sadness. "One of the Bane boys said something stupid, as boys do. But you know a Dimitri with a dragon doesn't leave home without it, and now—well, it's a mess out here."

Fear twisted in Hermione's stomach. But she managed to nod her head.

"You should head home. I don't imagine these streets will be too friendly tonight," the old woman said.

"Thank you, but I'm looking for someone," Hermione said softly.

The old witch nodded. "Alright, be safe, dear."

Hermione swallowed hard, her mind racing as she tried to come up with a plan. But as she walked farther along the street, she caught sight of something that made her heart race but also brought her some relief.

A massive, dead dragon lay sprawled across the street, its immense body crushing everything in its path. The once majestic creature was now a grotesque sight, its gray scales weeping fresh blood and its eyes vacant and empty. Its wings, torn and shredded, seemed to have been battered and sliced with a spell that was still wafting from its wings. Dark smoke drifted off them and disappeared into the asphalt.

She could hear the soft cries of injured witches and wizards trapped under the dragon's massive frame. Behind her were screaming shopkeepers, hysterical children, and angry citizens' voices, all clamoring over each other. The disspellers were all frantically trying to calm the citizens.

And Hermione was still trying to understand what she was seeing; this once-bustling street was now the remnants of a battlefield, where death and destruction had taken over.

Repercussions

October 24, 1971

It was as if the heavens had torn open, drowning the world in a relentless downpour. Hermione trudged along the sidewalk toward Pleasant Manor, her dress now a second skin, heavy with the weight of the storm.

Where are you, Christian? Where are you, she thought. The longer she walked, the less hope she had of finding her brother. She scanned the bodies, worried she'd find him among them, and was relieved when she did not. After a few blocks, the bodies became sparse, and as she rounded another corner, she only saw two. The first was directly in her path, and his coat bore a blue dragon. *Dimitri,* she thought, looking around. *The fight must've ended over here. But where?*

Hermione glanced around nervously, searching for somewhere to hide if she needed to. When she found a bush she could hide behind, she saw a young man sitting on the ground, propped up against a tree, his face slack.

Christian.

Hermione sprang to her feet and ran over to him. Her heart hammered in her chest as she knelt beside her brother, her hands shaking as she checked his pulse. He was alive. Her brother's breathing was shallow and irregular, and his skin was clammy, but he was alive. Hermione's mind began to race, trying to figure out what had happened and how to help her brother.

"I was wondering when I'd see you."

Hermione's heart leaped in her chest. She turned around to see Carmichael Dimitri standing a few feet behind her, a cold, cruel look in his eyes. If she were any closer, he would tower over her. His black cloak billowed behind him, likely shielding her from passersby's view. His ginger hair was wet and unkempt, framing his face in a fiery halo.

His olive skin was stretched taut over chiseled features as he bared down angrily, making his sharp cheekbones and angular jawline even more prominent. His long fingers—adorned with silver rings—wrapped around his wand, which was pointed directly at her.

How did he finds us?

"What did you do to him?" Hermione demanded, her voice shaking with anger and fear.

Carmichael scoffed. "He got in my way," he said, his voice dripping with malice. "I would have rid the world of Finley Bane if Christian hadn't killed Dougal's dragon."

He did what, Hermione thought.

Hermione shook away the thought. "You're a monster," she spat, standing up to face him. "What kind of person continuously massacres innocent people?"

Carmichael let out a bark of laughter. "Innocent? The Mandrake family protects their own, no matter the cost to others," he said, glaring at her. "Your family's first mistake was not creating treaties with mine. In a different world, you would be marrying me, not Mordecai Carmine."

Hermione's blood boiled. She couldn't let what had happened to Willowsby keep happening. But she refused to resort to blows. She took a deep breath, trying to calm herself down, and looked Carmichael in the eye.

"I would never have married you," she said, her voice firm and steady. "A man that would massacre thousands is hardly a man at all. And I'll stop you, no matter what it takes."

Carmichael laughed again, a cruel mocking sound. "Are you challenging me?"

Hermione didn't answer. But she stood her ground.

"Fine," Carmichael said. "Have it your way then."

Adrenaline pumped through her veins, her heart racing as she drew her wand. Suddenly, he launched a spell at her, but she dodged it, nearly tripping as she did so. She retaliated with a stunning spell, but Carmichael was quick to shield himself.

They continued to exchange spells, dodging and weaving, neither gaining the upper hand. And soon, the air was thick with energy, crackling with the remnants of magic. Hermione's muscles strained with the effort, her mind racing to come up with new strategies. But every blow she made was met with one of Carmichael's own.

Slowly the two began to circle each other, Hermione trying to find her second wind.

"Do you want a break, sweetheart?" Carmichael asked. "We can talk all about your uncle's betrayal. How quickly he was willing to promise your hand to me," he said with a smirk. "Or perhaps we could talk about your father's final moments surrounded by civilians begging for mercy in Fortuna Bay."

She'd heard enough. Finally, Hermione saw an opening, and as a spell leaped out of Carmichael's wand, she shouted, "Icio!"

A stream of black energy escaped her wand and collided with his spell, sending it back at him and striking Carmichael squarely in the chest. Carmichael cried out in pain, gasping and crumpling to the ground. Then moments later, he was still.

He's dead.

Hermione stood there for a moment, her heart racing with a mix of fear and exhilaration. Her mind raced with thoughts of what she had just done, but then, a car screeched to a stop nearby. She heard the doors open and a familiar voice shouting orders.

She heard someone rushing toward her, but she couldn't stop staring at Carmichael. She'd half expected to be looking down the other end of a disturbance. Instead, someone was shaking her by the shoulders.

"Thomas," she said weakly.

"Hermione, get in the car," Thomas ordered. "Newman will get Christian, but I need you to get in the car."

"But—"

"We can discuss that later," Thomas said, interrupting her. "For now, we're going to get in the car. The Magical Crime Unit is on its way."

Thomas led her back to the car, and she settled into the backseat, sitting between Thomas and her unconscious brother. She watched Carmichael's corpse through the window as the car engine sputtered on, and they sped away from the scene.

~

Hermione Mandrake. Mandrake. Witch. Fiancée. Murderer. She had never thought the latter title would belong to her. She was sitting with her brother's unconscious body, watching a mending elf administer yet another potion, unaware of the extent of his injuries. Mending elves typically provided assistance to doctors or healers, and they required only a fraction of the sleep humans need, meaning Wynn, the mending elf, was the only one available.

For once, Christian hadn't gone looking for trouble. Trouble had found him. She had wondered what impact Carmichael's death would have on the future as it hadn't appeared to affect the past. Upon their return, Thomas had called his spy who lived among the Banes and hadn't come to her with any particularly alarming news. The argument between the wizards was over something small. A bet in a tavern that had gone severely wrong, though no one could've predicted the amount of destruction left in its wake. The Banes wouldn't be going anywhere near Willowsby for a few weeks, and they didn't pick a fight with anyone bearing the Mandrake sigil. So whatever fight that had involved Christian was unsanctioned by the Banes family, which had been obvious enough for Hermione.

But according to Wynn, whatever wounds Christian had now were internal.

"The one I just gave him will keep his fever down," Wynn explained, setting the bottle back into his bag. "The doctor should come by in the morning, but it will be quite some time before Mr. Mandrake is ready to travel."

Hermione nodded and thanked the elf as he left the room. But when the door opened, two pale elderly witches stood in the doorway with Thomas behind them. Wynn nodded toward them and nodded at Thomas, thanking him.

The witches entered the room, setting their bags onto the dresser and opening them. Inside were potions and medical supplies. Neither woman introduced themselves; instead, they began to move quickly and efficiently, checking Christian's vital signs and assessing the extent of his injuries. Eventually, they shooed Hermione away so they could get a closer look. They scrunched their beak-like noses at her before turning their attention back to Christian. Hermione's heart pounded in her chest as she watched them work, hoping her brother would be okay.

She went to stand by Thomas in the doorway and turned to him. "Thomas, who are they?" Hermione asked.

"Those are the Blackwood sisters," Thomas answered. "Best healers among our loyalists and the only ones awake at this hour."

The Blackwood sisters began to whisper to each other bearing grim expressions. Each woman was lithe and hunched over, appearing to have more skin than bone as they waved their wands over her brother in unison.

"And you're sure they know what they're doing?" Hermione whispered.

"Positive," Thomas said.

Hermione couldn't help but wonder what conclusions the women were drawing. Finally, one of the healers turned to her with a solemn expression.

Thomas's expression softened. "How bad is it?" he asked.

"The damage is extensive. It's not safe for him to travel right now. He needs proper care and time to heal. It's best if he isn't moved," she said.

"His bones need to regain their strength," the other said, shuffling through her bag. "A hex has made them brittle. We will have to regrow them."

Hermione's heart sank. "No," she said, her voice trembling. "I can't leave him here. I have to take Christian with me."

Thomas sighed. "But you must—" he started, then lowered his voice to a whisper. "Regular travel would hurt him. Time travel would *kill* him, Hermione." His tone was sharp, and it pricked her ears as he spoke. "If you took him back with you, he would die. There would be no more Christian."

"But I can't just leave him here," Hermione protested. "How will he get back? Do you even have the materials to make another time trinket?"

"I can keep Christian safe," Thomas said. "I have the best healers at my disposal and magical wards set up to keep any unwanted visitors off the grounds. You have my word. No harm will come to him."

Hermione stared at her brother's still, motionless body for a long time. She knew he would be safe here, but it didn't ease her worry. She couldn't bear the thought of leaving her brother behind, vulnerable and alone.

"I don't know if I can do this," Hermione said, her voice barely above a whisper.

It almost felt silly to say, considering just a few hours ago, she'd murdered someone. But still, the weight of the decision lay heavy on her shoulders.

"It's not an easy choice to make," Thomas said sympathetically. "But sometimes we have to do what's best for those we care about."

Hermione bit her lip, feeling torn. If she left Christian, that meant facing Rowan on her own—he had to be the final disturbance. Stopping Rowan would create the tempest. But the thought of leaving without Christian was unimaginable—even if she knew deep down that it was the right thing to do, it wouldn't make it any easier.

"Get some rest," Thomas told her. "We'll talk more in the morning."

As Hermione made her way back to her guest room, she couldn't bear the idea of abandoning him. She felt an overwhelming sense of guilt and sadness at the possibility of never seeing him again. She wanted nothing more than to stay by her brother's side, to will him to wake up. But she also couldn't risk him dying by bringing him along. It was a cruel choice. Her mind raced as she searched for a solution, but her thoughts kept circling back to the same agonizing truth: she would have to leave her brother behind. Though the idea of it made her stomach churn, she took a deep breath, steeling herself for what was to come, and lay down for a fitful sleep.

Advice

October 24, 1971

Hermione sat at a table in the dining room, staring at the cup of tea in her hands. She had barely gotten a wink of sleep last night. She couldn't bear the thought of leaving Christian behind, but she knew she had no choice. As she leaned back in the chair, she heard a noise behind her and turned to see Alfred entering the dining room. In that moment, Hermione made a decision—an entirely selfish decision.

"Alfred, can I talk to you about something," Hermione said, her voice barely above a whisper. "Something important."

Alfred raised an eyebrow. "I'm listening," he said.

Hermione looked at him for a long moment. "You might want to sit down," she said.

He sat down across from her, and she took a deep breath. Then she told him everything. She told him who she was, where she was from, how she'd gotten there, the terrible truth about her brother's condition, the fact that Christian was the same son that was sitting in the living room, only older, and about her father's death—his death.

At first, Alfred looked stunned. Only after Hermione showed him his photo in the obituary section did his expression change. There was a flash of emotion on his face, perhaps anger, perhaps sorrow. For a moment, the clock ticking on the wall was the only sound filling the room.

Finally, he spoke. "I . . . I don't know what to say."

Tears pricked at the corners of her eyes. She had known she couldn't talk to Thomas about this. He wouldn't understand. She hadn't known if Alfred would. But now that she had told him everything, a strange sense of relief filled her.

"I'm sorry," she whispered, her voice shaking. "I wish I hadn't burdened you with this. It's just been weighing on me."

Alfred looked at her, his eyes softening. "You haven't burdened me, Hermione. If anything, you've given me a gift," he told her softly. "The gift of knowing that my future isn't as bleak as I thought it was."

Hermione's heart swelled with emotion. She had worried he wouldn't believe her upon learning the truth. But now, seeing the way he looked at her, she knew that she had made the right decision.

"I have children that believe that my survival could very well save the future," Alfred said, and then he smiled. "And I marry Isabel, and my family approves?"

"Well, there's some resistance from the stories she's told me, but everything works out in the end," Hermione said.

More or less, she thought. She faintly recalled how her father's marriage to her mother created the rift between the

Mandrake and a few other families. It was the straw that had broken the camel's back. That had created the circumstances for Rowan's deal with the Dimitris.

"I would've thought he would've gotten over the blueprints," Alfred said.

Hermione turned her attention back to him. "What?"

"The time trinket," Alfred answered. "I thought he would've given up. I didn't think it would actually work."

"He tried to bring back his leg," Hermione explained.

Alfred was taken aback by her answer.

"His leg? What happened to his leg?" Alfred said, staring at her blankly.

"I think it's best you don't know," Hermione said.

There was too much at risk to worry about her grandfather's leg.

Alfred shook his head. "Alright, I don't know what my father did to lose a leg, but I believe you. And I'll help you in any way I can."

Hermione smiled softly. "Well, I could use some advice."

She stared at him, waiting for him to say something, anything to make her feel better. But in truth, she wasn't expecting much. At the moment, he was only a few years older than herself. She needed his guidance, his wisdom, and his reassurance. At just twenty-five, he was still so cocky, but there was an unmistakable wisdom in his eyes. Hermione had come to see that he had more progressive thoughts than many of those around him. Alfred promoted the idea of a world where magicks and mundanes could coexist peacefully—they could marry without bias. His twenties were the years that had defined him as a leader, as Lord Mandrake. They were why his loyalists continued to follow him, even when his beliefs diverged from theirs. He had embodied the serpent, and she saw it in the way he moved. Every movement, every decision, was graceful and precise, like a snake winding its way through the grass. She wondered if he saw the same thing in her, if he recognized their family traits in her despite her use of dark magic.

"Do you know why we're represented by a serpent? It's a symbol of rebirth, transformation, and healing. It's fitting, really. Our family has been through so much, but we always emerge stronger."

Hermione rolled her eyes. "I've heard this speech before."

Alfred laughed and then shrugged as if unsure what other wisdom he could offer.

Hermione studied Alfred's face and then said, "What I know is that our family doesn't encourage the use of dark magic. Though your father has used it, and I have."

"The serpent also represents our cunning and adaptability," Alfred offered. His eyes bored into her own. "Dark magic is also a part of who we are, and we should never be ashamed of that. It's how we use it that matters."

Hermione was surprised by his words. She had always thought of dark magic as something to be feared and shunned, but Alfred's words gave her a new perspective. "A few years from now, you might not think that," she told him. "In fact, I'm quite sure you advised me against it as a child."

Alfred put his hand on her shoulder, and suddenly he reminded her a great deal of her father. "I know it's a hard decision, Hermione, but you have to look at the big picture. You have the opportunity to prevent a massacre and save countless lives—not just my own. Christian, even in the short time I've known him, would want you to finish what you two started. After all, temporal tempests are time sensitive."

Hermione stared down at her tea.

"I have to go back, don't I?" she whispered.

Alfred nodded. She found the will to stand and then stared at Alfred. For a moment, she wondered if this would be the last time she saw her father, and though he was younger, it brought her comfort.

"Thank you," she said, putting out her hand for a handshake.

Alfred took the hand but pulled her in for a hug.

"See you in a couple years, kid," Alfred said, still hugging her.

Tears pricked Hermione's eyes. "I hope so."

It's Time

October 24, 1971

Hermione knelt beside the bed and kissed her brother on his forehead. "I'll see you soon," she said softly as she stood back up.

She took his hand and squeezed it. Surprisingly, he squeezed back.

Christian slowly opened his eyes but didn't move to get up. "You take care of yourself," he said, his voice strained. "And of Rowan."

Hermione didn't know what to say.

"Thomas told me," he explained before letting out a cough. "When I woke up earlier, he was checking in on me."

She sighed. "I'm just glad you're awake," Hermione said, and then she couldn't hold it in any longer. "I wish you were coming with me."

"No, you don't," he joked. He gave her a weak smile as though he was trying to mask the pain. "You'll need that," he said, pointing to a glowing blue vial beside the bed. "Couldn't risk you doing it all on your own." His voice was just above a whisper. "Don't worry, I'll be waiting for you when you get back."

Hermione smiled through her tears, taking the vial. She knew her brother would be okay, but that didn't make it any easier for her to leave him.

"I'll let you get your rest then," she said, squeezing his hand. Though she wasn't sure whether the words were for him or for her. "And then I'll see you when I get back."

Christian nodded. "See you soon."

And with that, Hermione left the room, silently recalling every disturbance and wondering whether the last one would be as intense as the destruction of Amada's staff.

When she stepped outside into the backyard, the air was thick with the heady fragrance of roses and jasmine and freshly fallen rain. At the center of the garden stood a round table crafted from dark wood and adorned with intricate carvings of snakes. It was surrounded by chairs, and Thomas sat in one of them with a mug in his hand.

Various plants of both the magical and non-magical varieties were planted throughout the garden. There were also plants with medicinal properties, each one carefully tended to and nurtured. Hermione recognized the bluebell, whose roots could cure headaches, and the yarrow, which could stanch bleeding wounds. She even spotted a patch of mandrake, whose roots could be used in powerful spells.

Thomas stood up and smiled at her.

"Well, I guess there's not much left to say, is there?" Hermione said, approaching him.

He chuckled. "I would disagree," Thomas said.

Hermione furrowed her brow, hesitant to say anything.

Did he know about the temporal tempest? Had she and Christian finally been caught?

"Thank you," Thomas said.

Hermione pulled him into a hug.

"Thank you for believing in me," Hermione told him.

Thomas pulled back from the hug and held her at arm's length. "Thank you for reminding me of who I am," he said. "I always knew one of those ridiculous inventions had to work, and here's the proof."

Thomas waved his wand over his hand, and the time trinket appeared out of thin air. Then he whispered the incantation, "Reveler," as he waved his hand over the back of the watch. "You pull this switch down," he told Hermione, pointing at a small handle, and she heard a click as he pulled it down. "Afterward, you place the memory inside, stare into it, and, the moment you see a clear image, take a deep breath to keep yourself from fainting. Then you'll arrive in whatever time and place is attached to that memory. After that, the rest is up to you."

Hermione nodded, and Thomas took a few steps back.

"Goodbye, Thomas," Hermione said, looking at him.

She opened the vial and poured it into the pocket watch. As she watched the liquid swirl inside the time trinket, she began to hear a harsh-sounding *tick*, then it came again . . . *tick . . . tick.*

Suddenly she saw the image take shape and took a deep breath just as a powerful force pulled her forward. Then she felt as though she was being sucked through a tunnel at breakneck speed. The world around her blurred and twisted until everything went dark.

When Hermione opened her eyes again, she released the

breath she'd been holding, feeling relieved and disoriented. Her head was spinning, but she had materialized in a hallway. As she regained her senses, the smell of coffee and baked goods filled her nostrils, and the sound of voices and clinking utensils flooded her ears. She needed a moment to steady herself before she could fully take in her surroundings. So she made her way down the hallway slowly, keeping close to the wall as women rushed in the opposite direction to the bathrooms far behind her.

Hermione looked at the time trinket. Clearly, the magic that possessed it knew what it was doing. Christian's memory had spit her out somewhere inconspicuous.

The café was a quaint little place with exposed brick walls and wooden tables and chairs. Paintings and photographs adorned the walls, and a large chalkboard hung above the counter, listing the day's specials. Families and couples of all backgrounds filled the tables in the bustling café, chatting and sipping their drinks.

Hermione considered sitting at the counter but had to dart out of the way of a waiter carrying a tray of food. When she scanned the crowd, her mind racing, her eyes landed on a man sitting at a table in the corner, enjoying a conversation with a woman. It was her brother, Christian. He looked the same as he had when she had last seen him, well, except he was lacking the broken arm and scars.

Hermione's breath caught in her throat as she realized she couldn't let him see her. How could she have forgotten? She ducked behind a group of people huddled around the server podium, hoping that Christian wouldn't spot her.

She noticed a newspaper at a nearby table and quickly scanned the date: May 2nd, 1996. Hermione let out a sigh of relief. Even in his worst state, Christian had picked the right memory.

Hermione carefully made her way out of the crowded café, avoiding eye contact with everyone, and slipped out the door.

The moment she was outside, Hermione took a deep breath of fresh air and leaned against the building wall, closing her eyes.

Oh, thank Merlin, she thought. *Thank Merlin. Thank Merlin.*

She had made it back to the present, but now she had a new problem to deal with. Where the hell was her Uncle Rowan?

She had to find him before it was too late.

Where did Christian say he was? Where did he say he was? Think, think, think!

But no matter how much she racked her brain, the answer wasn't there. She still felt dizzy and was beginning to wonder how long the effects were going to take to wear off. But then Hermione had a gut feeling and she opened her eyes. Suddenly, she spotted a figure in the distance, dressed in a black coat with matching pants and flanked by two burly men.

Uncle Rowan.

Without hesitation, Hermione rushed toward them, weaving her way through the crowded sidewalk. She had to get closer. She had to stop him from getting to the Dimitris. But as she drew nearer, one of the men caught sight of her, and she bolted into an alley, hoping he wouldn't follow her. But as she stepped back onto the sidewalk, a jet of red light flew past her shoulder, and she doubled backward, nearly falling over.

"Lost, little one?" the man growled, his eyes narrowing as the other man stepped out from behind him.

She half hoped her uncle would appear as well, but he didn't. Hermione gulped, realizing that both men had a dragon embroidered on the breast pockets of their blazers.

Great, Dimitri loyalists, just what I need, Hermione thought, scorning herself.

She looked between the two men; the shorter man didn't seem as interested in speaking. Hermione pulled out her wand, preparing herself for the worst. She was outnumbered, but she couldn't let them stop her. Not when she was so close.

"Step aside," Hermione said, trying to keep her voice steady. "I don't want to hurt you."

The tall man snorted, his lips curling into a sneer. "You? Hurt us?"

Before Hermione could reply, the short man stepped forward, his eyes flashing with malevolent glee. "I say we teach her a lesson," the short man said, his voice dripping with malice. "A duel, perhaps?"

Hermione's shoulders tensed. She wondered if she could hold her own against two opponents, but she assumed she was about to find out.

Hermione stood her ground, her eyes fixed on the two men as they advanced. Her heart pounded in her chest, her breaths coming in ragged gasps. But she couldn't let fear overwhelm her.

The tall man lunged forward, casting a spell that was a sickly green light. Hermione sidestepped his attack and retaliated with a petrifying spell, hurling a bolt of searing blue energy back at him, which struck him squarely in the chest. He grunted in pain and stumbled back, clutching at his singed robes.

But Hermione had no time to savor her small victory. The short man was already closing in, his lips curled in a snarl, throwing a burst of energy at her.

She whispered, "Icio," redirecting the spell back at him. The short man's face twisted in agony, and he collapsed to the ground.

For a moment, the tall man hesitated, eyeing Hermione warily. But then he began launching a barrage of spells at her. Hermione was forced to dodge and weave around them, her body twisting and contorting as she evaded each one. She felt her strength beginning to wane as she grew more and more fatigued. But she refused to give up.

Finally, after what felt like hours of fierce combat, Hermione saw her chance. The tall man looked to be feeling the strain as well and left his back exposed. Hermione seized the opportunity and threw another spell, which struck him in his spine. He crumpled to the ground, his body writhing in agony.

Breathless and trembling with adrenaline, Hermione approached the fallen Dimitri loyalists and rifled through their pockets, searching for any clues that might lead her to her uncle's whereabouts. Her fingers brushed against a scrap of paper in the tall man's breast pocket, and she quickly pulled it out.

The paper was crumpled and stained with blood, but Hermione could make out a series of scribbled notes: a date, a time, and a location. It had to be the meeting place for her uncle and the Dimitris, and it was only a few minutes away—by car. But then Hermione had an idea.

Hermione pocketed the scrap of paper and rushed onto the crowded sidewalk, careful not to disrupt the flow of foot traffic. She scanned the street, her eyes darting left and right as she searched for a broom shop. If she didn't have a car, she could at least use a broom.

At last, she spotted a small shop tucked away between two towering buildings, a dazzling display of brooms filling its front window, with a placard declaring a fifty-percent-off sale. She pulled open the door, her heart racing as she stepped inside the shop.

The shop was cramped and dimly lit, with brooms of every shape and size hanging from the walls and ceiling like cobwebs. A balding brown man with a thick mustache sat behind a cluttered counter, his eyes fixed on a dusty book.

"Excuse me," Hermione said, approaching the counter. "I need a broom. The fastest one you have."

The man looked at her, his eyes widening in surprise as he took in Hermione's tattered clothes and messy hair.

"A broom?" he repeated, his voice tinged with skepticism. "What do you need a broom for?"

Hermione rolled her eyes and waved her wand over her clothes. The tears mended, and the seams wove back together. The shopkeeper *humphed* at her.

"It's a long story," Hermione said, feeling a twinge of impatience. "But I have money, I just need a broom."

The man hesitated, then shrugged and reached under the counter. He pulled out a sleek black broom, its handle wrapped in supple leather and its bristles gleaming in the dim light.

"This one should do the trick," he said, handing the broom to Hermione. Hermione looked at the price tag and set the money on the counter. The shopkeeper examined the money in the light, checking if it was real, and nodded. "Be careful with that one. It's a powerful model, but it's a bit temperamental. It can be tricky to control if you can't tame it."

"Tame it?" Hermione asked.

The shopkeeper shooed her away as he counted the money. Hermione thanked him and hurried out of the shop. She mounted the broom and kicked off from the ground, rising into the air with a whoosh of wind.

The broom vibrated beneath Hermione, its power coursing through her veins, pulsing through every nerve ending in her body. She had only flown a broom once before, and she'd been a little girl, but somehow it felt natural, as if she had been born to do this.

As soon as she gave it a nudge with her foot, the broom sprang to life. She had to hold on tight, her knuckles turning white as she soared through the air. She felt a sudden rush of wind as they soared over the rooftops, the broom twisting and turning as if it were alive.

Fight or Flight

Hermione gritted her teeth and tried to regain control of the broom, but the more she tried, the more agitated it became. It bucked and twisted beneath her as if it were a wild horse trying to throw her off its back. But she held on tight, feeling every bump and jolt as the broom through the air. The air shifted as the sun dipped lower, casting a final burst of warm radiance before slipping beneath the skyline. Buildings' shadows grew longer, stretching like ethereal fingers reaching toward her as night fell.

"Merlin, you're a tricky one, aren't you?" she muttered.

She had to stay focused or risk being thrown off and plummeting to her death. As they flew over the rooftops of the city, Hermione caught sight of a street sign and forced the broom low enough for her to see it.

We're getting close, she thought. She was almost downtown.

She urged the broom on, pushing it faster and faster as they closed in on their destination. The broom seemed to sense her urgency, and it responded with a burst of speed that took Hermione's breath away.

"Easy now," she said aloud as if trying to calm a skittish animal. "Easy."

The broom seemed to calm a little, and Hermione let out a sigh of relief. She could feel a sense of connection growing between them as if the broom was beginning to trust her.

As they flew over the city, Hermione marveled at the sights below. The broom was faster than anything she'd ever ridden before, and it made her stomach flip. But as they soared closer and closer, she could feel the broom's unease growing.

Though as Hermione flew farther, she had the most disquieting sensation that she was being followed. At first, she considered ignoring the feeling, keeping her eyes on the street signs so she could make her turn. But her imagination got the better of her, and she looked over her shoulder. She could make out the silhouettes of six people on broomsticks that were gaining on her.

At first, she thought they might be more Dimitri loyalists that were tracking her, but as they drew closer, she saw the emblem on their cloaks, a symbol of justice and order that had always made her uneasy.

The Magical Crime Unit.

Each was on a broom, and they were closing in fast. Hermione could see the determination etched on their faces. She wouldn't put it past them to be able to track her; after all, there were two of her in this timeline at the moment.

Okay, think Hermione, think, she told herself.

She wanted to convince herself they weren't following her, so she made a turn that sent her slightly off course. But the moment she did, a spell shot past her shoulder, and a flash of blinding light flooded her vision.

Then she heard a booming male voice shout from behind her. "Pull over!"

She didn't. She couldn't. The broom, however, didn't want to go any farther. It began to buck and twist again, and she nearly slipped off but quickly pulled herself back on. She gripped the broom's handle tighter and willed it to go faster, though it didn't change its speed.

"Pull over now!" shouted one of the disspellers as he flew up alongside Hermione on his broomstick. "You're in violation of several laws!"

Going against her better instinct, Hermione raised her wand.

"I don't have time for this," she said and tossed a hex at the disspeller, hurtling him backward until he crashed into another disspeller, and they both fell into the street.

The four other disspellers sprang into action, chasing after Hermione and hurling spells at her. The broom lurched beneath her, taking control and dodging each spell. She tried to withhold her shock and regain control of the broom, but her broomstick was already carrying her up and over the rooftops of the city.

The pursuit continued, with Hermione using every trick in her arsenal to keep the disspellers at bay while her broom seemed to make an uneasy truce with her, navigating around spells directed at it. She led them on a dizzying chase through the city, darting in and out of narrow alleyways and twisting around buildings, trying to gain an advantage. From the distance she was creating, it was a slim one.

The disspellers followed close behind, their brooms slicing through the air with deadly precision.

She let herself catch her breath as she stared at the watch on her wrist.

It's almost time, she thought.

She needed to catch up with her uncle, or this all would've been for nothing.

Suddenly, Hermione drew upon all her magical abilities, using every spell in her arsenal. She sent balls of fire at her pursuers, causing them to veer off course and narrowly miss her. She called upon gusts of wind, trying to knock them off their brooms. She shattered shop windows and hurled nearby objects back at them.

She fought with fierce determination, using her magic to its fullest potential. And one by one, the disspellers fell to the ground below. She turned around, her broom cutting through the air like a knife, counting the ones she could see lying there, dazed and defeated.

One. Two. Three, she counted silently. Then her heart lurched in her chest. Where was the fourth?

Hermione's heart pounded as she searched the sky.

Suddenly, a voice boomed from behind her, "You won't get away that easily, witch. Land your broom now."

Hermione turned to face the disspeller, holding her hands up in surrender. "I didn't want any trouble," she said, trying to keep her voice steady. "I was just trying to get to my destination."

The disspeller sneered at her. "Save it for the council," he said, his wand trained on her. "You'll pay for what you've done. I'll make sure of it."

She didn't say anything.

"Now land!" he commanded, pointing at a building's rooftop. "You're under arrest."

Her stomach twisted, but she lowered the broom toward the rooftop with the disspeller behind her, bridging the short distance to the roof.

When she got off the broom, it propped up beside her as if waiting for her to find an escape route for them both. The disspeller landed, his eyes darkening as they focused on her. He plucked her wand from her grasp, and Hermione didn't resist. Instead, she studied him. He towered over her, his expression fatigued as he clenched his jaw. He was about her age with a scar marking his right temple and a weariness that matched her own. But what would he do with her now?

Caught in the Crosshairs

May 2, 1996

The rooftop was littered with old and broken stone statues that had become wrapped in overgrown vines and moss over time. She guessed they'd been part of the wider collection of stone creatures that resided on the rooftop. There were griffins and a headless pegasus, harpies that nearly looked like angels if not for their decaying faces, which seemed to be watching Hermione and the dispeller. Each cast a shadow, which nearly drowned out the moonlight, leaving the flickering bulbs of rogue lamps along the rooftop's edges as their main source of light. The surrounding buildings loomed high above the rooftop, casting large shadows and leaving Hermione with a disquieting sensation that she was trapped.

Hermione had her arms crossed defensively over her chest while also trying to rub away the goosebumps on her skin. No matter how much she tried to ignore the cold, she couldn't, any more than she could ignore the rat that had scurried across her foot earlier. Though, that hadn't fazed the dispeller. His wand stayed trained on her as though he feared she would attempt to fight him for her wand.

But every minute she was with the dispeller was another minute lost. And she needed to find her uncle. Somehow, she needed to convince the disspeller to let her go. Though telling him she was from the future wasn't going to work—he knew that—two of her existed here, and they'd been tracking her for Merlin knows how long.

She needed to come up with a plan.

Hermione sighed, drawing the disspeller's attention.

"Look, I'm sorry for what I did, but I need to go. I promise I won't cause any more trouble," she said, stepping closer to him.

The disspeller tensed, aiming his wand at her chest. "And why should I believe you?" he asked, his eyes narrowing. "You've broken multiple laws today, young lady. Not to mention disrupting the timeline. Do you have any idea of the consequences we could be facing because of you?"

Hermione paused, trying to think of something that would make him let her leave. "Believe me, they would be far worse than if I wasn't here right now. So you need to let me go," she said, hoping the disspeller would take her seriously.

"What could possibly have gone wrong? Hmmm?" he asked angrily. "Did you break up an engagement? Stop a kid from drowning? Trust me, I've heard it all. The engagement is hardly ever worth saving, and the kid—the kid always ends up a serial killer."

"I'm trying to stop a massacre from happening," Hermione snapped, and the disspeller paused. "If you don't let me go, thousands of people will die! Thousands! What do your laws have to say about that?"

He rolled his eyes. "And you didn't think of reporting it? Why?" he asked. "Being a vigilante isn't the way to go about things—"

"The Magical Crime Unit doesn't interfere with the Big Three's battles," Hermione spat out harshly. "You all sit and wait to see who takes charge afterward, and your boss takes whatever money he's given. The whole system is corrupted. Your laws don't work. They never have."

The disspeller hesitated. But his expression had softened, his hand was wavering, and for a moment, Hermione thought he might lower his hand and let her off with a warning. But then, there was a faint sound, no louder than a whisper: A sound of paws scratching across stone, scurrying. Hermione turned her head toward the sound.

Rats tumbled over the rooftop's edges, falling clumsily onto the surface and scurrying toward the disspeller, eager and wild-looking, four-legged and tails flicking. Their eyes glowed red, whiskers twitching as the bewitched creatures rushed forward. Hermione leaped away and climbed onto the stone griffin's back, holding onto its neck as the vermin surged toward the disspeller.

Where are they all coming from? Who is controlling them?

She searched the rooftop but couldn't find any sign of the caster.

Then she turned her attention back to the disspeller as he let out a horrifying wail and watched as he doubled backward and fell over. The vile vermin took this as an opportunity to haul themselves up his legs, their tails swaying as they skittered over his chest, claws piercing flesh until they covered every limb of his body, including his face. He made another muffled noise as he thrashed wildly, trying to get them off him. Some flew off, others held on by their teeth, tearing his flesh, gnawing through muscle to keep him down.

Hermione's hand flew to her mouth as she watched in horror. She wanted to stop them, but she couldn't. Her body wouldn't let her move. She was high up on the stone griffin. Frightened but safe—at least for now.

A few seconds later, her wand slipped from the man's grasp, bouncing along the gravel until it skidded to a stop against the griffin's foot. She took a deep breath and tried to clear her thoughts, hoping she could drown out his screams of terror muffled underneath the river of fur. But after a few more minutes, she couldn't hear him screaming anymore, and she realized the disspeller had gone limp. But the rats continued their work on the man, seemingly not finished with him, likely until they finished feasting on his corpse.

Her first instinct was to stay on the griffin, clinging to the stone creature's neck. But a little voice insider her told her that she was next, and she needed her wand to defend herself. Though it hadn't done the disspeller any good, she figured she'd take her chances.

It took all her willpower to put one foot on the ground while keeping her eyes on the rats, and lowering her hand without looking. Her eyes never left the disgusting creatures consuming the corpse with their grubby little mouths. Each fattening with every bite they took.

Bile rose in her throat, and she forced herself to swallow it. She shut her eyes tightly, wincing as the chattering sounds rose to her ears. But then, a wave of relief washed over her as her fingertips felt the smooth wood of her wand and the rough rooftop beneath them.

Hermione plucked the wand off the ground and clung to the griffin, shielding her face from the sight before her. Tears stung her eyes as she clutched her wand tightly, listening for anything that might indicate the rats had grown bored of their present meal and were coming for her.

Then, from a few feet away, she heard a deep laugh that sent a chill down her spine. Hermione turned toward the source of the laughter and saw a man dressed in a dark cloak, his hood adorned with a single symbol—the sapphire-blue dragon of the Dimitri family. He was ghostly pale, and his dark eyes glinted in the dim light. He bore a sinister grin, seeming to relish in her horror. Then it struck Hermione who it was—Tanner Singleton.

Beside him stood her uncle. A wicked smile played at the corners of Rowan's mouth. In this lighting, he was a tall, regal figure, his brown hair bearing a sheen that wasn't common in the daylight. His eyes gleamed with malice as he looked at Hermione.

"And what might you be doing here, Hermione?" Rowan asked.

But she didn't answer. She'd balked at the realization of who the man was behind her uncle.

Cassius Barley, a man she had known for years. She had been friends with his son since she was ten. But Cassius had changed; his once kind face was now twisted with anger and hatred. The moonlight glinted off his brown skin, and he was dressed in dark leather clothing. A strap bearing metal pins crossed his chest, and his hand rested on a cane at his hip. The most prominent pin confused her—the surname beneath its crest was "Barley," but neither the colors nor the creature matched the Barley family's crest. The Barleys were represented by a griffin, not a hippogriff; their colors were violet and gold, not scarlet and silver.

"Enough of this, Rowan," Cassius stated. "We have a deal to finish, and you're making us late."

Rowan scoffed. "There's no rush, Cassius. The girl doesn't know anything."

"Then why was she tracking you?" Cassius asked.

"That is an excellent question," Tanner said softly. He pointed his wand at the rats, waving it once through the air, and the rats stilled. "I don't think it'd be hard for her to answer. Would it?"

Hermione gulped as the creatures' beady eyes turned toward her. Their teeth bared, fur soaked in blood, noses twitching in the air as if searching for their next meal.

This is it. They're going to kill me.

Tipping the Scales

May 2, 1996

For a second, she was frightened, but then she remembered what Carmichael had told her: part of their agreement had included marrying her off to him. So he couldn't kill her. Or could he? She wasn't exactly sure how this time travel thing worked. Would the Hermione here still exist if she didn't? She was determined to say yes, as one of them had to survive. If she didn't complete the temporal tempest, there would be no Hermione to replace because she would also be dead. She needed a plan and fast.

In her mind's eyes, she saw her broom by the edge of the building, hovering the same way it had when she first climbed onto it. But then a voice echoed inside her mind: It's not just about action. *It's about strategy, power, precision, and control.* It felt like an invisible hand was on her shoulder, as if Thomas was standing right behind her.

"How can you betray your own brother?" Hermione asked suddenly.

All humor drained from her uncle's face as he pointed his wand at her, gripping it so tightly that his hand began to shake.

"Betray him!" Rowan laughed. "Your father betrayed me when he chose Malicent as his head advisor. Your grandfather betrayed me when he selected your father to succeed him. The loyalists shame me and praise your father, yet we bear the same sins, but still, none of you can see him for who he truly is. I'm the one who will unveil your father's true nature. I'm the one who will protect our family from its impending doom. I am and have always been our family's greatest ally."

"And what do the Dimitris intend to give you that the Mandrakes do not?"

"Far more than your precious grandfather had ever offered, Hermione. Someone has to put an end to this charade. Believe me, I wish there were another way, but you'll have to trust me."

Hermione wanted to laugh. He was going to reveal her father's true nature? He had used his power, position, and her father's trust to take covert information to the enemy, and her father was the traitor? But she remembered their numbers were three to one, or far more if she counted the rats, so she held her tongue.

"How?" she asked. "What is it about my father's nature that I don't know?"

Tanner let out a laugh that made Hermione's blood run cold.

"Be quiet, boy," Rowan said, darting a glare at him. "I would much rather spare you the gruesome details. I hope you understand." He pointed his wand at her and smirked. "It's not for a woman's ears."

Hermione felt a jolt of revulsion but managed to suppress her reaction, persuading herself to listen. There would be time to react later.

"Tell me," Hermione said, her grip tightening around her wand, her nails biting into her palms.

In the moonlight, Rowan's glare appeared angrier and more determined.

But he didn't say anything.

"Your father's indiscretions date back long before you were even born," Cassius told her, looking at her as though she were a stranger. "Consider your uncle's decision to be an act of kindness."

"Why?"

"Because there are answers even we can't give you," Cassius said. He studied her for a moment. He took in her clothing and her wand, letting her appearance sink in before his eyes came to rest on her face. "But that is all I'm at liberty to say, and if your father were to beseech my forgiveness, I would tell him that he would have to do far more than a simple apology. The harm he has caused my family is unforgivable. I intend to seek justice for his wrongdoings, and I am sure the Dimitri family will give me that. I intend to help your uncle reclaim what is rightfully his and allow the loyalists time to grieve and adjust. But we aren't without mercy, we will let you and your brothers live. All we want is your father. And I will do everything in my power to make sure Alfred Mandrake is brought to justice." His voice was unnervingly calm as he spoke. But she saw the flicker of malice in his eyes as he tilted his head back to look at the sky.

"We are preventing Hampshire's ruin," Rowan said, running a hand over his jaw. "I can't—"

"Don't pretend this is about Hampshire's welfare. Especially when you intend to kill the man who has upheld peace for decades. Your brother has been maintaining order in Hampshire. Did you ever stop to think of what would happen if he was gone?" Hermione knew she should stop talking, control her emotions and be disciplined, but she couldn't help herself. "You don't intend to maintain peace. You intend to start a war."

She noticed Tanner's long fingers tighten around his wand.

"Honestly, do we really need her?" he asked. "It's eleven now—Horace isn't a patient man."

Tanner looked nearly indifferent but sounded so eager, so untamed, less a young man of ruthless ambition than a creature who believed his next meal was going to get away from him. The rats shuffled and chattered in response, and fear shot through Hermione, but she steadied herself and remained calm.

"Hermione will marry Carmichael after all is said and done," Rowan said softly. He glanced at her, assessing whether she was a real threat, and turned to Tanner. "Call off the rats. We'll erase her memory."

A knot formed in Hermione's stomach. She thought of losing her memory, every moment slipping away from her, so vivid that for a moment, she stood in Thomas's training room, facing off with a monstrous dark wizard, living the rest of his days as a wooden dummy. Thomas had shown her dark magic —not just a charm that could potentially save her as those she'd learned in school. Dark magic wasn't about offensive or defensive power. It was about control. And control was something that Rowan had always lacked.

Her spirits lifted as realization dawned on her. Dark magic was like any other magic. You called upon it, felt it stir in your bones, pulse through your veins—you let its power possess you and hold you in it. This was what Thomas had been trying to teach her. Magic couldn't control its users. She could never be a dark wizard because she was in control.

A wicked smile spread across Tanner's face as he gestured his wand toward the rats. There was a chorus of squeaks and chitters as they charged at her.

She didn't flinch, her wand hand steady, as she uttered a spell. A searing ribbon of light sprang from the end of her wand, flooding the dark roof with pure, unwavering light, shattering the darkness around them and vaporizing the engorged rats in midair.

Tanner had a hand over his eyes. He appeared confused, momentarily blinded by the light. Hermione narrowed her eyes, trying to see past the light, and she flicked her wand, casting another spell. It struck Tanner's chest, and he fell unconscious.

"Get rid of that light!" Rowan hissed.

He raised his wand, pointing it at the sky to destroy the orb of light she'd created, but with the flick of her wand, her uncle's wand leaped from his hand into her own.

Without a second thought, Rowan turned toward her and ran at full speed. Hermione remained calm, her eyes fixed on him. She pointed her wand at him and muttered an incantation. Rowan's body stiffened as if he'd been turned to stone, and he fell flat on his face.

Hermione quickly turned her attention to the third opponent, but to her dismay, she found that Cassius was gone, leaving only the sound of his retreating footsteps echoing across the rooftop. She let out a sigh of frustration and lowered her wand, waving away the light, her body trembling with the adrenaline that still coursed through her veins.

She pocketed Rowan's wand and slowly walked over to him. After crouching down, relief washed over her as she checked his pulse.

Still alive, she thought, and she smiled to herself. She'd cast the charm correctly. But instead of celebrating her victory, she placed both hands on her uncle's upper arm and pulled. She struggled to roll him over; his body was heavier than she had anticipated.

With a grunt of effort, she finally managed to get him onto his back, taking a moment to catch her breath.

Should've considered dead weight, Hermione thought. Hermione shook her head, pushing the thought aside as she focused on the task at hand.

As she searched her uncle's pockets, her fingers brushed against the smooth surface of a leather-bound pocketbook agenda. With shaking hands, she pulled it out and flipped through the pages, scanning the names and locations. For a moment, she wasn't sure what she was looking for, but then she saw it: an event circled—her father's name along with Fortuna Bay.

Hermione's heart leaped as she read the entry. She had half a mind to burn it but decided against it. With a sigh of relief, she closed the agenda and stuffed it into her pocket.

As she did, she felt a crumpled paper already there. She pulled out the paper and smoothed it. It was a clipping from the newspaper Christian had been carrying with them. *He must've put it in my coat*, she thought as she examined the clipping closely. As she stared at the headline, she felt a terrific stir in the air, like the world around her was shifting.

Suddenly, the newspaper transformed in her hands, the ink rearranging itself to form a new headline. Hermione read the words in disbelief, hardly daring to believe what she was seeing.

In big, bold letters it read:

DOWN TO THE WIRE: SENATORIAL CANDIDATES COMPETING FOR EVERY VOTE

Her father's picture sat beside his campaign opponent Vincent Hawthorne. She had never been so grateful to see news about her father's political career.

Hermione read it.

Senatorial candidates Vincent Hawthorne and Alfred Mandrake face off in fiery debate in Fortuna Bay as election day looms. Amidst accusations of dark magic and corruption, both candidates fight to win the hearts of Hampshire. Who will come out on top in this close race?

As she looked at her father's photo, a single tear fell from her eye and landed on the paper, smudging the ink. She couldn't believe it—she had saved the future. She wiped the tear away and smiled as a sense of relief and accomplishment washed over her.

The doubts that had plagued her for so long began to wane. She had spent so many years doubting she'd ever successfully produce a charm; it was as if she'd forgotten that she too was a descendant of Merlin.

Magic flowed through her veins, untamed and wild. Her worth as a witch was not defined solely by her ability to master charms or any other spell. It was not tied to the constraints of an arranged marriage. No, it was her courage, her unwavering determination, and her ability to wield the power she'd been blessed with that had led to this moment. As she stared at the newspaper, knowing she was going to return to a brighter future, her heart swelled with anticipation. The world shimmered with possibilities, and she, a beacon of untapped potential, was more ready to embrace the future than she had ever been.

As Hermione stood up to her full height, clutching the newspaper clipping tightly, a sudden gust of wind hit her, making her stumble. Looking up, she saw dark clouds gathering overhead. Lightning flashed across the sky, illuminating her surroundings for a moment. She could see her broom out the corner of her eye, suspended in air as if waiting for her, shouting at her to hurry. As she made her way across the rooftop, lightning crackled in the distance, illuminating the darkest corners of the roof and casting eerie shadows on the ground. Hermione tried to keep her nerve but had the most disquieting sensation that something was wrong.

Her heart pounded in her chest as the sky overhead grew darker and the wind began to howl. Suddenly, a bolt of lightning struck a few feet away, causing her to stumble and lose her footing. She caught herself on the edge of the rooftop, her fingers clinging to the cold stone as she fought to regain her balance. But the winds grew stronger, pushing against her, and she knew she was in trouble.

Desperately, she reached for her broomstick, hoping to use it to steady herself. But just as her fingertips grazed the handle, another bolt of lightning struck, this one much closer, and she was thrown backward. Suddenly her broomstick was far away, and she was hurtling toward the ground.

Fear consumed her as she fell, the wind rushing past her ears like a banshee's wail. She kicked and screamed and twisted her wrist, trying to cast a spell, positive that she'd injured it when she did. But just as she was about to crash into the ground below, her broomstick raced toward her, and she grabbed hold of it.

For a moment, she hung in the air, arms wrapped around her broom, panting and trembling in fear. But then everything went black as if a switch had been flipped and the world had gone dark. She couldn't see anything, couldn't hear anything, and could barely feel the broomstick beneath her fingers.

Panic seized her chest as she realized she was no longer in control, that an invisible hand had taken hold of her and was dragging her down into a dark abyss. She tried to scream, but her voice caught in her throat, choked by the crushing weight of the darkness.

Hermione felt herself falling at unimaginable speed, the wind whipping at her hair and clothes. Every instinct told her she was about to hit the ground, but as she braced herself for impact, she felt a jolt as if something had caught hold of her from behind.

The End and the Beginning

She opened her eyes, trying to see what had saved her, and saw a figure emerging from the darkness. Hermione blinked a few times to clear her vision. It was Gianni. He was staring down at her, his face twisted in a mixture of fear and concern.

"Hermione, are you all right?" he said, his voice calm.

She slowly sat up, panting and sweating, and stared down at her lap. She was in bed. Her comforter pooled at her waist. *No wind*, she thought, looking out a nearby window. Outside, it was bright and sunny. It was a new day.

It took her a few moments to realize she was back in her room, though there was something off about it. The room looked different. The walls were painted a soft shade of green, and the large windows were draped with sheer curtains that allowed the sunlight to filter in gently. The floors were made of polished birchwood, and antique paintings hung on the walls. She lay in a four-poster bed with a canopy, and the bedding was made of the finest silk. Several pillows were available to prop her up, and an emerald throw blanket was draped over the foot of the bed.

A cozy sitting area was in one corner of the room with two armchairs and a small table between them. The chairs were upholstered in light green fabric and decorated with gold tassels. A vase of fresh flowers and a crystal decanter of water with two glasses sat on the table. And to her right was a spacious walk-in closet beside the bedroom door, where a large vanity was visible. This room oozed luxury and demure but had an old-fashioned feel to it.

It worked, Hermione thought, trying to gather her wits. She couldn't help but wonder what this version of herself had been like. But she wasn't sure it mattered now—she'd already stolen the other woman's life.

"Hermione?" Gianni repeated.

For a moment, she struggled to remember his question. She was still dazed from the fall.

Hermione nodded weakly. "What happened?" she asked, her voice trembling.

Gianni shrugged. "I don't know. I was downstairs, and the next . . . well, I heard you screaming." He gestured toward her, indicating that he'd woken her.

Hermione shuddered, remembering the rooftop.

"Humph, new broom?" Gianni asked, looking past her.

She followed his line of sight and gasped. She assumed the broom must've followed her from the past, and beside it, peeking from underneath the bed, were the clothes she'd been wearing, dirty but neatly folded, and the time trinket sparkling in the sunlight.

Before Gianni could notice, a knock came from the door.

"Enter," Gianni said, and a tall serving elf with pale skin entered the room. "Ah, Petal, what is it?"

"The guests are arriving downstairs," Petal said.

"I see," he said, turning to Hermione. "It seems we have to get out there. I'm sure Father is eager to introduce you to Mordecai." He smiled and stood from the bed.

Hermione said nothing. She blinked a few times, then turned and found herself looking at the calendar. *It's July*, she read, staring at the date. Small hearts surrounded a note on a particular date: *Betrothal Announcement.*

"Do me a favor," Gianni said, and Hermione looked up at him. "Don't dress like you're going to a ball. You don't want to overwhelm him."

"Really?" Hermione said, caught off guard by the comment. She looked at the closet. "What do you suggest I wear?"

Gianni was nearly standing beside Petal now. "I don't know," he said with a small laugh. "But I'd rather you dress like you're going to a funeral than scare him off with a neon green dress."

Hermione laughed nervously. "Perhaps a dark green dress then."

When she finally reached the bottom of the stairs, Hermione saw a flash of movement out of the corner of her eye. She turned her head and saw a figure looking himself over in the mirror. Her heart lifted in her chest.

Christian.

She nearly leaped from the stairs. She raced over to get to

him in her dark green cowl dress, which was one of the few dresses available in the closet that Hermione liked. But she didn't care as much about that as she did her brother. She wondered how much he remembered—if he remembered anything at all.

"Good morning, Hermione," Christian said with a smile as she approached him. "Are you feeling all right? Nightmare?"

Hermione forced a smile. "I'm fine, Christian. Just a bad dream."

Her brother nodded, then gestured toward the mirror. "Sorry about this," he said. "I can't get my hair quite right."

She was beginning to wonder if this was her Christian or this timeline's Christian. She was growing impatient waiting to find out. Hermione looked past the staircase, where a sea of people were funneling themselves into the garden. In her mind's eyes, she knew the partygoers were dressed in their finest clothes, sipping champagne and chatting merrily, awaiting her arrival. And as Hermione stood there, she could feel her hope slipping away.

"So, Dad's campaign," she said weakly as she stared at her feet. "Do you think he'll win it?"

She knew this Christian was still too busy fussing with his tie, and she couldn't look at him. She couldn't let him see the tears in her eyes.

"I'm sure he will. After all, it's better than the alternative," he said.

Hermione shook her head, quickly wiping the tears. "Here, let me," she offered, looking up at him.

For a moment, looking into his eyes, she thought she saw a glint of something. But she knew better and forced herself to focus on the tie. But as she worked on the tie, memories flooded back to her—their short time as the Singletons, the laughs they had shared, the battles they had fought, and the losses they had endured. Tears stung her eyes as she thought about all the sacrifices they had made for their family. What hurt most was that she knew the next time she looked up at her brother, she'd realize, in a cruel twist of fate, that it wasn't him standing in front of her. It was someone else entirely—a stranger who looked remarkably similar to her beloved brother.

She tried to compose herself but couldn't stop herself from shaking. Then she felt his hands grab onto her own. Hermione looked into this Christian's deep blue eyes.

"Because the alternative is our father being dead," he whispered, and Hermione fell into his arms.

"Christian," she said, her voice cracking with emotion. "Oh, Christian."

He squeezed her tightly. "I told you I'd be waiting for you."

Hermione hugged him tighter, and she couldn't imagine letting her brother go again.

"I'm here, Hermione. It's me," he whispered, rubbing her back soothingly. "I know it was hard for you to leave. I just had to make sure you were you."

Hermione nodded as she pulled out of the hug. "I know," she said, wiping away her tears. "I just thought—"

"The worst," he finished for her, taking her hand. "Nope, I'm all patched up. Turns out Thomas knows a thing or two about healing."

Hermione took a deep breath to steady herself. "Of

course he does," she said, her voice trembling slightly. "How long have you been here?"

"About a month," he whispered. "Thomas thought it would be best if I arrived before you—with this." He pulled a small pocket watch out of his inner breast pocket.

Hermione smiled, looking down at it.

"Thomas felt I should have my own," Christian said with a smile. Then he looked toward the staircase. "I guess we should get this over with then," Christian said, offering his arm.

Hermione nodded, steadying herself. "Let's go."

As they made their way out of the room, Hermione glanced back at the hallway and the stairs, knowing her brother walked beside her, alive. She was afraid to believe it for a moment, but when she touched his hand gently she knew. *It's him,* she told herself. *He's here.* A wave of relief washed over her.

She wasn't alone anymore.

The Mandrake Family Legacy

July 1, 1996

The morning sun bathed the garden in a dreamlike glow, making the dew-kissed grass almost shimmer. As her gaze swept over the blooming flowers and verdant foliage of the garden, Hermione's eyes landed on a welcome sight—a white gazebo nestled amidst a cluster of towering trees. The gazebo was new—or at least new to her. Its intricate lattice work complemented the garden, but it reminded her that this home was not her own. Though her brother stood beside her, he'd had some time to adjust to it. She, however, had the most disquieting sensation churning in her stomach. But the sensation stilled when she spotted three of her siblings sitting beneath it: Gianni, Ares, and Achilles.

She considered leaving them be and joining her grandfather on the bench as she had before but decided against it. She wasn't ready to ask him about the dummy just yet.

"Things may be a little different than you remember," Christian said lowly.

Hermione stared at him blankly. "Bad or good different?" she asked.

Christian hesitated, and Hermione sighed.

She wanted answers. She had just saved their father and subsequently eliminated another Hermione from this time-line, so the least her brother could do was give her something to go on outside of things being *different*. Of course they'd be different. This wasn't their world.

Hermione rolled her eyes and began to make her way toward her siblings, her brother in tow. The breeze swept through her hair, carrying the scent of blossoms with it. Each step brought her closer to their familiar voices and warm laughter. Strangely, the siblings were wearing matching ensembles, each in a dark green suit.

Hermione had never known them to match.

"Christian, you're just in time! Achilles was just telling us about a nightmare he'd had," Ares said, wearing a self-satis-fied smirk. His posture exuded arrogance, emphasized by a subtle tilt of the head and a raised eyebrow. "Go on then —repeat it."

Achilles's shoulders hunched slightly as if he were trying to make himself smaller. "I've already told you, Ares, it didn't feel like a dream." He hesitated and began avoiding direct eye contact as if he feared saying the wrong thing. "I swear our father died at Fortuna Bay . . . I remember going there after-ward to search the area with Uncle Malicent. Children lay burned on the ground. Buildings had fallen, and the smell . . . it was *sweet*, it filled the air, choking our lungs—"

"It was a nightmare, Achilles," Gianni said in a stern voice. "Nothing more, nothing less. Perhaps it's the books you've been reading."

Achilles nodded in silence.

Hermione stared at Achilles and swallowed hard. *Was that even possible?*

She searched his face for an answer and found more than she'd like to admit. The bright green eyes she remembered now held a hint of sadness, casting a shadow over his youthful face. Dark circles were nestled beneath his eyes, like smudges of exhaustion. Lines of strain and fatigue traced the corners of his eyes, adding years to his face and hinting at the silent battles he had fought. In group settings, Achilles often positioned himself as the jester. He joked and laughed, occasionally pranking his siblings. He'd once charmed Hermione's hairbrush to turn her hair sky blue, and she'd been angry. Her father had grounded Achilles. But when it returned to its normal shade a few days later, Hermione and Achilles had laughed about it. But the differences in *this* Achilles were evident; his spirit had been dampened, his natural exuberance was stifled by a past she knew nothing about.

"Yeah, don't read horror novels before bed," Christian said, piping up and resting a hand on Achilles's shoulder. "It might help."

"Yes, maybe you're right," Achilles said before turning to Hermione. "I hope I'm not putting a damper on your day. I know it's important to you."

Hermione smiled. "It's perfectly fine, I wouldn't want you bottling up your feelings, Achilles."

"It's just . . . after what happened to Uncle Rowan—"

"Rowan was a traitor," Ares said, interrupting his younger brother. "Whoever killed him did us all a favor. He was plotting with the Dimitris and the East to kill our father."

"The East?" Hermione whispered to Christian.

Christian gave her a look that said, *later*.

"He's still family. We could've at least given him a funeral," Achilles said. "An attempted murder is shocking, no doubt, but he was hardly the worst of us. When you consider our family's history is tainted by dark deeds, starting with the numerous atrocities committed by our own flesh and blood. We're bearing the weight of our ancestors' sins."

"Like the dummy," Hermione stated, her voice just above a whisper.

But from the look on Achilles's face, he'd heard it.

"Yes, Sir Reginald," Achilles said. "Was it really warranted for our grandfather to turn him into that *thing*?" His voice carried a hint of bitterness. "Rowan's posthumous charge, as terrible as it is, pales in comparison to the full extent of the malevolence that exists within our family's legacy."

"*Enough,*" Gianni said sharply. "I'm not in the mood for another one of your lectures, Achilles. If you're so opposed to being a part of this family, perhaps you should defect to the East."

Achilles clenched his jaw, and Gianni glared at him in warning. For a few moments, they stayed that way, eyes boring daggers into each other, then Ares laughed.

"As if Achilles would have the gall to defect and join up with the Eastern Barleys," Ares said with a smile. "Perhaps he should give Father a blood oath—to prove his loyalty."

Hermione's heart skipped a beat as the proposal hung in the air; the weight of Ares Aristotle's words made her stomach churn. A chill crept up her spine, and she hoped he was joking, but Ares didn't budge. The very notion of a blood oath sent tremors through her body. How could he joke about that?

A blood oath required the oath taker to surrender a piece of their soul to another with dark magic, forever binding them to the promise to the receiver. If the wizard, witch, or conjurer ever broke their oath, their life was taken by the same dark forces that bound them to the receiver. It was a pact that forever altered the oath taker's existence. The thought of willingly inviting dark forces to hold sway over her being made her sick to her stomach.

"I thought you were beyond such juvenile behavior, Ares," Gianni said, a stern expression on his face. "Have you not outgrown your childish ways?"

"It was a joke, Gianni. Lighten up," Ares said, defensively. "You've always been the righteous one, haven't you? Always lecturing us about morality and responsibility? Then tell me how that applies to Achilles. Do we not have a duty to uphold our loyalty to our family?"

Gianni shook his head. "It's not about righteousness, it's about decency. Achilles may voice his concerns, just not in *mixed company*. It's best that we keep these conversations within our family. We wouldn't want our loyalists to doubt our family's strength. We are bound by Merlin's law. We should use our position to guide and defend, and to empower, not to tear down our own flesh and blood." Then Gianni turned to Achilles, and his eyes softened. "Our grandfather did what had to be done with Sir Reginald. You may have your doubts, but we are all well versed in the dark arts. Our tutors upheld our father's belief that mastering the dark arts was the only way to overcome them, and I know that you've seen some of the worst of it, Achilles. But might I suggest seeking out a therapist to discuss it, brother. It may be difficult now, but we must endure."

Achilles's eyes grew vacant as if fixed on some unseen horizon, but there was no recognition the world around him.

"Must we?" Achilles said abysmally.

Hermione looked at him, hoping to draw his attention. But there was a haunting stillness in his eyes, an eerie detachment that caused a twinge of pain in Hermione's heart. It was as if Achilles had retreated inward, leaving behind an empty vessel tethered to the physical realm.

His pain was clear. His pain was her pain—and her guilt. In that moment, when he seemed lost in a world only he could perceive, lost in the memories that held him captive, she saw the repercussions of her actions. In her past, their family was held in high regard; she understood the depth of what it meant to embrace the Mandrake family legacy and the power it bestowed. But now, flickers of doubt crept into her mind, staining the pristine image she had cherished. Where she'd come from, her father was against dark magic. The dark arts weren't meant to be meddled with.

But here, Merlin's law, or more likely, Merlin's desire for control, for dominance over others, whispered from the shadows of the Mandrake family's history. And what part had she played in it? Was it that moment she had told her father about the future? About his untimely end. Had the young Alfred Mandrake decided to change his ways?

As she looked around at her brothers, she sensed a level of detachment between them, perhaps a coping mechanism developed over time. This world was tainted. The bright tapestry of their familial bonds was now threaded with betrayals and atrocities. Hermione yearned for clarity, for a way to reconcile the conflicting emotions that gnawed at her conscience.

What have I done? Hermione thought, an inexplicable unease settled deep within her bones. Her instincts tingled with a silent warning, whispering to the deepest depths of her soul, and a flicker of fear ignited as a question forced itself to the forefront of her mind: How far would Alfred have gone to change his fate?

The Skies Run Red

Date Unknown

Seeking solace and clarity, Hermione retreated indoors, eventually wandering into Castle Mandrake's library, hoping to clear her head. Bookshelves towered over her, brimming with books of all shapes and sizes.

She took a deep breath and inhaled the rich scent of aged leather and parchment as she made her way to one of the many tall ladders that were scattered throughout the room. She hoped that for a few moments, she could escape the *other* Hermione's life. She was still feeling unsettled, as though there was something undeniably wrong with this world that she wasn't seeing.

The library was lit by the soft glow of chandeliers hanging from the high ceiling, casting a warm golden light on the bookcases that lined the walls. The shelves were made of a dark wood that seemed to almost absorb the light, and a few of them had intricate carvings of serpents and other mythical creatures.

As she walked deeper into the library, she passed by upholstered chairs and sofas, perfect for curling up with a good book, and small tables with reading lamps that beckoned her to stay a spell.

Finally, she arrived at the section of history books and began searching for the one she needed. The titles were written in bold script, making it easy to read them. She ran her hand over the spines, feeling the raised lettering, until she found the book she was looking for. She stared at the title and its dulled gold letters: *The Forgotten Histories of Noble Houses: The Mandrake Legacy.*

Hermione rolled her eyes. It was meant to be an autobiography on the Mandrake family legacy, though she wasn't quite sure her grandfather ever approved of it. She pulled the book off the shelf and sat down at a nearby table, taking in the view of the garden outside the large windows. She opened the book, thumbing through the pages. Her fingers traced over the words as she searched for any mention of the Barley family.

The pages were filled with illustrations of crests and descriptions of their origins, and Hermione's eyes widened as she finally found what she was looking for. There were two separate crests for the Barley family—one belonging to those of the east and another for the west.

She read the words aloud, her voice echoing through the vast library.

As I sit in the dimly lit museum within Castle Mandrake, surrounded by rows of dusty books and ancient artifacts, my mind can't help but wander to the whispers and rumors that have plagued this family for generations.

The most recent being the claims of Atreus Barley, who dared to speak out against the ruling Mandrake family and claim that Alfred Mandrake the First had fathered a bastard child within the illustrious Barley family. It was a bold move, one that ultimately halved their house, dividing them along their eastern and western borders.

Now, as I thumb through the pages of history books and old journals, I can't help but take note of Thomas Mandrake and his sons and the whispers that surround them. Some say they are the spitting image of their father, with his piercing eyes and sharp wit. Others claim they are nothing but pale imitations, lacking the strength and conviction of their patriarch.

But there are darker whispers as well, ones that hint at secrets and lies buried deep within their family tree. Whispers of betrayal and infidelity, of hidden children and illicit affairs.

The Eastern Barleys were exiled, and the halves hold an uneasy treaty to prevent a civil war betwixt them, as those in the east are no longer allowed in their ancestral home territories of the west. Left only with the eastern territories, and yet they thrive. Though the Mandrake family denies any wrongdoing, the rumors follow Alfred Mandrake, and the weight of them has only grown heavier with each passing year. The hold of the Mandrake family has shrunk, yet they remain the most power-ful, but a fourth family has risen to prominence. The noble houses of Mandrake, Dimitri, Bane, and the Barleys of the East.

As I trace my fingers over these yellowed pages, I can't help but wonder what truths lie hidden within these walls.

What secrets have been buried deep beneath the ground, waiting to be uncovered by those brave enough to seek them out?

But for now, all I can do is sit and read beside Thomas Mandrake, my heart heavy knowing the weight he carries, bearing the truth of this family's past. For in this world, the truth is often a slippery thing, and the secrets we keep can be the most dangerous of all.

The adventures are just
beginning!

If you'd like to follow along sign
up for my newsletter at
www.aminahfox.com/newsletter,
where you'll receive updates as
new books in this series are
released and much more!

I also hope you'll consider
dropping a quick review at the
retailer and book review site of
your choice.

Thank you and happy reading!

TURN THE PAGE FOR

THE ELEVENTH HOUR

BONUS MATERIALS

MANDRAKE
DESCENDANTS OF MERLIN

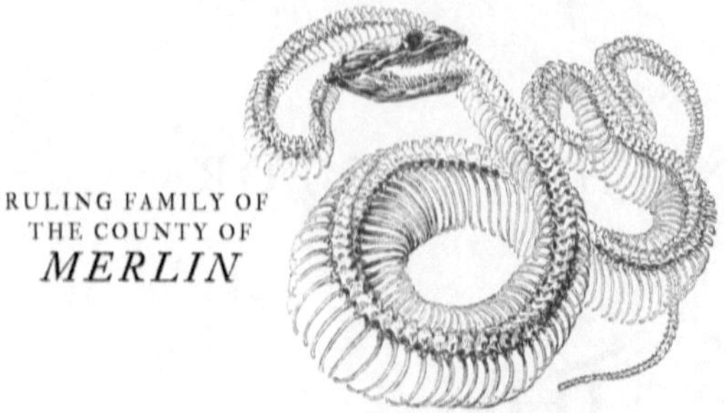

RULING FAMILY OF
THE COUNTY OF
MERLIN

HEIR APPARENT
GIANNI MATIAS

HEAD OF THE FAMILY
ALFRED MANDRAKE

ISSUE

♂ GIANNI MATIAS

♂ DORIAN

♂ CHRISTIAN CARLISLE

♂ ARES ARISTOTLE

♂ SEBASTIAN (✝)

♂ CORNELIUS

♂ ACHILLES

♂ REMY

♂ ALFRED II

♂ ELDERIC II

♂ FILLIAN

♂ FREDICK

♀ HERMIONE

WIVES AND MISTRESSES

Fonda Abbot [Wife 1]: Mother of Gianni Matias, Alfred II, and Elderic II

Alison Mandrake [Wife 2/Mistress 3] (Deceased ✝): Mother of Ares Aristotle and Achilles

Isabel [Wife 3]: Mother of Hermione

Laoghire Mandrake [Mistress 1]: Mother of Dorian, Cornelius, Filian and Frederick

Kassandra Graves [Mistress 2] (Deceased ✝): Mother of Christian Carlisle and Sebastian (✝)

Phaedra Price [Mistress 4]: Mother of Remy

his father and mother, Thomas and Leigh (✝)

his brothers:
Aidan (Deceased ✝)

Rowan and his wife, Renee Hughes
    their three children; two daughters and one son: Talia, Evelyn, and Brody

Malicent and his wife, Fey Graves
    their four children; twin sons and twin daughters: Randall and Boris, Lenea and Delphine

Damien and his wife, Chelsea Van Dorenss
    their five children; four sons and one daughter: August, Phineas, Flynn, Thomas II, and Diana

THOMAS MANDRAKE

LEIGH MANDRAKE
(NÉE ROUX)

At the age of thirty-seven, Thomas married Leigh Roux, a woman fifteen years his junior. Their marriage was a known diplomatic alliance. Thomas had a loving marriage with his wife. Their devotion to each other was unwavering, and when Leigh's untimely death occurred, Thomas was left heartbroken and in mourning.

Together they have five children. Twin sons Aidan and Alfred, were born in the first year of their marriage. Followed by three more sons: Rowan, Malicent, and Damien.

While Thomas's relationship with his eldest son, Aidan was characterized by warmth and mutual respect, the same could not be said for his interactions with his other sons. They, unfortunately, bore the brunt of being seen as a "spares" in the eyes of the world.

Tragedy struck when Thomas's firstborn son lost his life in a devastating firefight between two dragonriders from the Dimitri family. Despite not being the intended target, the young heir met his demise within the city where the fierce battle unfolded.

In the wake of his firstborn's tragic passing and Thomas's ongoing mourning, a decision was made to strip Thomas of his title, passing it to his second-born son, Alfred. This sudden change in leadership not only marked a significant shift in the family's legacy but also strained the already complex relationship between Thomas and his surviving sons.

The Mandrakes hold the loyalty of fourteen noble magical families. Their sworn loyalists are: Carmine, Barley, Sutter, Graves, Hawkins, Hughes, Abbot, McCoy, Van Doren, Augustine, Roux, Fauntleroy, Thistle, and Price.

These families are fiercely devoted to the family and its ideals. They assist in maintaining order within the borough, safeguarding its secrets, and supporting the Mandrake family's endeavors.

Acknowledgments

I would like to express my heartfelt gratitude to my family for their unwavering support and encouragement throughout the long journey of writing this book. Their belief in me and their willingness to stand by my side, even during moments of doubt, provided the motivation and strength I needed to see this project through to its completion. This book would not have been possible without their love and support.

To my editor, Jeanine Harrell, whose keen insights played a pivotal role in shaping and refining this story. Her constructive feedback and insightful suggestions not only improved the book but also helped me grow as a writer. I'm immensely thankful for her hard work and dedication to this project.

A special thank you goes to my talented cover designer, Gabriella Regina, for creating a beautiful cover that captures the essence of the story. Her creativity and artistic vision have given this book a beautiful and eye-catching identity.

To all my friends, beta readers, and everyone who offered feedback and encouragement along the way, I extend my heartfelt thanks. I am deeply grateful for their involvement in this project. Their input helped shape this book into what it is today.

Thank you to each and every person who played a part in

the creation of this book. Your support and belief in my work mean the world to me!

Finally, to the readers who pick up this book, I am humbled and honored that you have chosen to spend your time with my words. Your curiosity and engagement with this story mean the world to me.

OTHER NOVELS FROM
Aminah Fox

AMINAH FOX

THE
MOURNERS

THE DEADLY ELITE

THE FIRST NOVEL AN ADULT DYSTOPIAN FANTASY SERIES WHERE A MUTE TWENTY-ONE-YEAR-OLD WOMAN MUST MASTER A POWER SHE DIDN'T KNOW SHE POSSESSED OR RISK THE DESTRUCTION OF EVERYTHING SHE HOLDS DEAR.

After the American Civil War ends in a stalemate, the southern states become a separate nation and their government is overthrown by Minister Samuel Davis, later known as the Apostate. Over a century later, his followers, the Apolites are thriving in the superstate of Scopus, a seemingly utopian society where a fundamentalist regime has kept their subordinate states in line and more importantly the people themselves, equal. Once a year, all twenty-one-year-old Apolites must take an aptitude test to be assigned their life's work and consequently their place in society.

Elide Hester, a mute, studious young woman living in dystopian Texas, who has spent all of her life preparing for the test, is relieved when she receives a high score. But when she is suddenly selected by a deadly pseudo-religious organization to be initiated into their ranks, she discovers that nothing is as it seems, including the country's enigmatic leader himself. And with war threatening their borders, Elide must stay alive long enough to unravel the secrets of their past and master a power that could be the key to ending the war—or risk the destruction of everything she holds dear.

Prologue

Cyrus

The search team had been dwindling for several months, the hunt for the harlots had surpassed average commuting distance by fourteen miles, and they had been forced to set up camp approximately forty-nine paces south of where he stood now. Cyrus Coin, who had lived all his life being the least attentive of his siblings and rarely remembered passages of Holy Writ, never expected to find proof of Him in an angel number, but seven was everywhere. In the fingers of sunlight that woke him in the mornings spent in his tent to the omens of death that clung to the trees, tarred and feathered during their searches at night. He was a God-fearing, Christ-haunted man as all Seekers were trained to be, though Cyrus could not have had worse luck; he had been the one to find the harlots.

"A moment longer," Cyrus urged as the sky grew darker above them. "The harlots are dead ahead."

"Does a harlot's bosom frighten you?" Ezra asked with a slight chuckle.

Cyrus didn't entertain the jab at his character. He was younger, entering his late twenties, and he had once heard Ezra shriek when a branch touched his shoulder.

"Harlots are harlots," he said. "We are all purveyors of sin if we learn nothing from it."

"You empathize with them?" Ezra asked. "With those who tempt men from their proper houses? Is that not treason?"

"Cyrus would never commit treason," Jakob said softly. "If he empathizes with them, then it's due to him being the son of a reverend elder."

Cyrus had intended to be silent on the final day of the search. He meant to pray for the harlots the night before as once they were captured, they were to be auctioned to the bawds without trial—Apostate's orders.

"My father would vote in favor of them getting a proper trial," Cyrus added lowly.

"My uncle would wish for the same in his old age, Cyrus," Ezra replied. "Though he's not as sharp as he used to be, and he's not the head of state. There are men meant to enforce the law and men meant to abide by it. And women follow men in doing so."

"We've waited long enough," Jakob said. "I want to be home before tomorrow night, maybe morning. Where is the page whistle?"

Cyrus watched as Jakob searched his pack for it, his brow knitted tightly together above his weary eyes. Jakob was twenty years his senior, far more accustomed to the ways of the Seekers than himself and had married lower than his station. A humble man with more to lose. Paired with a fool and a youth, neither with enough sense to remember a page whistle. Under suppressed anger, Cyrus could sense a manner of urgency in the man. It permeated off him.

Cyrus bore the weight of it. He had spent all his life in Texas, but this was his sixth year as a Seeker. His first time near the border.

The harlots were a mere twenty minutes from freedom, all they had to do was cross, but they slept around a fire, huddled together. He had counted them, young and middle-aged women, all would be convicted the same. For years Cyrus had been plagued with watching executions a thousand times over, and there was no new guilt for men like him. Or so he thought.

"Here, I've brought a light," Ezra said, offering Jakob a flashlight. "The old ways serve us just as well."

Jakob took it. "Aye, they do," he said, using the light to cast a signal south.

Cyrus watched as the signal was repeated by another Seeker, and then they waited.

"We've done our part," Ezra said with a yawn. "The men will load up the horses and file out before long, only a matter of time. There's no need to watch, boy. You'll only frighten yourself. I remember the first time I saw them do it, still thought of them as women then. But that's the trick. Demons possess the body, they sneak up on you quieter than any mouse, Cyrus, and at first, you sneeze, and you may shiver and try to run from it and tell yourself it's a bad dream. But once it gets inside you, it makes you feel warm like your mother's love until you begin to burn. You'll think it's fever, but no, and you'll start to drown in it. Struggle as you might, you won't have the strength to fight it. Before long, you'll slip away, thinking you're in pleasure, begging for more, but you're in pain. Though you don't know it yet, and you start tempting others to sin as well, and then you're sinking into a pit of darkness. Weak and weary."

"Don't frighten the boy, Ezra," Jakob said apathetically. "Those harlots can't be helped unless they find it in their hearts to repent."

"When have you heard of a harlot rebuking her demons?" Ezra said, stretching out and propping his head up on his pack. "They're out all night dancing with them. Selling what's not theirs to give."

Jakob grimaced. "Don't speak in such a way, or the lord will judge you as harshly."

Ezra shook his head and yawned again. "I only speak the truth, Jakob, they'll have them soon enough, and we'll all be on our way back in time for breakfast, I hope."

Within moments of Ezra speaking aloud, the Disciples rode out, bearing the Apostate's famed raven on their war flags, set forth by rage and driven by the will of the lord to see the women apprehended and justice executed. Forty in total, moving two by two across the glen, their horses' hooves roaring like thunder, and as they descended on the harlots, shrill screams rose into the night.

Chapter 1

Elide

"I, Hansel Hester, violated the sanctity of my marriage bed and that of Reverend Elijah Stone, knowingly, foolishly, and regretfully," Hansel said, lifting his eyes to meet those of the reverend elders. "And I have come to make amends."

Hansel stood like a soldier, and the loyal follower of God's law could have been one, had he not retired those dreams years ago upon her birth. Their ancient laws had served the Maleficarum family for ten generations, as had the Hester family. Growing up in Texas, as part of the Apolitian commune, Hansel had faced temptation often, thinking the men of their family were plagued more than all others. Elide knew little of the temptations men faced, only that her own were few and far between. At the moment all she wanted was her winter coat as the courtroom was exceptionally chilly.

The elders' heavy black robes protected them from the cold, though each of their brows were furrowed due to Hansel's request. Reverend Warner, the eldest reverend and overseer of Baptiste, looked irate by the request. The old man's jaw was clenched so tightly, Elide thought it might snap. Last week the floors of the church shook when he'd read Juliette's penalty for adultery. Elide had been shaken as well, concerning those around her, and she'd hoped to never be on the other end of his wrath.

"Juliette has already faced the penalty for your co-conspiracy," Reverend Elijah said, grimly. "Her auction is sanctioned for October."

Hansel winced at the statement. "And what of my penalty?"

Elide's instincts were telling her to grab her brother, but she didn't move. She didn't want to dishonor him by interrupting his act of repentance. No matter what her instincts told her.

"Of your what?" Reverend Warner stated.

Hansel took a deep breath. "Forgive me, I—"

"All is already forgiven," Reverend Warner interrupted, clasping his hands together. "You have sought for something you've already earned, Hansel. A man needn't seek a gift that has already been given. Tell me, has your wife's retraining not been going well?"

"It's going well, but—"

"Would you rather be rewed, perhaps to a lina or baroness instead?"

"No, I—"

"Then there is nothing more this council can do to serve you," Reverend Warner said.

Elide could hear the warning in his voice and reached for her brother's arm, hoping not to vex them further. Hansel pulled his arm away.

"Is there no penalty I must face?" Hansel shouted.

The council looked among each other, communicating wordlessly and coming to the same conclusion.

"Young man, there's no need to fuss," Reverend Coin stated, as he appeared to be the most levelheaded among the reverend elders. "You have made a mistake, as many of us do, and as head of your household, I would expect you to be relieved. It is the decision of this council that your guilty conscience should suffice and there is no need to ruin two futures with our verdict."

Hansel didn't speak. For three days, he had paced the length of Elide's living room plagued with guilt, declaring his sorrows to her, and this was their conclusion. No matter what he had felt or did feel now or how long it had taken the search committee to find Juliette beforehand. The hunt for her was over, their standing in the commune remained intact, and regardless of the morbidity of the circumstances, Hansel was forgiven by everyone but himself.

Elide watched as Hansel nodded obediently, accepting the verdict.

"Your sister is approaching her assignment year, is she not?" Reverend Coin asked with a smile.

Hansel nodded, glancing at Elide.

"Dear girl, where is it you hope to be assigned?" Reverend Coin asked, turning to her.

Elide hesitated. She often wished to be among the more scholarly linas, walking the aisles of Library Decaturian in Blackburn, exploring their peerless selection of books on a winter's day. But, at times, she was drawn to dreams of being a baroness, living off an endowed fortune in Hickory, on her own property, surrounded by the arts, and able to select her future husband.

She could have a library built for her, she reasoned. There were no foreseeable issues—or more accurately, Elide would have to get a high score on the LAT to make either option available to her. There was one application, therefore, one chance at happiness.

"Elide is mute sir," Hansel said.

"Oh, my apologies, Elide," Reverend Coin said kindly. "I'm afraid my ability to sign is rather lacking."

Elide gave him a small smile.

"Very well then," Reverend Warner stated. "This meeting is adjourned. You are dismissed, Hansel."

Hansel bowed lowly, and Elide was relieved. Then she had the oddest feeling that someone was staring at her, and in the corner of the courtroom, perhaps they were. Three spectators in black veils and dark, long-sleeved dresses stood like shadows along the wall; the eldest clutched a cane with both hands.

"Mourners," Hansel whispered, guiding Elide out of the courtroom with a hand on her upper back. "Never look them directly in the eye. I hear they can smell fear."

Elide swatted her brother the moment they stood outside the courthouse.

"Ow! It was only a joke, Elide," Hansel said, trying to flag down a carriage.

"What if they'd heard?" Elide signed, gesturing back at the courthouse. "What then?"

Hansel sighed. "I wouldn't let anything happen to you," he said softly. "Hell, you wouldn't be staying at the house —*your* house—alone if it were up to me."

"It's not my house," Elide signed. "It's Dad's."

"Well, Dad left it to you."

"Reverend Warner says—"

"It doesn't matter what Warner says," Hansel said. "Dad left it to you, and that's that. He can't overrule another reverend's will, even a dead one. And if he tries, I won't let him. Okay?"

Elide rose to her toes and hugged Hansel.

She knew he meant it and that he meant well, but in protecting her, he would bedevil the council again, and she couldn't let that happen. Hansel was struggling with newlywed life; Elide knew he wouldn't have selected Lilah of his own volition. Their grandfather had matched them a week after their father's death, and as the patriarch of the family, he had final say in most things, including who they wed.

"We should get you home; it'll be dark out soon," Hansel said, holding her at arm's length.

He flagged down a horse-drawn carriage with a pug-faced driver that grumbled as he stopped.

"Thanks for stopping, Fred," Hansel said with a hint of a smile.

The old man grumbled. "Least I could do for you getting that Timber boy to fix my wheel," Fred said with a chuckle. "Though I would've preferred he'd matched it with the set, bit odd for my customers to see one black wheel. Some have joked that it's an omen."

Elide couldn't agree more. The newer metal wheel gleamed brightly in contrast to the duller silver wheels. She imagined it would have made a fine set of four, but the black wheel made the others look shoddy.

"Then let's hope it's a harbinger of good luck," Hansel

said, eliciting a raspy laugh from Fred as her brother helped her into the carriage.

"Where you headed then?" Fred asked.

"The only place that's ever brought me peace, 42 Mansfield Street in Baptiste," Hansel answered before stepping into the carriage himself.

Chapter 2

Mansfield Street, Baptiste, Texas

Half an hour after their departure from the courthouse, they traded the large red brick buildings of Central Prospero for the small, overcrowded houses of Baptiste. Most families had lived in the area for generations and were nestled within a few streets of each other, allowing their children to wander freely between houses for meals and baths. Parents could work while children stayed with aunts or grandparents. Whether work was near or far, they could get by with horse-drawn carriages, which were plentiful. In Texas, there were no cars because cars were too modern, and modern amenities that were deemed as overt luxuries went against the faith—as did initiating war.

But war was scarcely spoken about in pleasant conversation, though men went off daily to fight it, to protect them from the outsiders who wished to rob them of their faith. The bombings hit southern Baptiste the worst, leaving behind burned balconies and buildings half standing, half fallen.

Their family was one of the lucky ones. Their homes hadn't been robbed from them; they would rest their heads on pillows tonight, not dirt.

Elide sighed as they passed another pub. She looked away the moment she saw staggering men, because they reminded her too much of their late father, who was a long time dead but had left quite an impression. She never wished to wed a man that struggled as he did. When they were some distance away, she braved another look out the window and smiled when she saw her home roll into view.

"All right, out we go," Hansel said, getting out and helping her out of the carriage as he always did.

As soon as they were out, Fred took off without another word, the carriage kicking up dirt behind it.

"Well, Fred was in a hurry," Hansel said. "You can come over for dinner if you'd like."

Elide smiled. "I'm going to stay in tonight," she signed. "They're allowing a new film to air at six."

"Really? I hadn't heard, though with everything going on, it's a bit hard to keep up with recreational activities. I wish I had more time," Hansel said with a sigh. "You sure I can't convince you to come have dinner with us?"

"I'm going to study after the film," Elide signed.

"Oh, right, the LAT. When is that?" Hansel asked.

"Tomorrow," Elide signed.

"Wow, that's right," Hansel said lowly. "Twenty-one's the year. It's always the year. I swear my head is in the clouds today. I still remember teaching you how to tie your shoes. I forget some days how much older we are now."

"Speak for yourself," Elide signed with a hint of a smile.

Hansel laughed. "Oh, very funny, mock your poor brother," he said, hugging her goodbye. "I love you, and good luck on your exam."

She hugged him tightly to assure him that the feeling was mutual, and then the two went their separate ways. She into 42 Mansfield Street, their childhood home, and him into 41.

Elide stepped on three letters upon entering her home, so the first she looked at had mud caked onto it. It was the smallest of them and was from her friend Fiona, who lived several streets away, but typically used all seventy-two hours of designated cellphone time within the first week of the month. Perhaps calling Gabriel Timber, who was six months their senior and engaged to Fiona when they were both eighteen with her parents' permission. Elide was not envious of her friend; she was happy for Fiona. Having never experienced true love herself, Elide knew nothing of the trials or temptations that came with it. Sometimes she wondered if she, too, would falter and use her entire monthly allowance of cellphone time on one man. For her, there were only two contacts: Hansel and Fiona. Though she rarely had a reason to use her phone, as she never had any critical emergencies, nor did she need her brother to chaperone a date. Men who had pursued her in the past were of unsavory character and curious—or more specifically, questioning what it was like to have sex with a mute woman.

She attributed it to the area. There weren't many hopeless romantics in Baptiste aside from herself. Most were easily paired off. But it didn't upset her because she would make a life for herself through the examination. The Livelihood Assessment Test was her ticket out, as it was for most people that lived there. Gone were the days that they'd have to continue to live in squalor, living from check to check, rather than having vacations as those higher up could afford. The aptitude test would measure her skillset as it had those before her. Score too low and she'd likely stay in Baptiste and work as a scrubber, subjugated to clean up after others, or be a packer, packing and shipping packages throughout Texas. Neither job fit her. Though the employment rate in those jobs was high, wages were low. She would need a particularly high score to be either a baroness or lina, but she was confident in her abilities. Or at least her ability to study. Her brother was lucky to have inherited the title of Mart from their father; he received monthly stipends from the commune as a leader of the people. He covered his household's expenses and hers.

That, however, hadn't prevented him from risking his position over the temptation that drove him to bed Juliette in 41 Mansfield Street. Elide questioned whether it had been cupid's arrow or foolishness that had struck him, though she was sympathetic for both parties. She couldn't reconcile why their grandfather hadn't selected Juliette to be Hansel's wife. The ways of men were a mystery that she, a woman, had no right to question. Or, more so, questioning them aloud would sooner cause her tongue to be cut out. Faith was against her in that instance. Though, she was one of the lucky ones. God had given her the gift of being speechless on the day of her operation. But God had also given her Hansel, and he, common as he was, had often given answers to her questions that no man had to give a woman as deemed by the faith.

Chapter 3

The night was filled with nightmarish sounds. Most nights, Elide slept through them; she never had the urge to check the source of them, sensing her fear was unfounded, but mostly because she was already anxious. The first bang in the walls could have been a demon or merely the water shifting through the pipes. The same way the creaking floors were the house settling as the old house did every night—rather than a burglar lurking around the house. Today was the most important day of her life, so it was only right for her to be nervous about it. The weight of it was dreadful to think about.

Her morning was no less wild. The first four hours she'd been awake were chaotic, to say the least, and she was short on time.

Elide had placed her flashcards on the kitchen counter in a plastic index card holder, which she had been gifted on her twentieth birthday. She had set the holder beside the toaster. She was positive she had. Today it wasn't there.

She opened all the cabinets in her kitchen, even the cereal cabinet, and hadn't found it there. She was checking under the dining room table when the front door opened, startling her, and causing her to bang her head on the table.

"What happened here?" Hansel asked. "It looks like a tornado's gone through the place."

Elide got up and rubbed her head, trying to alleviate the pain.

"I can't find my flashcards," Elide signed. "They were by the toaster."

"Well, Lilah had said she'd popped in last night," Hansel said. "Perhaps she moved them."

Elide shook her head and flung her bag over her shoulder. "I have to go, or I'll be late," she signed, growing increasingly angry by his response.

"Sorry, Elide. I know, boundaries," Hansel said. "I'll tell her not to touch the key from here on out."

Elide nodded as she grabbed hold of her coat and binder and quickly left the house before she could lose her temper. She flagged down a carriage and handed him a note with her destination. Elide tucked her phone into the coat and zipped the pocket to keep it safe. Her chauffeur wasn't concerned with her not speaking, though he wasn't her usual driver. Most people didn't speak to drivers outside of giving them money. In some ways, this was beneficial for her as it didn't indicate any difference between herself and anyone else, though she wouldn't have minded having a conversation with him.

Inside the carriage, there was nothing but silence to keep her company. Outside, a storm had started with gossiping clouds, speaking in dark tones and flashing like camera bulbs. But the most talkative was the rain rushing down the carriage window that showed no sign of slackening.

After they'd ridden a few miles on the dirt roads, she stepped out onto the sidewalk in front of Miller Hall. Elide had studied here all her life, taking numerous classes and testing often. She'd even had her height measured here when she was six, but today would decide the rest of her life; whether she would be trapped in Baptiste or would thrive in Prospero. She covered her head with her binder and rushed inside the building so eagerly that she crashed into someone and landed on her back on the floor.

Elide gathered up her binder and went to mouth an apology, but when she looked up, a hand was waiting for her. It was a Seeker man that didn't look nearly as angry by the error as the four fellows he was with.

The Seeker men wore brown suits with black ties—Seeker formal attire. There to collect early initiates and begin their training as apparently being taught to search and protect took priority—if this was what Second Class soldiers looked like, she was afraid to see First Class.

Elide took his hand, and he helped her to her feet while saying, "Easy," as though she was a skittish horse.

"Sorry," Elide signed.

She blushed and then mouthed the word.

"It's all right," he said aloud while signing back. "I know some from my time in the west."

"Watch where you're walking, girl," a larger Seeker beside him stated harshly.

The Seeker man turned to him. "No need to be uncivil, Ezra," he said. "Accidents happen, don't they."

He gave Elide a warm smile that made her cheeks grow warmer.

She was almost certain she recognized him from a photo

in Hansel's yearbook. He had distinct features; his dark hair and pointed nose were both familiar though his green eyes couldn't be captured in a black-and-white photo. His jaw was sharper now than it was then, but she couldn't remember the name beneath it.

"Cyrus, making friends, I see," a voice coming from behind Ezra said, and Elide pulled away her hand.

"Reverend Coin," Ezra said, quickly bowing his head to the reverend elder. "We weren't told you would be making an appearance today."

"Well, it's quite rare that a man my age gets to see his son and he's not on his deathbed," Reverend Coin said.

"I had been meaning to visit," the Seeker beside Elide told the reverend elder. "But we've been rather—"

"*Busy,* tracking those harlots," Ezra finished for him. "That your boy managed to find all on his own."

Reverend Coin smiled with pride as though he had made the discovery himself and patted his son on the shoulder. Elide tensed as she felt immediately out of place. And yet she couldn't think of a way of excusing herself, but she didn't mind it. She would likely never step foot in this building again after today— once they were assigned, everything else would fall into place.

She would miss sitting in classes together with Fiona, they would be trading that for morning tea and brunches soon, which was difficult to envision, but the easiest pill to swallow. Her anxiety was the least of her worries now.

"Excuse me! Excuse me!" someone said in a melodic tone, her voice growing louder as she pushed through the crowd. "There you are! I've been looking all over for you," Fiona said.

Her best friend, Fiona, stood in her best dress, holding a binder close to her chest as though it was a shield. Her blond bob was curled, and her small nose wrinkled at the sudden realization of the men around Elide. There was a hint of nervousness in her green eyes, and she let out a nervous laugh. When they were younger, Fiona looked like a porcelain doll, but now she looked much more like the plastic dolls women bought their daughters in stores. If she wasn't already promised to Gabriel, she would have another suitor waiting for her among these men.

"Sorry, if you'll just excuse me and Elide. We need to have a little last-minute review for our tests," Fiona told them, quickly hooking her arm into Elide's and pulling them far away from the Seekers and Reverend Coin.

When they were a few feet from the exam door and well out of earshot of the Seekers, she stopped in her tracks.

"Okay, spill! Tell me absolutely everything immediately, Elide," Fiona said giddily.

Elide stared at her blankly.

"Oh, come on, Pansy wouldn't shut up about how you were talking to Cyrus Coin of all people," Fiona said, cocking a brow.

"I bumped into him," Elide signed. "It was an accident. What's the big deal?"

"The big deal is that he's basically a celebrity," Fiona answered, sighing. "If I weren't already spoken for, I'd go for him."

"Reverend Warner says we're all equal and—"

"Yeah, yeah, no celebrities," Fiona said, rolling her eyes. "You know I heard on the radio that the lands across the water have celebrities. We ought to go visit someday if you ever get a passport."

"I'm working on it," Elide signed and Fiona laughed.

"I'm only teasing," Fiona said with a giggle, hooking their arms together again. "You worry too much. Soon we'll take the test and be up in Prospero together. Gabriel will be a tom, messing with all those fancy doctor's instruments and I'll be married to him as a baroness, and you'll be right there with me, even if you choose to be a lina. Best friends forever. No exceptions."

Elide smiled at her friend's candor. There were often days she wished that she was nearly as bold as Fiona. Elide was honest but had never been able to openly express feelings, though she was sincere whenever she declared them.

"All right, everyone," Tutor Mackenzie said, clapping her perfectly manicured hands together. "Time to line up and remember what we say is nearly as important as what we do. Your oral test will be worth forty percent of your score. For those requiring different testing procedures, your proctor has been made aware. Any questions?"

She waited a moment. "Yes, Mr. Anderson?"

"Is it true what they're saying about the North End?" he asked.

And the students stirred, whispering frantically about a rumor that hadn't reached Elide's ears. The North End was a trade route built by construction workers from Baptiste who'd volunteered to travel north with military protection to establish trade with the lands across the water. They started in the center of what was once called Houston—now called Prospero—and planned several other routes bridging from Texas to other trade routes until they stopped working on them.

There weren't any trade routes in Baptiste, there were plenty of dirt roads, and the city may as well have been left to rot after the first civil war.

"Mr. Anderson, keep all questions not pertaining to the test for the end, please. And I assure the rest of you that there is no need to panic about the North End. We are well protected within our great state," Tutor Mackenzie said confidently. Instilling confidence in many around Elide, including Fiona. "Now, what do we say?"

"Our fate is not our own to decide," they all recited in unison—all who weren't mute.

Tutors passed out numbers to students. Then they were told to go down one of twelve hallways. Fiona was sent down Hall 2 as a man directed Elide to go down Hall 3. When she stopped, she stood silently against the wall. Her neighbor across from her, Lorraine, was sweating and pale.

Lorraine was always nervous, though she typically received high marks in everything: her eyesight, her hearing, her mathematics tests—her results were exemplary—and yet she was shaking. Perhaps she feared the idea of abandoning her family, or she feared them finding out it was what she wanted. Though she was likely projecting as she had failed to tell her brother her hopes for the future.

The proctors were paid volunteers, mostly from Baptiste —their uniforms were all white—women in dresses, men in dress shirts and dress pants. There were three Scout women —they were Seekers, but the name changed with gender— and they had tattoos on their wrists. Soldiers were the only ones allowed to have tattoos; the swallow meant they saved someone, but no one told Elide what a mouse meant.

"Lorraine Hoss and Elide Hester," a volunteer said sharply.

The volunteer who called Elide was from Prospero—his shoes were too nice for him to be from Baptiste. She couldn't be tested by someone from Baptiste because it went against the rules and would nullify her result. If she were put in a room with a Baptiste proctor, she would have to ask them to move her.

Elide stepped forward obediently, walking behind Lorraine into the room he pointed to.

Inside, the room was halved by two offices built from stanium, a white metal that neutralized sound—they used it in buildings in Baptiste so people couldn't hear their neighbors.

Lorraine looked back at Elide, gave her a small smile, and went into the first office and shut the door behind her. Elide was frozen to the spot. Her breath caught in her chest. She had half expected them to take the oral test last and wasn't sure what she would say. She'd not practiced any form of pitch for herself, though Tutor Mackenzie had never spoken of what the subject of the pitch would be.

The second office's door creaked open, and a woman with round glasses poked her head out. She was thin with brown skin and curly hair that was in a tight bun and wore a white pantsuit—it was the first time Elide had ever seen a woman in a suit—and tall shoes. She signaled Elide to come to her, and Elide obeyed. Then she quickly got Elide into the office and shut the door behind them.

"You've really got to be careful," the woman said, "it is

bad enough to have liberty men take notice of you, but it is worse to not be able to speak if they do something."

It took Elide a moment to register the insult and another for her to realize the woman was a lina. A lina's stagecoach had broken down by a pub when Elide was seven. The woman was wearing "kitten" heels and a tweed dress. She stuck out like a sore thumb among the Baptiste women. Calling someone from Prospero a "liberty" was an insult that held a lot of weight, because it was undefined, at least to a Baptiste woman like her.

The woman took a deep breath.

"My name is Angelique, and I'll be your proctor for the oral test," she said calmly. "Your multiple-choice test will be taken in another room."

"What do I have to do for the exam?" Elide signed.

The room was empty aside from the desk and the two chairs that accompanied it, hardly an effective testing environment, Elide thought.

"You'll take one of these," Angelique said taking a seat and setting a bottle on the desk. "And then we'll begin."

Elide eyed the two pills in the bottle curiously. They were the same color. Angelique pulled out a blank sheet of paper and a pen.

Elide looked at the pills again. There were no obvious differences between them, aside from their shape. The weight of the bottle seemed about even. Perhaps the test itself was whether she would pollute her body with drugs. Or the test was literal, and, therefore, she had to select a pill as instructed. She could feel her heartbeat in her chest. Elide had never taken drugs. Hansel was the adventurous one, and he'd chosen to stay in Baptiste.

"What happens when I take it?" Elide signed. "Do I have to take one?"

"Yes, either of them. Neither will harm you."

Elide's mouth felt dry, and she swallowed hard. She took the bottle, opened it, but hesitated and set it down.

"What's the difference?" Elide signed.

"Both will take you places, but only one will take you where you want to go," Angelique said. "Choose whichever one calls to you."

Elide took a deep breath and looked between the two pills again. And then pulled out the circular pill and swallowed it.

Testing had lasted all afternoon. Now it was growing colder and darker, and Elide couldn't remember the LAT at all. All those weeks she'd spent studying, and she couldn't remember a word from her oral test or the multiple-choice test, though she had taken both or at least been told that she had. Elide had taken a seat at a cafeteria table outside the testing room, in front of Hall 2. Her head was throbbing, likely a side effect from not having eaten this morning—or the pill. Either way, she'd be home soon. It was getting dark out, and she and Fiona were supposed to head back to Baptiste together.

"My proctor thinks I'm a shoo-in for baroness," Fiona bragged as she took a seat beside Elide. "What's wrong? Are you worried about your score?"

Elide groaned. She felt as though she would faint if she stood back up.

"I think that pill gave me a headache," Elide signed.

"I'd rather have a headache than fishy burps," Fiona said. "Which one did you take?"

"Hey," Gabriel said happily. "What's wrong?"

Elide looked up at him. He had dark hair, brown skin, and brown eyes and was wearing a dress shirt with jeans.

"Those pills are what's wrong," Fiona answered.

"What pills?" Gabriel asked, looking between the two women.

Fiona sighed and rolled her eyes. "Figures, the guys would get off easy," she said, then she toyed with a strand of her hair. "We had an oral test, and apparently, the women had to take pills, which they completely failed to mention in the LAT prep book. And I nearly slept through half the multiple-choice test. It's a miracle I finished in time."

I'd rather be tired than nauseous any day, Elide thought to herself.

Gabriel laughed. "Well, neither of you could have done worse than Lorraine Hoss. I heard she vomited during the oral test, and they had to escort her out."

Elide was sure it was meant to make her feel better, but it didn't. She could only imagine how having her LAT score slip through her fingers would've felt. Elide felt a pang of guilt in her chest—she couldn't even remember leaving Angelique or the office—but she wasn't sure how much of a test those pills were. They were just pills.

"Well, I've got something that'll take the edge off," Gabriel said lowly to Fiona. "Some of the others and I are thinking of heading into the woods for a little celebration. Nothing impure, honest."

Elide was skeptical of the offer, but Fiona looked giddy.

"Come on," Fiona begged. "It'll help you relax. And

tomorrow, we'll find out our scores and be spending the rest of our days in Prospero."

Elide sighed. She was tired, but she could feel her head clearing.

She wouldn't mind spending time with a few of her class-mates before they likely never crossed paths again. So, she nodded in agreement, and Fiona hugged her tightly.

By the time they'd reached the forest, the party had already started, and Elide's head was clear. Gabriel paid off the stage-coach's driver, and he agreed to wait for seven hours, but no more.

"Don't worry," Gabriel told Elide. "Everything will be fine. If any Seekers show up, Rob here will text me, and we'll be out of here before you know it."

"She can't help but worry," Fiona said teasingly. "Elide was raised to be a proper young woman with good morals and sound judgment. And I would've been too if I wasn't engaged to you, Gabriel Timber."

"Oh, hush," Gabriel said, kissing Fiona's forehead. "Come on, I see the guys over there."

Elide followed them and took a seat on a log where a few boys were playing cards. Neither looked up when they arrived.

"Hey, what are you two playing, James?" Gabriel said, sitting down across from Elide with Fiona beside him.

"Don't know what it's called," the younger boy answered. "Just know I have to put the numbers in order and empty my hand."

Elide could count on one hand the number of times she'd heard James Anderson talk while his twin brother talked much more. Ryder was the older of the two. He had blond hair like his father, with his mother's silver eyes and pale skin. He always wore clothing to emphasize that he was from Prospero, preferring to stand out in a crowd. He had no interest in being a tom, and though he didn't declare it, Elide would guess he had his eye on becoming a Disciple while James wanted to be a Seeker.

Disciples were the personal guard of the head of state, the Apostate, who led the First and Second Class armies that stood for freedom above all else. The Disciples were all male and wore black from head to toe with a gold crest of a raven embroidered on their uniform's breast pocket.

"So, how's everyone feeling about the test," Ryder asked as he set down another card.

"Great, I'm sure my mother will be pleased," Fiona said. "I studied day and night, and it finally paid off."

"I'm just glad it's over. If I knew it was going to be that easy, I would've taken more breaks," Gabriel said. "At least we're done with high school."

"How about you, Elide?" Ryder asked with a hint of a smile.

"Good enough," Elide signed.

"She says—"

"I don't need you to translate, Fiona. I've been working on it," Ryder said. He let out a laugh. "I'm sure Elide crushed it like she always does."

Elide blushed. Ryder was being kinder to her today, perhaps he was in a better mood than usual, or it was simply because he was beating his little brother at the card game.

"No fair, Ryder, you cheated!" James shouted as Ryder set his last card down.

Ryder laughed. "Come on, James, don't be a sore loser," he said playfully.

After a few hours, more partygoers showed up in the forest with wine and beer to drink, and some began exchanging more than words. Elide knew kissing wasn't against any laws if it didn't lead to sinful behaviors, but she still felt it was a slippery slope. Fiona and Gabriel were relatively careful. They'd left to kiss and fool around at a lake nearby. They always avoided being seen, unlike some others present. Public gambling, however, went against a few laws, though James was in high spirits now that he was winning card games.

"You want a drink, Elide?" Ryder asked, shoving a beer into her clumsy hands.

Elide rarely drank wine. And if she drank anything it was usually with Hansel and his wife. She didn't want to drink.

"What? You think I put something in it," Ryder said accusingly.

Elide shook her head. And while she didn't want to offend her friend, she set it down.

"I don't want any, but thanks," Elide signed.

Ryder shrugged and said, "Whatever." He drank his beer before downing Elide's too.

Elide pinched her lips together. She was tired and wanted to go home, so she grabbed her coat and waved goodbye to Ryder. Elide had to walk up the hill before she could reach the parked stagecoaches, all the while hoping one of them could bring her back to Miller Hall so she could contact Hansel to pick her up. But as she walked, she had the strangest feeling she was being followed. And the more she tried to ignore it, the more anxious she was.

She didn't hear anyone behind her but could feel her heart pounding in her chest. *Everything is fine*, she told herself. *Everything is fine*. But she couldn't shake the feeling. She sped up, rushing with her coat in her arms, and made it a few feet before she fell forward.

"You all right, Elide? You took quite a tumble," Ryder said, helping her up.

Elide nodded and turned to go, but Ryder didn't let go of her arm. She felt her stomach turn. She was sure that she'd left him by the campfire.

"Aye, what's the rush?" Ryder said. "The party isn't even over yet."

She was taken aback by his statement. She tried to pull away again and sent them both tumbling back down the hill. When they stopped rolling, he was on top of her, and she tried to shove him off.

"Damn, Elide, just relax," Ryder said. "I'm not going to hurt you."

But he didn't get off her. He just looked at her, and as she looked at his face, she saw something that looked worry-ingly like desire. His pupils were dilated as he stared down at her, panting heavily, each breath reeking of beer. She flinched and instinctively hit his chest, but like a man possessed, he ignored her. Then he grabbed one of her arms and used his free hand to slide up her dress, and for a moment, all she could hear was the sound of his breathing.

His fingers traveled her inner thigh, and then, "You. Come here!"

The voice was gruff and angry as Ryder was lifted off her by two men in black. Elide's heart pounded in her chest as she saw the crests on their coats—Disciples. *Thank God*, she thought. She sat up and was immediately pulled up onto her feet.

"You two are under arrest for attempted fornication and eliciting temptation," the Disciple said angrily.

"I didn't do anything, it was all her," Ryder stated.

She couldn't believe what she was hearing. He was blaming her? Elide shook her head furiously.

"All right, then what's the story," a brawny Disciple asked, signaling the Disciple to release her.

He waited a few moments. Elide fidgeted, but her hands were bound behind her back. She tried to mouth "him," but neither man seemed to understand. After two more attempts, the brawny Disciple ordered, "Take her away."

About the Author

Aminah Fox is an American author and graduate student studying an MI in Library & Information Science. She was born June 1998 in Oakland, California. Her sophomore novel, The Mourners: The Deadly Elite, released on November 11, 2022. She lives in Texas (USA) and Toronto (CAN).

www.aminahfox.com